THE LOVE
I COULD
HAVE HAD

The perfect uplifting story to read this
summer full of love, loss and romance

C.J. CONNOLLY

W0007916

Joffe Books, London
www.joffebooks.com

First published in Great Britain in 2023

Cover art by The Brewster Project

ISBN: 978-1-80405-937-1

To my best girlfriends — Shona, Sarah B, Libby, Becky, Jo, Rach, Sarah J, and Nicla-Picla. No matter how near or far our lives may be from each other, there's no universe where you don't mean the world to me.

CHAPTER 1: OLIVIA

May 27

I trace my finger over his bare chest, playing for a moment with the smattering of sandy hair in the center, damp with perspiration and gleaming gold in the midday sun. The square diamond on my ring finger glitters, and through my half-closed eyes it shoots out tiny rainbow prisms of light. I rest my head below his shoulder, his thudding heartbeat slowing after the exertions of a few moments earlier. Even though it's not yet June, his skin is already seeing a tan from two months of shirtless surfing off the North Carolina coast.

"You're so much browner than me already," I murmur into his chest.

Jake gives a low chuckle that rumbles through him, reverberating through me. "Time to get you out on the water. This is the summer I finally teach you to surf, right? I promised you I would after the reno was done, and now it is, so . . ."

I lift my head to look at him. His sandy mop of hair is becoming golden. Since we moved to our fixer-upper nine months ago, he's been out at the nearest beach almost every day except during the harshest weather.

"Are you serious? With all my new clients? And the wedding less than three months away? Honey, maybe *next* summer."

Jake twists his lips. "Really, Liv? I thought the wedding was all sorted. Everything booked—"

"Sure, it is." I kiss his smooth shoulder. "But business is ramping up, so I'll be working early mornings and late nights right up until we take the month for the honeymoon. I mean, we'll have a few weekends together at the beach, but I don't see me learning to surf anytime soon. Sorry, honey."

He blows out a resigned huff, knowing I'm right. My interior design business has taken off in the last couple of years, giving us the extra income we needed to buy our little house and renovate it ourselves. Well, mostly *my*self. And if Jake wants his dream job *and* the renovated house a few minutes from Wilmington's best surfing beach, *and* for us to have the wedding we've always wanted, he needs to support my working hours. Jake may be a lawyer, but since I encouraged him to work for a non-profit helping undocumented refugees, his salary has been less than half what he earned in private practice.

Jake props himself on his elbows, his naked body stretched out on the blanket, unabashed. We've been coming to this secret spot since we were eleven, ever since Jake's dog, Ginny, disappeared from the trail and we followed her through the gap in the wire mesh. That moment of awe on finding this old quarry with its turquoise swimming lake has barely waned for me in the seventeen years we've been coming here. It's so beautiful.

Surrounded by birch forest and completely inaccessible by road, it doesn't even have a hiking trail. It's marked on maps as a disused quarry, not a lake, and it's surrounded by fencing. In fact, we've only ever seen another person here a couple of times.

The quarry's steep rocky sides drop into milky-aqua waters, accessed by scrambling down the old quarry road or — for the bravest of hearts — taking a running jump from the highest cliff into the deep end. I've only done that a couple of times, as I'm always scared I won't jump far out enough to clear the jutting rocks near the bottom. Jake, utterly fearless and at one with any body of water, does it with ease every time.

This is our place. We grew up here. We shared our first kiss in the water, aged fourteen. We lost our virginity to each other on this very spot, at the tender ages of sixteen-and-a-half (me) and just-turned seventeen (him). We even got engaged here. A year ago today.

I sit upright, my stomach churning slightly after the mention of our upcoming wedding. Sure, it's all booked and planned to the last detail, but that doesn't make me any less nervous. That's another thing Jake is so fearless about, which I don't necessarily share. His certainty about me. Us. Our forthcoming marriage. He's told me many times I'm the love of his life, and it doesn't matter that we've never been with anyone else.

He knows I'm The One.

"Didn't you ever want to play the field, like your buddies?" I used to ask him all the time when he was home from Princeton. And, it's come up again, since our engagement. "What if you meet someone better after we're married?"

He'd pull me close, and kiss my hair. "Not possible. There *is* nobody better. You're the loveliest, sweetest, coolest, and most beautiful of them all."

Then why do *I* feel the niggle of hesitation?

I love Jake: there's no doubt about that. I've never met anyone better — not smarter, not kinder, definitely not more handsome. So what makes me wonder what else is out there? Not so much in terms of men — more like life in general.

Everything is familiar. Jake and I grew up near this spot in a small, rural town just outside of Wilmington, and we've both lived in the city since our early twenties. Jake went off to Princeton and law school for several years, but I studied design locally, not wanting to be far from my parents and sister. I've never lived more than fifty miles from here.

When people meet us and find out we were childhood friends, they often ask how old we were when we each realized we found the other attractive. The truth is, I don't remember exactly. Jake just looks like, well . . . Jake. Always has. There's never been any newness, any . . . *excitement*, I guess. That thrill of the unknown.

My skin prickles. Either with trepidation or, perhaps, the effects of the sun on my still-untanned skin. Probably both.

I sit up, reach for the sunscreen, and apply it liberally to my arms and bare legs, before passing the bottle to Jake. "Do my back?"

He pushes my chestnut hair aside and trickles cold lotion onto my shoulders and back, rubbing it in with strong, firm hands.

"I meant to tell you, Dad said yes to being my best man. He was so sweet, got kinda choked up."

"Aww. Your dad is the best."

"Is your sister happy about being maid of honor?"

"Yeah, Charlotte's totally into it. She's already planning a bridal shower. And I have all the dresses and flowers ordered, so she doesn't have to do anything except on the Big Day."

Jake pulls a strand of my hair aside. "She'd probably like to be given more to do. I get the impression she's at a loose end, now she's single again."

I nod, pulling my hair out of the way. "She's so disappointed it didn't work out. She's desperate to be a mother, which, I dunno . . . It's a bit soon, right? I mean, she's six years younger than me. Twenty-two. And I know even I'm not ready to be a mother yet."

Jake's hands still — and I know I've hit a nerve. It's a bone of contention between us. He's more than ready to be a father, hoping there will be a baby before we're thirty, but I'm not so sure. I want to travel the world first, and I'm not convinced our month-long honeymoon in Asia will satisfy that itch.

He puts the bottle down. It's obviously an effort for him to stay quiet, but I know he won't say anything more about it — not today. Not when we're celebrating our anniversary, with a picnic and champagne. Followed by a skinny dip that got very heated, and some spectacular clifftop lovemaking. For somebody who has been making love to me for twelve years, Jake never fails to impress me with his skills. Anybody inadvertently coming across us today would've gotten a real show, that's for sure.

It's a wonderful life. What more could a girl want?

"You wanna finish the strawberries?" Jake asks.

"No, my stomach is starting to feel weird."

I swing my legs to the side, nearly squishing the white roses Jake surprised me with earlier. They've been my favorite flowers since I was a kid, and Jake always remembers to buy me them. He's so sweet. So thoughtful . . .

And maybe a little unoriginal? Something different, once in a while, would be nice.

Still naked, I stand and reach my arms toward the sun, stretching. My engagement ring casts glittering fairy lights on the rocks.

Jake looks up at me, shading his eyes. "You okay?"

I force a smile. "Yeah. Just going to stretch my legs for a minute. Along the cliff. Would you mind packing up? I have a call at three and I need my swatches."

A tiny crease appears at the top of his nose. He can always tell when I'm feeling off. "Sure. Just be careful on those loose rocks. I'll never forget having to save you when you slipped over the edge. It was terrifying."

I scoff a little. I was twelve and barely remember the incident. But the way Jake tells it, I fell off the side of the highest rock, and was clinging perilously onto a ledge, when he hauled me back up, saving me from plunging to certain death on the rocks below. I don't recall exactly what happened, but I'm sure it wasn't that dramatic. Jake just loves to be a hero.

"I'll be fine."

I leave Jake packing up our picnic as I tread over the rocky ground, heading straight for the high point Jake warned me about.

He's not the boss of me.

This is my favorite section of clifftop, anyways. It's where I've watched Jake for years taking those huge, scary leaps into the deep pool. I'm always drawn to it, to that side of him. The fearless adventurer. The man I love, the one I want to adventure with. Less so the guy who wants to settle down and have kids while we're still so young.

I need to talk to him again about putting our plans for babies, and maybe even our careers, on hold for a couple of years. This wedding, our steady jobs, and our newly settled life in a finished home has me feeling antsy. Perhaps a year or two traveling the world would fix that.

I reach the highest point and lean over, my bare feet gripping the warm stone. How far out would I need to jump to clear the rocks at the bottom? How fast would I have to run before jumping? I did it when I was sixteen, moments before I gave myself to Jake for the first time. But that was twelve years ago. I'm not so fearless now.

The cliff I'm on juts out, obscuring my view of the pool below. I shuffle sideways onto some loose stones to get a better view of the bottom. The stones are sharp on my soles.

"Ow," I mutter, lifting a foot to see if I've drawn blood. As I adjust my weight onto the other foot, the scree shifts below me.

Time slows. It slows enough for me to realize I'm off-balance and, as I begin to return my raised foot to the ground, the other is sliding out from under me.

It slows enough for me to understand I'm not getting my balance back, and that my only hope is to fall onto the clifftop rather than over the precipice.

It slows enough for me to know it's too late to fall onto the clifftop. I'm definitely going over the edge, and there's nothing but air below, as I desperately claw around for a ledge to save me.

It slows enough for me to realize Jake was right about needing to be careful, and to be irritated with him for it.

It slows enough for me to acknowledge I'm in free-fall, and to recognize this is what it feels like to have your last moments. I'm almost fascinated by the experience. So unexpected.

It slows enough for me to think about how much I love Jake, and my family, and my beautiful life. I see Jake's clear blue eyes, and the devotion in them.

And it slows enough for me to notice my body isn't dashed on hard quarry rocks, but instead plunged into cold water. Instantly deep, instantly dark. Down and down. So much deeper than I thought.

But I don't come up again. I keep plunging. Darker, colder, the noise of rushing water and bubbles intensifying, the pressure increasing.

Maybe I am dead, after all. Maybe this is what death feels like, and my body is in pieces on the rocks above.

Then total darkness.

Total silence.

Time stops.

CHAPTER 2: OLIVIA

May 28

I'm ascending again. Pushing upward. Breaking through the surface into brightness.

But I'm not where I thought I was. I'm lying in a bed, light dazzling me.

I turn my face away from the glare.

A wide window reveals an urban view, which I immediately recognize as downtown Wilmington and Eagle Island, divided by Cape Fear River. If I could see closer, I could probably pick out Jake's office building from here.

A machine to my side beeps a steady rhythm, and an orange plastic chair sits empty by my bed.

On the other side of me, a green curtain is closed, and somebody is talking — a low, male voice. Jake? No, even lower than Jake's.

The curtain swishes to one side, and a stocky nurse in green scrubs emerges. He glances at me and raises his eyebrows.

"You're awake." His smile is wide, bright against his dark skin. "Welcome back." He sits on the chair beside the bed. His badge reads *Marcus Deneil, Nurse Practitioner.* "You're quite the mystery. You came in yesterday without any ID.

And you've been asleep ever since," he adds. "What's your name?"

What? That's weird.

"Olivia Grainger," I reply, frowning. "Call me Liv. Where's Jake?"

The nurse's eyebrows lift. "Jake?"

"My fiancé. He must've brought me here. We were at a quarry lake together and . . . I don't know. I fell, I guess."

Marcus shakes his head. "A hiker named Kirk found you yesterday afternoon at the quarry. In fact, his dog led him to you, otherwise you might never have been found. The hiker didn't even know the quarry was there. You didn't have any clothes, or any items nearby that could ID you. There was nobody else around, he said."

"But — no." I shake my head. "I was with my fiancé. Jake Johnson. He must've been nearby. We were picnicking. He was packing up when I fell."

The nurse pats my left hand. "It's okay. Jake was probably somewhere looking for you when you were found. Now that we know who you are, we can call your fiancé for you, let him know you're here. Do you have his number?"

My left hand feels odd, empty. I flutter my fingers. My engagement ring is gone. "Uh, yeah, his number's on my phone. I don't know it by heart. Do you have my cell?"

Marcus shakes his head. "You had nothing on you, not even clothes. I guess it's still at the quarry. Or your fiancé has it all. But that's okay. We can track him down. Where does he work?"

"He's in-house counsel at Refuge Advocacy International — he works from their downtown office. He is supposed to be back at work today. You can find their number online—"

I stop.

This can't be right. They're saying I fell *yesterday* afternoon. So where is Jake? Did something happen to him?

"But I wouldn't think Jake's gone to the office, if he thinks I'm missing and doesn't know I'm here. But maybe call them anyways, I guess, and tell them what happened?"

Crap, Mom and Dad will be wondering what's happened to me, too. "And if you could contact my parents — they'll be panicking. Tilly and Burt Grainger. Mom's cell number . . . oh, it's on the Ten Thousand Roses charity website — she does a lot of fundraising for them."

Marcus makes notes on a little pad from his top pocket and gives me another smile. "Great. Jake Johnson, at Refuge Advocacy, you said? Okay, got it. We'll have you connected with your family in no time. I'll send Dr. Connor in to check you over, but you seem to be doing well physically. Back soon." He rises and disappears around the curtain beside me.

This is *bizarre*.

Why wasn't Jake at the lake when the hiker found me? Did he not see me fall? Was he searching for me in the forest? Is it possible Jake and the hiker missed each other? It makes no sense.

A doctor appears in the doorway — Dr. Connor, I presume. She gives me a once-over, examining my limbs and torso, carefully, under my hospital gown, then stares at me, one eyebrow raised.

"What?" I ask.

"You fell off a quarry cliff?"

I nod.

"It's amazing. You don't have a scratch or a bruise on you, except for the soles of your feet."

"What's amazing is I missed the rocks at the bottom." I still can't believe that. "I slipped. You'd usually have to take a running jump to clear them. My fiancé loves to terrify me by doing that," I add.

The doctor gives me a sympathetic half-smile. The same kind of smile I'd give a child telling me about their imaginary friend. My hackles rise. Jake is real.

Dr. Connor turns away. "Hopefully when your family arrives, we can find out more about what happened. Once they're here and we've figured out your identity and your insurance details, you'll be cleared to go."

"Thank you, doctor."

As she leaves, she crosses paths with Marcus the nurse. They exchange glances, Marcus giving the doctor a tiny shake of his head.

What's *that* about?

Marcus sits beside me. There's a deep crease between his brows.

"Okay. So, I called Refuge Advocacy International to get your fiancé's cell number, and there seems to be some misunderstanding. They said they have no record of a Jake Johnson, or Jacob Johnson, ever working there. So, I was unable to get hold of him."

I scoff. "Well, he definitely works there. I visit him at the office all the time. We went to their Memorial Day barbecue last week. You must've got some clueless new receptionist who doesn't know all the staff."

Marcus sucks in a breath. "I was transferred to the CEO, David Ackerman. He said he'd never heard of Jake Johnson . . . Nor Olivia Grainger."

What?

I shake my head. "Jake and I both know David very well. They've worked together for three years."

"Here's where I'm worried, Liv." His tone is gentle. "I found your mom's number on the charity website like you said, and called her. I explained her daughter, Liv Grainger, was here at New Hanover Regional, and . . . well. She pretty much screamed and broke down. Next thing I'm speaking to Mr. Grainger, and he's asking me who I am and what's going on. When I tried to explain his daughter was here, unhurt, but needing to be picked up, he started shouting at me, things that made no sense."

A wash of bile builds at the back of my throat. I try to sit up, but my body is weak with fatigue. Marcus sees my struggle and levers my bed into an angled position.

"What was Dad saying?" I have to force out the words.

"Things like, 'what kind of scam is this?' and 'how dare you try to exploit our grief' — that kind of thing. Called me a liar. I repeated that you were here and asking for them."

Marcus takes my hand, his expression kind. "He said, 'It's not possible. Our daughter Olivia died sixteen years ago, when she was twelve.' Then he hung up. So, I checked the city birth and death registry database and, well, I found an Olivia Grainger who died in the mid-2000s, aged twelve."

I suck in a breath, swallowing hard. Leaning my head back, I try to make some kind of sense of this.

"You must've got the wrong Olivia Grainger? Obviously."

In my periphery, I see Marcus shake his head. "There's only been one born in the nineties to a Burt and Tilly Grainger. Do you have any siblings?"

"My sister, Charlotte. She's twenty-two. She manages a branch of Zara downtown. You could call her."

"I can try that later, but I think for now we need to figure out what's going on here," he replies. "I only mention siblings to check you're talking about the same family. And yes, there's a sister named Charlotte. She's been an only child since her older sister Liv died aged twelve."

My head is reeling so much I can barely see. I turn away from the nurse and retch, a thread of sickly saliva spilling from my mouth. My stomach is nothing but acid. Marcus scurries to my other side, placing a metal bowl under my chin. He crouches by my bed, holding my hand.

"Look, I don't know what's going on here. You don't seem to be lying, but obviously you can't be a person who died sixteen years ago. You have no ID to back up your story, and the people you say are your parents tell me you're dead, which the city data confirms. I have to ask you. Is Olivia Grainger really your name?"

"Yes!" A tear slips down the side of my cheek. "I'm not lying, I swear. Why would I lie about who I am?"

"It happens. Con artists, scammers, identity thieves. Although this would be a really weird scam, to pretend to be someone who died as a child, and notify the family they're taking on that identity—"

"I'm not a scammer." The tears fall harder. "I swear I'm Liv Grainger. I'm twenty-eight. I'm *close* with my family

— I have dinner with my parents and sister at their house at Landfall every Sunday. Usually also with my fiancé, Jake. We have a house near Bradley Creek — we bought it last year after we got engaged and fixed it up. We're getting married August 20th. I . . . I run my own interior design business, Living Inc., and Jake works at Refuge Advocacy. We were together yesterday at the quarry. He'll be so worried about—" A sob catches the rest of my words.

Marcus passes me a tissue. I blow my nose as he stares at me.

"Okay," he replies finally. "I'll track down your Jake Johnson and see what he has to say. I'll also call Charlotte Grainger at Zara, maybe she can shed some light on this. The downtown branch?"

I nod, wiping mucus from my nostrils. "Thank you."

He gives me a kind smile and rises. "I'll be back. Hang in there."

My head throbs painfully, my thoughts racing too fast for me to catch up with them. Nothing makes any sense.

Why the hell would Mom and Dad claim I died as a child? Have they gone nuts? I've never even broken a limb, much less had a major accident or serious illness. Why would Jake's boss deny knowing us? Why isn't Jake here at the hospital with me right now, or calling all the hospitals to track me down? Where did he go when I fell?

I'm almost in a trance by the time Marcus returns, the swirl of nonsensical information descending into a nightmarish blur.

"Liv?"

I open my eyes, not realizing I'd closed them. I start upright. Marcus sits on the orange chair, taking my hand, his face grim.

"I got through to your sister at the store. As I suspected, I got the same reaction I got from your father. First accusing me of being a spam caller, and then, once I'd explained more, telling me that you must be a scammer or identity thief of some kind, since her sister Livvie died when Charlotte was six. But I did manage to get Jake Johnson's cell number from her. Charlotte does know him, although she says he's not your fiancé."

I let out a fresh sob, mixed with a strangled cry.

Marcus continues, "Charlotte said she knows him through a friend, and he works at a private law firm downtown. I called Jake, and explained what you've been telling me. He was as perplexed as the rest of them, telling me that he did know you as a child, the two of you were best friends throughout childhood until you died aged twelve. He's sure you can't possibly be who you say you are, as he was there when you died. And he said he was sorry he couldn't help me identify you further. That was it — he hung up after that."

I hear Marcus's last words as if through fog or underwater. Unclear, their edges blurred, the sound distorted.

I'm slipping again, falling. Back into the deep. Back into the darkness of the lake, the water enveloping me. Wrapping its comforting, cold arms around me.

Back to the place where time stops.

CHAPTER 3: OLIVIA

May 29

My body is convulsing. Or rather, something is convulsing my body. I'm being shaken by the shoulder. I twist away from the stranger's hand, sitting upright, suddenly awake. Two men are beside my bed.

One speaks. "Sorry, ma'am. We need to speak with you."

I push my greasy hair off my face. I haven't washed it in days. I had managed to stand up late last night, unstick the pads on my skin linking me to the bedside machine, and hobble to the shared bathroom in the corridor. I had looked terrible — gray, drawn, free of make-up, my hair lank and lifeless. I'm fully aware of how wretched I must look to these people after another night of restless sleep.

They're police officers, both young, male. The one who was shaking me is around my age, maybe a couple of years older. Very short cropped dark hair, tan skin, friendly features, good-looking. A little stocky, probably no taller than my five-foot-nine frame. Not tall, like Jake. The other guy is a lot younger, skinny, his face covered in acne. He's holding a notepad and pen.

"I'm Detective Adam Banks, and this is my trainee, Officer Gary Phelps," says the older one, sitting beside me. "We need to have a conversation with you to clear up your identity. Are you good to speak with us now, ma'am?"

I straighten up, plumping a pillow behind me. "Sure, I guess. Please call me Olivia, or Liv."

Detective Banks looks skeptical. "Thank you, ma'am," he replies, ignoring my request. "We're here because we had a complaint from a Burt Grainger, who said he received a call from a nurse here saying that you claim to be his deceased daughter, Olivia. We verified this with the nurse practitioner this morning. He confirmed this story, and that you have no ID to corroborate your claim. Is this correct?"

"Yes. It's correct that I'm saying I'm Olivia Grainger, and it's also correct that I *am* Olivia Grainger. Also, that I have no ID to prove it — I came here with nothing. My purse must still be at the quarry lake, I guess." I shrug. "But it's not correct to say that Olivia Grainger is deceased. Because I'm her, I'm Burt and Tilly's daughter, and as you can see, I'm very much alive. I have absolutely no idea why they would say I died as a child — clearly I didn't. I'm right here, always have been. I've never been away for a long period, never gone missing, never lived anywhere but Wilmington. It makes no sense that they would say this. Or that Jake says he hasn't seen me since we were kids. We live together — we're engaged. It's so crazy . . ." I can't go on. I don't want to break down again in front of these cops.

"Okay, ma'am. I understand you're upset." The detective's voice is low, soft. "Here's the thing. We went to the quarry lake this morning — which, by the way, is private property. There was no sign of anybody's personal possessions. The man you say is your fiancé, Jake Johnson, does not have your purse or your ID — we called him, too. He told us about the accident at the same quarry lake when he was twelve years old, when young Liv Grainger fell from the cliff and died. He was the only other person there. We've checked his story, and it matches the police and city records.

Olivia Grainger died at that lake sixteen years ago. Her body is buried in Wilton Cemetery, close to the Graingers' former family home.

"So tell me, ma'am." He leans in. "Why are you pretending to be Olivia Grainger? Who are you, really?"

An unwanted tear slips down my cheek. I brush it aside with the heel of my hand.

"*I. Am. Olivia. Grainger.* I can't explain my family's response, nor Jake's. *I* know who I am. I'm not lying. Why would I lie? It's not like it would be an effective scam. People who steal identities do it secretly, without alerting anybody. Why would anybody publicly claim to be a dead twelve-year-old?"

Detective Banks shakes his head while his young trainee scribbles furious notes, one eyebrow quirked.

"Ma'am, I have no idea. But this is the claim you're making. The doctor told us it could potentially be . . . some kind of personality disorder. A neurological condition caused by your fall. Except that you had no identifiable head injury. I'm told you'll be undergoing a psych eval soon. Okay, then, next question — where do you live? Assuming you're, erm, remembering wrongly about who you are, if we can take you home, we can see if there's ID and correspondence at your home that will tell us more."

"I live with Jake Johnson. In the house we bought together last year — 878 Bradley Road. Near the creek. But if Jake is saying he doesn't live with me . . ." I shake my head, trying not to let my face crumple.

Could the doctor be right? Am I really somebody else? Do I live somewhere else?

No.

I am Liv Grainger.

I remember everything about my life.

My wonderful, blessed life.

Detective Banks twists his mouth. "Yeah, Mr. Johnson lives in an oceanfront condo on Wrightsville Beach. He's been there three years, he said. We can visit that Bradley

Road address to double-check. But I'll be honest, ma'am. I think we'll find somebody else living there." He hesitates. "You told hospital staff you're self-employed, but there's no record of an interior design business called Living Inc. registered, and no online presence. Is that the correct name?"

I nod, miserable. I can't look him in the eye. "The website is www.livinginc.com."

Detective Banks nods toward his trainee, who taps something into his iPhone. The younger officer frowns, giving Detective Banks a tiny shake of his head, shows his mentor the screen.

"That domain name is available for sale," Detective Banks tells me. "Okay, how about your cell number? You know that by heart? Maybe we can try calling it."

"Sure. 910-555-3554."

Officer Phelps taps at his phone again and holds it to his ear. "Hello . . . this is Officer Gary Phelps with Wilmington PD. May I ask whose cellphone this is? We're trying to ID the victim of an accident . . . No, sir, nothing wrong. May I take your name? . . . And you've had this number for how long? . . . Thank you, sir. That's all I need. Thanks for your time, have a great day." He hangs up. "Number belongs to a Fred Crocker, he's had it at least seven years."

I push out a breath. "You definitely dialed 555-3554?"

Officer Phelps checks his phone. "Yes, ma'am."

I bristle. "I'd really love it if you guys would stop calling me 'ma'am'. Makes me feel ancient. Can you please call me Liv, even if you don't believe I'm her?"

Detective Banks ignores me. "Is there anybody else who you can think of who could identify you. Some other way to show us who you are?"

"I can try other friends, but if Jake and my family don't know who I am . . . Plus I don't have any of their numbers memorized — I'd need my phone." I bite my lip. "Oh, what about social media? I'm Liv Grainger on Facebook and Instagram. And Living Inc. has a Facebook company page."

"We already checked those," Detective Banks replies. "There are some Liv and Olivia Graingers on social media, but none living in the area, and nobody who looks like you. You'd be pretty easy to identify, visually speaking."

What does *that* mean?

He notices my frown but continues smoothly, "Clearly you're not Liv Grainger, but it also seems to me you genuinely believe your story. You're not deliberately lying. Hopefully the psych eval will tell us more. We may have to treat you as . . . an amnesiac, and hold a press conference with your photo. We could potentially say you can't remember who you are, and ask people to come forward if they recognize you." He pauses for a moment, obviously thinking it through. "We can also circulate your photo on social media, since many of your real friends will be on those platforms. We wouldn't be able to say you think you're Liv Grainger, though. Many people will remember that tragedy and accuse you of lying, of being a scammer."

"Like my parents."

"Mr. Grainger thinks you are, yes. But Mrs. Grainger . . . well, she told us it could be a miracle. I understand she's become a very religious woman since her daughter's death."

Religious? *Mom*?

"Wow. Okay. Well, maybe she'd believe me. If I could just see her? I mean, I look exactly like her daughter, just grown up. She'd recognize me, even if she thinks she hasn't seen me for years. I have the same scar on my eyebrow, from falling into a coffee table at Jake's house when we were ten. Ooh," I sit upright, excited. "DNA! We could have a test, right? We could find out who I am that way — prove I'm related to the Graingers."

Detective Banks nods slowly. "We could see if the Graingers would be willing to take a DNA test. Even if not, we can do a test on you to see if it throws up any name in the system. Fingerprints too. Even take a mold of your teeth and compare that to dental records, if it comes to that." He nods to his young colleague, who scribbles more on the notepad.

"But in the meantime there's the problem of what to do with you. You have nowhere to go. We'll check the address you gave us, but I'm not optimistic that's your home. And there's the issue of how to pay your hospital bill."

"Oh, crap." I rub the heels of my hands against my eyes. "I'm on Jake's insurance. Have been ever since I became self-employed."

"Well, you're not, as he doesn't know you. You're about to get a sizeable bill that I'm guessing you have no means of paying. Since you don't know who you are or where you live, we can't trace any bank account or credit cards." He sighs as the young officer continues to scribble away in his notebook.

"We can't let you go out into the community until we know who you are. You have no money, home, or income. You wouldn't even be able to get a job. There's no Social Security under the name you're claiming." His brown eyes meet mine. "One way or another, we have to figure out who you really are."

I'm Liv Grainger.

But, crap, he's right. In this nightmarish version of my world, I don't exist. I have no money. No health insurance. No home. No business. No family or friends. No ID, no phone. Not even clothes. If my family and Jake don't come to their senses, outside this hospital, I'll be a beggar on the street. A naked one.

But there's one thing I'm sure of.

I. Am. Liv Grainger.

CHAPTER 4: JAKE

May 27

Jake lay back on the picnic blanket, blissful, spent. Above him, nothing but blue, a few wisps of airplane trails and dark tips of the forest in his peripheral vision. Liv was tracing light swirls on his sweaty chest, moving dangerously close to his genitals, which needed some downtime after their recent exertions. Damn, she was good. Maybe they'd have a short rest and then go for round two. Although, didn't she say something about having to get home for a conference call? She was always busy now, with her design consultancy doing so well.

The blazing sun caught the diamond on her finger, a prism of light, momentarily dazzling him. Closing his eyes, he smiled softly, even though a stone was digging into his back under the blanket. He could stay like this with Liv forever.

She was a little antsy, though. More than just preoccupied with the time and her work call. She sat up and passed him a bottle of sunscreen to do her back, and he recognized it as a distraction. He knew her well enough to know she was feeling jittery about the wedding. Sure, she loved him, she wanted to marry him — he wasn't worried about that. But having only ever been with each other — which, to Jake, was the best possible scenario — Liv seemed afraid of somehow missing out. Or maybe of him missing out on other women, and therefore being tempted by them further down the line. Which he never would be. But she didn't seem to believe him when he told her that.

She'd be okay, though. He just needed to give her a little space, maybe ease back on the talk about kids for a while. Yeah, she was twenty-eight and they didn't have forever if they wanted three, which he did, for sure. But there were still several years before they'd be pushing it, biological clock-wise. Maybe he'd start figuring out how to take a sabbatical so that they could travel the world together, for a year or something, and bring it up before the wedding. That would calm her nerves. She'd love that.

Jake finished rubbing sunscreen into Liv's shoulders. She stood up and stretched her naked body to the sky above him, fingertips seemingly brushing the dispersing plane trails. Her chestnut hair and smooth skin gleamed in the bright-ness, the moles on her arms and back adding character and warmth. Her butt curved perfectly down to long, toned legs that would make her a natural surfer if she'd just give it a go.

God, she was gorgeous. How Jake ever got to have a kind, smart, generous woman with movie-star looks all to himself for an entire lifetime was beyond his understand-ing. One thing was for sure, he wasn't about to mess it up. Whatever she needed, he'd give her. After all, she'd always given him everything he needed.

Liv turned, smiling down at him, although it was the smile that meant "give me a minute".

"You okay?"

"Yeah," she replied, although she didn't meet his eyes. "Just going to stretch my legs for a minute. Along the cliff. Would you mind packing up? I have a call at three and I need my swatches."

Too bad. Round two was definitely out.

"Sure." Jake frowned. "Just be careful on those loose rocks. I'll never forget saving you when you slipped over that edge. It was terrifying."

His stomach churned just thinking about it. They'd only been twelve, and he'd nearly lost her. He'd underplayed it, but in truth it had been the scariest moment of his life by far, and he'd been in some hairy situations caught in big swells and riptides since then.

Life without Liv? Unthinkable.

He watched her walk away, then began packing up the sandwich wrappers, half-eaten box of strawberries, and empty champagne bottle and plastic cups, setting aside the bouquet of white roses. They were her favorite flowers. So why had a shadow passed momentarily across her face when he'd produced them earlier? She'd smiled, of course, kissed him, given effusive thanks, but he knew something was off, had missed the mark. He didn't want to ask, though. Not today. Not when they were celebrating. Maybe he'd buy her different flowers next time and see if that worked better. Maybe it was all part of the sameness she seemed to be worrying about. Maybe he just needed to switch things up a bit.

Still, sex in the open air on a quarry clifftop was *definitely* exciting. He chuckled, turning to view his beautiful, naked fiancée on the high point of the cliff.

But he couldn't see her. She'd been walking along the ridge just a second ago.

Where was she?

Jake's stomach tightened. Where the hell was she? Had she gone off to the woods instead? *No.* Why would she do that?

Ignoring his own nakedness, Jake made his way across the rocky surface to where he'd last seen her, just ahead of the highest part of the cliff — the section where he'd done a running jump into the water an hour or so earlier.

"*Liv?* . . . *LIV?*"

Silence.

Jake twisted his head, scanning the outskirts of the surrounding forest. No way would Liv scramble, naked, through that undergrowth.

"*LIV*!!"

Nothing.

Blood pounding in his temple, Jake traversed the last section of the cliff to its highest point. The point where a twelve-year-old Liv had once slipped. The stones were loose and slippery here. Even he was having trouble walking. Ignoring the rubble biting into the soles of his feet, he carried on. Surely she couldn't have fallen? Not when he'd just warned her, literally moments before, to be careful?

"*LIV*??!!" he screamed.

He leaned out a little over the cliff edge, peering onto the flat rocks below, terrified of seeing Liv's beautiful body, broken and bloodied, twisted at improbable angles, her hazel eyes wide open and empty.

Nothing. Thank Christ. He blew out a breath.

Wait.

Narrowing his eyes, he looked again. There was something down there on the rocks, glinting impossibly brightly in the sun. What was it?

He scanned the rocks, the water. Was she in there? Drowning, right now?

Without even thinking, Jake turned, ran away from the cliff, turned again, and ran toward the edge, jumping into the void. Time seemed to stop, Jake suspended momentarily above the turquoise lake. Then cold water, teal with pale bubbles, engulfed him as it had done so many times before. Always in exhilaration, never panic.

Jake pushed up, up, up, through the surface, desperately hoping to see Liv clambering to the side of the pool. But there was no one there. He sucked in a lungful of breath and kicked his way under the surface again, his eyes wide, searching for her, reaching for her soft limbs. He kicked further down into the deep.

There she was. His fingers touched her floating hair—
she was near the bottom, her body limp. He grasped, but the
hair became slimy and slipped through his fingers.

Not her hair. Just soft reeds, teasing him.

He panicked, losing air in a cloud of bubbles, and was
forced to kick back up to the surface once more.

"*LIV*??!!"

Silence.

Again and again, Jake dove under, his usually strong
limbs weakening from lack of oxygen. After the fifteenth
time, he was forced to give up. Exhausted, he hauled his
body onto the warm, flat rocks beneath the cliff.

If Liv were down there, she'd have drowned by now.

But he couldn't think that.

He hadn't found her, plus she was a strong swimmer,
so if she wasn't in the water and she hadn't fallen, she was
somewhere else. It would all become clear. It was a misunderstanding. They'd laugh about it.

Maybe she'd taken her clothes with her, had got dressed,
and was waiting for him at the car? Maybe he'd misunder-
stood about her walk along the cliff and she'd been expecting
him to pack up and follow her through the forest?

He sat upright with a half-laugh. That would be it. He'd
panicked unnecessarily. It was some weird mistake. These
things always were.

Ouch.

He'd put the heel of his hand on something sharp. It
was digging into him. Small but vicious. He lifted his hand.
Beneath it, a square diamond ring sat innocuously winking
in the sunlight.

Liv's engagement ring.

What the fuck?

Jake let out something between a cry and a yelp, his face
breaking. Had she left him? Thrown her ring into the quarry
and walked away without a single word of warning?

No.

Jake needed to get up to their picnic spot to see if she'd taken her clothes and the car key.

As he rose, the crunch of footsteps on stones came from above — along with, weirdly, a dog's bark.

Thank Christ. He smiled with relief. Liv was still up there. She'd probably hidden when she heard someone coming and been found by some hiker's dog, or something.

"Hello?" It was a man's voice.

"Hey," Jake called back. "I'm down here. Wait there, I'm coming up." He scrambled up the quarry's access slope to the lower cliffs, running toward the direction of the voice, where a dog was still barking.

A man with graying hair, about his dad's age, and a large Alsatian stood by the picnic spot. Both spotted Jake at the same time.

"Oh!" The guy turned away. The dog barked again, doubling its volume.

Shit. Jake had entirely forgotten he was naked.

"Sorry, man." Ignoring the excited dog, he rushed to dress quickly in shorts and a T-shirt. Liv's clothes were still there, where she'd left them, her burgundy lace underpants entwined with Jake's briefs.

"That's okay." The hiker was still turned respectfully away. "My dog came across this quarry and we found your stuff. I just wanted to check everybody was okay."

"Thanks, yeah, no, I . . . I can't find my girlfriend. My fiancée, Liv. I guess she must've maybe seen you coming and hid somewhere, as she wasn't wearing any clothes either. There's never anybody else here," Jake added apologetically. "Have you seen her?"

The guy turned to Jake with a half-grimace, half-smile. "No, sorry. No naked women. Last time I saw a naked woman was in 1996, so I think I'd notice."

Shit. Where was she?

"She must still be hiding, since you're here." Jake was struggling to keep his voice calm. "She's probably embarrassed.

Did you see our car on the track? A silver Audi with a roof rack?"

"Yeah, I parked next to it. There was nobody there, though."

Fuck.

"Would you mind sticking around here for a minute while I go look in the forest?"

The hiker nodded, with a kind smile. "No problem. This is a beautiful spot. I'd be happy to chill here a while, anyways." He looked about him appreciatively. "Strange, I had no idea it was even here." The guy sat down on the ridge, his dog settling beside him. Both looked up at Jake.

"Thanks, man. Help yourself to strawberries."

Jake gathered Liv's clothes so she could dress before facing the stranger, and began scouring the edges of the forest. He called out into the trees. "Liv? It's me . . . I have your clothes. You can get dressed and come out. The guy with the dog is cool. Where are you? . . . Liv?"

Surely she had to be here somewhere?

But she wasn't.

And Jake knew this, even as he completed the circuit of woodland surrounding the quarry. Even as he'd spoken to the hiker and his dog. Because if Liv was around, her ring wouldn't have been down by the water.

"No luck?" the hiker said as Jake returned, concern etched over his sun-battered face.

Jake shook his head, blowing out a breath, trying to control the resurfacing panic. "No. I have no idea what the fuck's happened to her. I even went into the lake. I thought maybe she'd fallen in . . . It happened before," he explained at the older man's expression. "Then I heard you and figured she'd hidden from you. But she'd have come out by now." His expression brightened. "Maybe she's at the car now?"

The hiker shrugged. "You wanna go check, and I'll stay here?"

"Thanks, man. I really appreciate this. I know it's not your problem. If I run, it'll take me twenty minutes there and back."

"No sweat. I'm in no hurry."

Jake grabbed the car keys and pushed his way through the undergrowth, the wire mesh fence and along the wooded trail, increasing his pace to a sprint at the last section that met the track. The car was parked where he'd left it, a blue Toyota now beside it. But no sign of anyone else.

"*LIV*!!"

Silence, but for birdsong and the rustle of the breeze in the silver birches.

He opened up the car and grabbed a pad and pen from the glove compartment, scrawling a note for the windshield.

HONEY, I LOST YOU! STAY HERE AT THE CAR. GET IN, IT'S UNLOCKED. BLANKET IN THE TRUNK. STAY WARM. I'LL COME BACK. LOOKING FOR YOU AT QUARRY.

It was an invitation for thieves, but the chances of anybody other than the hiker coming along seemed extremely slim.

He ran back, making it to the quarry in less than ten minutes—record time. The dog began barking, the hiker turned and rose from his sitting position.

"Any luck?"

"Nothing," Jake shrugged. "I left a note in case she goes to the car. But it doesn't make sense. It's a twenty-minute walk, plus she's naked. *Shit.* I don't know what the fuck is happening." The adrenaline coursing through Jake's body made him shake, his legs suddenly turning to Jell-O. "Fuck."

He collapsed onto the rocks at the guy's feet, the Alsatian stopped barking, nuzzling him gently instead.

The hiker crouched down beside Jake, putting a comforting hand on his shoulder. "Dude. I think maybe it's time we called the police. She might have gone into the water."

"I found her ring down there. Her engagement ring." Jake's body was beginning to shake. The hiker looked even more concerned, the dog began whimpering, looking from his owner to Jake and back again.

It took Jake a moment to realize that his shaking was actually sobbing.

The hiker stayed in his crouch, producing a cellphone from his pocket and dialing, just three digits. Three little beeps. The last two the same tone.

"Police, please . . . Hi. Yeah, we have a missing person, a woman has disappeared, but she may have been swimming and met with an accident . . . That's right . . . We're at a lake in an old quarry . . . Yeah. It's through the woodland at the end of Travers Lane, between Rocky Point and Long Creek. It's marked as McMahon Quarry on Google Maps — I guess it's private property as there's a mesh fence. I've never seen a gate, I think it's been disused for years."

He stopped, listened for a few seconds, his eyes flicking to Jake. "Yeah, just an overgrown trail at the end of the lane, but I can meet you at my car and guide you here . . . It's been maybe twenty, thirty minutes. I know that's not long for a missing person, but I'm concerned she may be in the water and her boyfriend is very distressed . . . Name? I'm Kirk Evans. I'm just a bystander, the woman is . . . uh . . ." He nudged Jake, his eyebrows raised in question.

"Liv," Jake choked out. "Olivia Grainger."

"Olivia Grainger . . . yes . . . here with her fiancé. Please hurry, he's in a bad way and it's not, uh, looking great . . . Yes, I'll be by the car in twenty minutes." He looked at his watch. "Say . . . 2.35. Okay, thanks." He put his phone away.

"Okay, dude — uh, what's your name?"

Jake rubbed his face into his elbow. "Jake. Jake Johnson."

"Okay, Jake. I'm Kirk. So, Jake, I'm gonna go meet the police at the trailhead, okay? You sit tight here, in case she shows up. I've got a hoodie in my backpack, so I'll keep calling out for her too, and if I find her, I can put the hoodie over her. She'll be safe with me, don't you worry." He looked

29

unsure whether to leave Jake or not. "Sit tight, Jake. I'll be back with the cops as soon as I can."

Kirk rose and jogged away, his dog trotting behind him.

Jake lay back, finally allowing his body to dissolve into anguish, twisting into a fetal position. How could it have been only half an hour ago when Jake was lying right here, feeling Liv's fingertips running over his body? How could their celebration turn so quickly into a nightmare?

He lay curled up for goodness knows how long, the late spring sun beating down on him like a whip, brutally unrelenting. The salt water dried on his face, his skin shriveling with dehydration and over-exposure. Sunscreen, Liv would always tell him.

He sat upright, opening the factor 30 lotion he had applied to Liv's back earlier, inhaling the scent deep into his lungs, coating his insides with it. Coconut, summer, surfing, Liv's soft skin. He squeezed out a large, drizzly mound onto his palm and applied it liberally to his face, arms, and legs, but it didn't soothe him.

Maybe now this smell would always remind him of the day Liv disappeared.

A rustle in the undergrowth behind him.

"Liv?"

But it was the guy, Kirk, again, and his dog, leading a pair of cops. The hiker was pointing to Jake, saying something, then gesturing to the clifftop, the water below.

Jake fell back against the rocks again. It was their job to find her now. He'd done everything he could. And failed.

When the officers spoke to Jake, trying to get him to sit up, he could barely acknowledge them. He'd lost all capacity to speak. He heard things: words, jumbled sentences, mutterings.

"Not in a good way, officer."

"—last time you saw Miss Grainger?—"

"Purse is still here, clothing too, so—"

"—would be long dead by now if she'd fallen in the—"

"—Her engagement ring? Ah, okay—"

30

"—can't drive like this."

At some point, somebody shoved their shoulder under his armpit and led him through the forest, back to the track. Not into his and Liv's car — the one with the note on top. Instead, he was guided into the back of the police car, a hand on top of his head.

Like a criminal.

CHAPTER 5: OLIVIA

May 31

"I'll be honest. I've never seen a case like this."

I shift uncomfortably in the creaky leather chair in the doctor's large office. The gray sweatshirt and sweatpants Marcus had handed me from the hospital's spare clothing stash are hot and oversized. "You'll still look great in them," he'd reassured me, generously. He'd given me some shampoo and conditioner so I could wash my hair in the shower room. It was the only highlight of an otherwise very bleak day — the darkest of my life, despite the bright sunshine outside my big window. A day spent lying in that hospital bed, staring out over Wilmington and the river, the sun sparkling on the water. Wondering where Jake might be, among that view. He works at some private law firm downtown, they'd said.

The doctor performing my psych evaluation, Dr. Stephens, clicks the end of his pen, his barrage of questions apparently over. "I've discussed it with colleagues. None of us has ever seen a case of amnesia combined with a personality disorder that results in a patient believing they are somebody else — somebody who exists in reality, or once existed. Fascinating." He examines me like I'm a specimen.

"We think it might be a multiple personality disorder," he continues, "potentially one you've been living with for a long time. Somehow the trauma of your recent accident has gotten you stuck in a false version of your identity. One thing I feel sure of is that you believe you are telling me *your* truth — there's nothing to indicate otherwise. Hmm." He clicks his pen again.

"Maybe you were friends with Liv Grainger as a child, and the tragedy of her death stayed with you in ways you never dealt with, so you adopted a version of her as part of your split personality. However, until we know who you really are, we can't source your medical records to figure that out . . ."

I tune him out. My appointment in the behavioral health building today was something I'd been dreading, but at least I'm out of the ward. At least I'm talking to somebody new. It's only been a few days, and already I feel imprisoned by these hospital walls. Already sick of the food. Already wary of anybody in authority. But also, already terrified of what may lie beyond these walls.

Already institutionalized.

"—You're getting your DNA swab and fingerprints today, right?" Dr. Stephens is asking. "Perhaps that will help our identity problem."

Our identity problem? I nod, a sullen teenager. I know who I am.

The doctor raises his eyebrows. "Well, I'll write this up, but I'll need to keep monitoring you for any changes. If you do have multiple personality disorder, we can hope you'll . . . switch back and give us some clarity."

I purse my lips. "I don't know how long I'll be able to stay here and keep having these appointments. Apparently, in this nightmare version of reality, I don't have any health insurance."

Dr. Stephens tilts his head, clicking his pen again. "That's interesting. You didn't mention that earlier. The idea of this being a 'nightmare version of reality.' Is that how you feel about your situation?"

I laugh, humorlessly. "Sure. One minute I'm Liv Grainger, happy, engaged, successful in business, loved by my family and friends, safe, financially secure . . . The next moment, I'm in a world that doesn't want me, accused of being an identity thief, and the people I love most say they don't know me, apart from as a child who is supposedly dead."

My throat thickens.

"I have literally nothing in this world. I don't even know how I'm going to eat, once I'm no longer being handed this hospital food. I'm wearing a stranger's clothes. I'm not an official refugee, or in any kind of social group that would entitle me to go to a specific charity for help. If I have to leave this hospital, I'm a panhandler on a street corner." My voice hitches and I stop, trying not to cry. Again. "Yes, this is *absolutely* a nightmare version of reality."

The doctor makes more notes, nodding, his brow furrowed. He seems both fascinated by me and detached. The wedding ring on his left hand glints, taunting me. Tonight, Dr. Stephens will go home to his spouse and talk about what an interesting case he is working on. My desperate situation makes his life better, gives him something to share with his loved one over a glass of wine. *He* will sleep soundly tonight.

I may never sleep soundly again.

"Do you think this is a different version of reality than the one in which you are Liv Grainger?" Dr. Stephens asks. Click. Click. "Some kind of parallel universe, or alternate timeline?"

The silver birch tree outside his window ripples in a gentle breeze. I huff, more at the tree's innocent beauty than at the doctor. "That would be crazy. It's impossible. And I'm *not* crazy."

The doctor puts his notepad and pen down. "Of course. Well, thank you for sharing with me today, Olivia. I'll file this report and Dr. Connor will let you know when your follow-up will be." We both rise and I follow him to the door. He pauses as I step through.

"Have a good rest."

"Thank you, doctor. And thank you for calling me Olivia. You're the first person to do that."

He nods, closing the door behind me.

I can't go back to my bed, not just yet. Now that I'm finally dressed, I can wander around the grounds. I step out of the building's main doors and take a left along the green space that divides it from the main hospital building. There's a shady area with benches, where I sit for the sake of sitting, wishing I had a book or my phone or something to take my mind off this terrible reality I'm in.

In this world, I don't own a single book.

The breeze blows my hair across my face, and I brush it back with my hands, twisting it over my shoulder.

Or a hair tie. Not even a piece of elastic.

I let out a breath, shaking myself out of it. The list of what I don't have could go on forever, and the woe-is-me, I-have-nothing attitude is getting old fast. I have to figure out how to fix this.

In the meantime, the brown-eyed police detective and his sidekick are coming back this afternoon to take my fingerprints, after which Dr. Connor is going to take a cheek swab for a DNA test that Detective Banks requisitioned. Maybe the fingerprints or DNA test will help prove my identity. And as for reading, I'll bet there's a hospital library somewhere.

One step at a time.

I get up and wander back into the main building, wandering aimlessly down the corridors on my way back to my room. There's a gift shop — which I can't buy anything at — and a café, the smells of which make me hungry. I'd *kill* for a croissant.

I check the wall clock. 2.43 p.m. Nearly time for the cookie round. They might not leave them if I'm not in my room, so I scurry along the corridors and up three flights of stairs. I'm back in bed, and in my hospital-issue gown, before my cellophane packet of chocolate chip cookies arrives. Craving the comfort of sugar, I devour them in seconds, bereft when the last crumbs are gone.

Detective Banks and Officer Phelps show up at my room a half-hour later, taking their previous seats at my bedside.

"How are you holding up?" Detective Banks asks, a kind smile in his eyes. "You're looking a little brighter."

"I washed my hair, thank goodness. That's probably the difference." I make an effort to smile back. "And I had my psych eval today. That went fine. Except the doctor has no idea what's wrong with me. But hopefully all this," I wave my hands about, "can help us figure it out."

He nods. "Okay, then. Gary," he turns to the young officer, who reaches into his bag and takes out an ink pad, a card with ten empty boxes, and a swab kit. "So, there's nothing to worry about. Gary's just going to ink each of your fingers and thumbs. Then you'll press them down into the boxes on this card, okay? And we'll swab your cheek for DNA. Then our team runs the results to see if you're already in the database. In case you're someone that police have come across before."

"I see. That makes sense."

The detective turns to his younger officer. "Start with this one."

Officer Phelps guides my hand with his own, gently pressing each of the pads of my fingers and thumbs onto the inky sponge tray, before maneuvering each one to his finger-print card. He gives me a wet wipe to help remove some of the ink, then asks me to open wide as he swabs the inside of my cheek with a large cotton bud.

"All done." Officer Phelps places the swab in a clear tube and seals it.

Detective Banks nods his approval and turns back to me. "The fingerprints will be analyzed in the next twenty-four hours. And the DNA sample will be sent directly to the lab, and they'll have a pattern for us to check against records in a couple of days."

I try not to feel despondent. I've never been arrested, or even hospitalized. And how else would I be in the system? But I can't think about that now.

I attempt to smile, but it feels more like a grimace. "What about my parents? Have they agreed to take a DNA test?"

"We asked them if they'd consider it. No decision yet." Detective Banks rises from his chair, and his young charge follows. "We'll keep you posted, I promise." He lays his hand on my bare arm, and my skin prickles. He looks directly into my eyes, hesitating a moment. "Just hang in there. And try to stay positive. We'll figure it out. It's just taking a while, is all."

I do a better job of smiling this time. "Thanks, Detective. Both of you." I nod at the other officer. "I appreciate the help."

"You're welcome, Liv," Detective Banks replies. He hurries to catch up with his trainee, who's already walking away.

Liv.

He called me Liv.

Maybe he believes me.

CHAPTER 6: OLIVIA

June 2

I lift my feet onto the window ledge, sitting back, examining cloud formations and the constantly shifting shadows they cast over the city. The book I'm reading from the hospital library is a fun, chick-lit read — the kind I like — but today it sits unopened on my lap. It doesn't suit my dark mood. I should probably take this time to read *War and Peace* or something else serious, depicting troubled times. It's too hard to read about beautiful people falling in love right now — their beach houses, their jobs, their cars, their fancy dinners. These people aren't even real, yet I'm desperately jealous of them. They feel more real than I am.

I'm a non-person. An anomaly. A glitch in the Matrix.

I've been spending most of my time sitting at the window these past days. I refuse to lie in bed — I may be stuck in hospital indefinitely, but I'm not sick. Marcus found me a much better-fitting pair of jeans and a faded Whitesnake T-shirt yesterday, along with a battered pair of ballet flats. They are tight, but at least better than the flip-flops I wore to my psych eval.

I've created a little routine of sorts — showering before breakfast, spending the morning journaling my thoughts with a notepad and the plastic Bic pen Marcus provided, followed by a walk in the hospital grounds after lunch, and an attempt at reading before dinner.

That has been thrown off by this morning's news. It was delivered by Marcus after a call from Detective Banks, saying my DNA results had come in, and there was no trace of me in the system. Of course, this is no surprise to me. Why would my DNA be in their database? In this world, I died when I was twelve.

But at least the police know I'm not some registered criminal trying to pull a scam, I suppose. Although I could still be a criminal, just one not in their system.

My only hope is that Mom and Dad agree to a DNA test to compare mine against. Although, I'm terrified of that too.

What if it comes back and we don't match?

What if I'm *not* who I think I am, after all?

What if I really am an unidentifiable amnesiac with multiple personality disorder?

My gaze is fixated on the distant converted warehouse office building Jake works in — at least in my world. But I don't see it. I only see me, as if from above, sitting day after day in an institution like this one, only with more bars. Fading away in a state-run psychiatric hospital filled with other impoverished, mentally disturbed people.

Or living on the street, eating at soup kitchens, and begging for change.

Yep, things are not looking great for me right now.

I turn back to my novel. I've got to distract myself, even if it's with these sickeningly fabulous characters and their lobster dinners.

I've barely made it a few sentences when some heavy footsteps alert me to Marcus's presence. It's not his usual time. I turn and smile in a way that I hope passes as cheerful.

Marcus pushes aside the curtain by my bed. It's hard to read his expression. "You have visitors."

My smile drops and my jaw slackens as I take in the people stepping tentatively into my space.

Mom and Dad, followed closely by Detective Banks and Officer Phelps.

I emit something between a cry and a yelp, my face crumbling as Mom's eyes widen, her mouth opening in shock.

"Mom," I manage, my voice breaking. "Dad. You came." I stand, trying to greet them, but my legs are unsteady and I have to lean on the bed.

Mom doesn't look the same as when I last saw her, less than a week ago. She's let her hair go fully gray, as if she didn't have me around to encourage her when she wanted to dye it, and it's shorter and finer than before. She looks older, thinner, seemingly even more petite. Dad, on the other hand, tall and usually lean, has put on weight.

They don't make a move to hug me. Dad's brow is deeply furrowed, while Mom looks like . . . well, like she's just seen her dead daughter rise from the grave. She's ashen-faced, staring at me.

Marcus pulls two plastic chairs forward, and turns my leather chair to face them. He guides me back down into my seat, his hand supporting my arm. Detective Banks does the same for Mom, who has been frozen in place. The detective steps to the side, standing with his young colleague, as Marcus stands beside me. Our official chaperones to this bizarre meeting.

Detective Banks turns to me. "Mr. and Mrs. Grainger decided they wanted to come meet you, to see you for themselves. I hope that's okay with you."

I nod, my tongue too solid in my mouth.

Mom is leaning toward me, her eyes reddening, the lashes damp. Dad sits beside her, his face stern, jaw set hard.

He speaks first, in a flat monotone that sounds so different from his usual warm, engaging voice.

"Okay, then. You say you are our daughter, Olivia. But you also know we lost her when she was twelve. So, who are you? And why are you pretending to be Livvie?"

I shake my head, a tear escaping down my cheek. "I don't know how to explain it." My voice is thick. "I know I am your daughter. I'm Liv Grainger. I'm twenty-eight, and I live with Jake Johnson, who is my fiancé, and we have dinner with you at your house in Landfall every Sunday. I'm very close with you, with Charlotte, too. In my . . . version of events, I didn't die at twelve. I lived. And we're happy. We love each other—" That last bit does it, and I have to stop, my eyes filling with tears. Marcus hands me a tissue from the side of the bed.

Mom is sitting even further forward, her hands on her lap almost reaching my knee. She speaks at last. "You look *just* like our Livvie," she mutters, almost to herself. "Just like she'd be now, if she'd grown up to be a woman. And a lot like Charlotte, only taller. We always knew Livvie would have been tall. Just like you, Burt."

"I *am* her, Mom. I am. I'm not lying."

I lean forward, taking her hands in mine. Her fingers are cold. I search her face for some glimmer of recognition.

"Look at me. Don't you know me? I don't just look like her, I *am* her. You know it." I lift one finger to my left eyebrow. "See this scar here? Remember? That's from when I was ten and Jake was chasing me round the Johnsons' glass coffee table. I slipped and hit my face. There was so much blood. Jake's dad had to take me to the ER. You were so mad at him, remember? For not stopping us running around."

Mom's face crumples, tears welling up. "I remember . . . I remember."

"And these moles on my arms," I continue, encouraged, "when I was—oh, about eight, we connected them with a pen and this one was like the Big Dipper? But we didn't realize the pen was a permanent marker so I had arm constellations for weeks."

Mom is nodding, crying hard now.

"How could I know all this, if I'm not really her?" I continue, squeezing her hand. "I can tell you a thousand things from my childhood that you'll remember. Why would I even lie about this? I know how impossible it sounds."

"To scam us out of our money, that's why," Dad interjects, his voice cold. "A good con artist does their research,

41

and preys on people who are wealthy — and vulnerable, like someone grieving. And yes, we're still grieving our daughter, even after sixteen years. Our daughter is *dead*. I held her lifeless body in my arms." His voice breaks slightly but he carries on, his expression resolute. "We buried her." He takes Mom's other hand. "You're either delusional or a liar — there's no other option."

I let out a breath. "I get it. I know that's what makes sense. But I'm telling you, there's another option. One we can't understand. One that seems totally impossible, yet true. There has to be. Me being alive in this — this, well, other timeline where you lost me as a child, that's the third option. You always said, didn't you, there are things . . . what's that quote? Something like, '*There are more things in heaven and earth . . . than can be dreamt of—*' something. Right?"

"'*Dreamt of in your philosophy.*' Hamlet to Horatio," Dad huffs.

"Burt." Mom's voice is small. "Just look at her. *Look*. It's her. It couldn't be anyone else."

Dad crosses his arms, turning away.

Mom's grip on my hand tightens. "Detective Banks said you've had a DNA swab taken. You want us to have one too, is that right? To prove you're our daughter?"

I glance up at Detective Banks, who is staring at me. He blinks and looks away, as if waking from a dream, then nods.

"Will you do it?" I ask Mum. I don't even look at Dad.

She musters a smile through her tears. "Yes. We've got to find out for sure if this miracle is true. If our Lord has truly answered my prayers and given us back our daughter."

My brow creases. Neither of my parents is religious, although both grew up with churchgoing families. But then, the Tilly Grainger in my version of life didn't tragically lose her twelve-year-old daughter.

For the first time, I wonder what else might be different. What did my apparent death at twelve change, in this world?

I push the thought away. First things first. "The police already have my results, so all their lab needs are your swabs for comparison. But," I shake my head, "I'm scared, Mom. What if I'm some crazy person who doesn't know who she really is? I'm scared of what we'll discover."

Mom squeezes my hand at this, especially my use of the word 'Mom'.

Dad turns back to me, his eyes cold, hard. "All the more reason to get this test done. We have to figure out who you really are."

Mom wants to do this test to prove I'm her daughter, miraculously resurrected. Dad wants to do it to prove I'm not. To prove I'm a psychotic con artist.

Either way, I guess we'll find out.

CHAPTER 7: JAKE

May 28

Jake woke at dawn, in the wrong bed, but one he wasn't entirely unfamiliar with. That must be what the deep-rooted, twisting feeling in his stomach was about. He was just in an unexpected place. Nothing else bad. Merely temporary disorientation.

Where was he?

He sat up, looking about the room, noting the green curtains, the palm prints framed on the wall, the pale green sheets with a tiny floral print he was lying on. Ah, right. The guest room at Tilly and Burt's, his soon-to-be in-laws. He'd stayed over. He blinked, rubbed his eyes. They had come to his and Liv's place for a while last night, then taken him home with them. But why?

Something weird.

There had been police.

No. *No. No, no, no, no.*

Liv disappearing at the quarry.

Him screaming her name, searching for her, underwater, through the forest. Hair, reeds, slipping through his fingers.

That can't have really happened. It was all a nightmare. Just vicious, pre-wedding dreams.

She would be in the ensuite bathroom right now. In a moment, she'd come out and smile at him. She'd be naked, gently lit in the cool morning light. She'd let him admire her body for a moment, the full swell of her breasts, her generous nipples, the hourglass of her waist and hips, which always made him want to play her like a cello. She'd laugh at his rapt expression and slide into bed, kissing him, running her fingertips down his stomach, shushing him when he groaned so her folks wouldn't hear. They'd silently make love, her on top of him, rocking her body to fulfilment. She'd muffle a cry into a pillow as she came, and they'd chuckle again, holding each other.

He sank back onto the bed. Waited for the sound of water running in the bathroom, the flush of the toilet.

And waited.

And waited.

Silence.

She wasn't in there.

She wasn't anywhere.

His keen ears picked up a more distant sound. A strangled sobbing cry, high-pitched. Tilly, Liv's sweet mom. A man's voice, low tones pleading. Burt. Liv's poor parents.

Jake pulled on shorts and a T-shirt, wondering when he'd last seen his cellphone. Liv might be calling him. Where was it? He had to find it.

He padded lightly down the wide stairs of the Graingers' elegant home, making his way to the great room, immaculately decorated in the beachy blues and grays Liv had designed. In the white kitchen, clutching the marble island counter, Tilly was exhaling controlled breaths, her blonde hair uncharacteristically unkempt. Burt, ever gruff and practical, was making green tea by the kettle. They both stared at Jake blankly, as if they had no idea what he was doing in their home.

"Uh, hi." Jake walked over the island and took a stool. If he looked directly at Tilly he might start blubbing like a baby all over again. He'd done enough of that yesterday. Tilly didn't seem able to look at him either.

"Morning, Jake," Burt replied. "Coffee? Green tea?"

"None, thanks. Have you guys seen my cellphone? I don't want to miss . . . any calls."

Burt nodded to the sideboard. "It's charging. How did you sleep?"

"Like I was drugged," Jake admitted. He slipped off the stool, crossing the room to unplug the phone. Glancing at it, he saw several missed calls, but nothing from Liv. Sucking in a breath, he walked back to the island and resumed his seat. He murmured, "I barely remember anything after the cops arrived at the quarry."

Burt placed a mug of tea in front of his trembling wife. "We had to bring you home after the police left your place. You were kind of out of it. Not quite catatonic, you were responsive, but barely. I gave you and Tilly each an Ambien. You've had a terrible shock, son. We all have."

"I can't feel anything. I've no clue what's happening." Jake gripped the counter tightly, just like Tilly was. "Where *is* she, Burt? I don't understand any of this."

Burt's expression was grim. "I dunno, son. The police are coming here this morning. They want to talk to us some more. The way she disappeared, without even any *clothes*, her engagement ring left behind . . . They're taking this very seriously." Liv's imposing father stared down at him.

Deeply uncomfortable, Jake broke eye contact. *Yes, Mr. Grainger, Liv was naked. We did have sex in broad daylight just moments before she vanished off the face of the earth.*

He nodded. "Good, I'm glad they're taking it seriously," he replied. "We need a major search party in the forest, right now. The only thing I can think is that she ran to hide in the trees, and somehow got hurt and couldn't respond to me, or was unconscious or . . . something. She could be out there. It wasn't a cold night, right? She'd still be okay. That's the only possible solution. Aside from . . ." Jake stopped.

"Aside from if she's in the lake," Burt finished for him.

Tilly, silent until this moment, let out a strangled noise. She rushed from the kitchen up the stairs, her tea untouched on the counter.

"We've got to be strong for them," Burt said in a low tone. "No matter what has happened to Liv. Right, son?"

But Jake didn't want to be strong. He wanted to sob and wail like Tilly. He wanted to beg the police to find her. He wanted to plead with the universe to give him his Liv back.

"Of course," he managed. "Hey, what happened to Liv's stuff? Her purse, her cellphone, her house keys?"

"We have it," Burt replied, putting Tilly's mug in front of Jake. "The police gave it to us last night. So we know Liv doesn't even have her phone." He nodded to where Liv's sleek gold iPhone was lying on the coffee table.

Shit.

Jake drank Tilly's bitter tea and spent an hour texting all his friends and immediate family members, especially those who were closest to Liv, starting with Nicole, her closest friend.

JAKE: Hey Nicole. Have you seen or spoken to Liv in the last 24 hours?

NICOLE: Nope. What's up? Did you guys have a fight?

JAKE: No. We were at the quarry yesterday, celebrating our engagement anniversary. Liv went for a walk and, there's no easy way to say this, but she basically vanished. I couldn't find her and she didn't come home last night. The cops are involved now. We have no idea where she could be.

NICOLE: WTF Jake?! That's awful! Does she have her phone?

JAKE: She didn't take anything with her. I have her cellphone and house keys. I was hoping she'd been in touch with you. We're all super worried about her. I'm at her folks' place, and the police are coming round soon. Hoping they'll send out a search party.

NICOLE: OMG. No, I've heard nothing. Of course, I'll call you immediately if I do. Fuck!! So sorry. Please let me know if there's anything at all I can do, and keep us all posted, okay? I'll call around. Talk to you soon. Hugs x

JAKE: Thanks Nicole, yeah, I totally will. Hopefully she'll turn up and there'll be a good story. Talk soon.

At just before 10 a.m., Liv's sister Charlotte banged on the front door, tears streaming unchecked down her cheeks as her dad let her in. After giving her a kiss, Burt made his excuses, quickly escaping to the terrace. Tilly hadn't come downstairs after her tearful breakdown, so Jake and Charlotte were alone.

"Hey, Char," Jake said, already exhausted.

She stood facing him. "What the hell? Jake! Oh my God!"

It hurt to look at her. Charlotte was fully six inches shorter than his fiancée, but her shoulder-length hair was so like Liv's. Just the thought of those soft chestnut locks was enough to crush him.

"What happened? Mom said you guys were at the quarry and she just vanished. Without taking any of her stuff? How is that even possible?"

Jake shrugged. He had no words. His face began to crumple again.

"Oh, Jake, honey." Charlotte led Jake to the couch like a child, sitting down with her arm around him, hugging him tight. Both of them were sniffing back tears.

"There's got to be a good reason, we just don't understand it yet," Jake eventually replied, more to himself than Charlotte.

"And you found her ring? On a rock?"

Fuck. Did he still have it?

Jake dug around his shorts pocket, feeling the hard stone, the coldness of the platinum band. Thank Christ. It was as if he'd found a tiny piece of Liv. He pulled it out and handed it to Charlotte.

"Okay, we gotta keep this somewhere safer than your baggy pockets," Charlotte muttered, staring at it. "She loves this ring. I got this for a while, okay? Just for safekeeping, until we find her."

"Thanks."

The doorbell rang, singing its overly cheerful little tune.

"That'll be the cops," Charlotte said, as she headed towards the door. "Dad said they'd be here at ten."

She let the two men in, as Burt came in from the terrace. "I'll go get Mom — she'll want to be here for this."

The cops stood awkwardly, taking care to keep to the hardwood floor and not step on the whiter-than-white rug.

"Mr. Grainger, Mr. Johnson," the older one said, "How are you? I hope you folks managed to get some sleep."

Burt gestured for them to sit. They were both young. The older one, clearly in charge, was a stocky, dark-haired guy of no more than thirty. His companion was an acne-covered, skinny young man in his early twenties who looked alarmed at the entire situation, shifting uncomfortably in his seat.

"Thank you, Detective," Burt replied. "Not much sleep, no. We're all still in shock. Have you got any news? Hopefully my wife . . . ah, here she is now."

The normally well-groomed Tilly was led into the great room by her younger daughter. She looked disheveled, her eyes red-rimmed, nose scarlet from crying. Charlotte sat her mother in the armchair across from Jake, perching herself on its arm before nodding at the policemen.

The detective politely half-stood while the women settled. "I'm Detective Adam Banks, and this is my trainee, Officer Gary Phelps. Thank you all for being here this morning. I know it's difficult." He looked enquiringly at Charlotte.

"Hi, I'm Charlotte, Liv's sister. Do you have an update?" She looked at the detective hopefully.

"Nothing has been uncovered yet, no," he replied. "We would like to ask Mr. Johnson some more questions, if you're up to it." He gave Jake a half-smile. "It's been less than twenty-four hours, so we still have plenty of cause for optimism. These cases are usually a matter of a misunderstanding. There's often a good explanation for what's happened — perhaps something that isn't yet obvious. That said, it's unusual for someone to disappear without their clothes or any of their personal possessions — cellphone, credit cards, and such. So, we want to move quickly on this."

Charlotte frowned. "What? She had no *clothes*? Dad, you didn't tell me that." She turned to Jake. "Why would she have no clothes on? What were you . . . ?"

Jake raised his eyebrows at her, and Charlotte stopped, instantly understanding.

"We were celebrating the anniversary of our engagement," Jake explained to Detective Banks. "There was nobody else at the quarry. It was kind of our secret place."

"Of course," Detective Banks said, as his trainee scribbled away, blushing. "Although I should mention you were on private property. Anyways, the circumstances do mean that Ms. Grainger likely couldn't have gone far, and it probably wasn't premeditated on her part, given she left her purse and phone."

He looked at the Graingers, his smile kind. "This is helpful. It means we have a reasonably defined search area, at least to start. Our team is already on their way, right now, and Officer Phelps and I are heading out to join them. We will cover it in a grid system, combing through all the surrounding forest, in case she's in there and has been injured, or there are any clues as to her whereabouts."

Detective Banks glanced back at Jake. "If nothing turns up in our initial search of the forest, we also need to look at the lake, which will involve divers and potentially a dredging system. We understand you found her engagement ring at the bottom of a cliff, is that correct?"

Jake nodded. "Yeah, on the flat rocks below the highest point of the cliff."

"And where was she when you last saw her?"

"Taking a walk, heading along the ridge toward that the highest point. I was packing up the picnic, giving her a minute. She was wearing her ring at that time, but . . . you know. Nothing else."

Detective Banks twisted his mouth. "That would suggest she took the ring off at the high point of the ridge and dropped it, or even threw it over. Mr. Johnson, did the two of you have a fight? Why did you need to 'give her a minute'?"

"No. No fight. Nothing like that," Jake replied, aware that Burt's eyes were narrowed, and Charlotte and her mother were staring at him. "We'd been talking about the wedding, and she was . . . antsy, I guess. Maybe a little nervous, but nothing to be concerned about. As far as I knew." His last words fell into silence.

"And the ring couldn't have fallen off accidentally? It wasn't too big?"

Jake shook his head. "We'd had it resized — it fit perfectly."

Detective Banks turned to Charlotte. "Perhaps your sister confided in you about having cold feet?"

Charlotte frowned. She was stroking her mother's arm. "No, not really. I mean, I always tease her about how she'll never know what it would be like to be with anyone other than Jake, and she'll get defensive. One time she asked if I thought Jake might get bored with her — feel he was missing out." She half-smiled. "I told her she was an idiot. Anyone can see you're mad about her," she added, nodding at Jake. "Generally she seemed excited about the wedding, wasn't she, Mom? Liv had it all planned down to the last detail — like, I'm her maid of honor and I really don't have anything to help out with, except plan a bachelorette party. Everything's already booked and paid for."

She wrinkled her nose. "Plus, even if she was having second thoughts, she would never just run out on Jake. Not in a million years. And not *naked*. No," she shook her head, her voice thickening, "something must've . . . happened to her."

Tilly emitted a small sob, and Charlotte kissed the top of her head.

"Okay, then," Detective Banks said, rising, gesturing for his colleague to do the same. "That's all for now. Obviously the next twenty-four hours will be crucial, and we'll keep you informed. You can expect several phone calls today as we go through our search. But you folks need to stay put, in case she shows up. You can keep her cellphone for the moment, and we'll let you know if we need it. And we'll keep hold of Olivia's clothes for now, until we know more.

"Mr. Johnson." He turned to Jake. "I recommend you go home, in case she manages to make her way there. But please don't go anywhere else. Or leave town." He nodded to Burt and Charlotte. Tilly was weeping into her shoulder. "We'll speak later."

Burt stood and ushered the officers out.

Don't leave town.

That sounded ominous.

In these situations, it was always the boyfriend or husband, right? Was Jake under suspicion? Did the Graingers think he'd done something to Liv?

"I've got to get home," Jake muttered, to nobody in particular. "He's right. If Liv managed to make her way there, she didn't have her keys, and I've been here all night—"

"I'll drop you." Charlotte picked up her car keys. "We can bring Liv's cell. Keep both your phone and hers charged and on full volume, in case we need to call you, or in case somebody calls Liv, and they know something."

Charlotte was packing up Liv's leather purse. Tilly was still crying. "Dad," Charlotte said to Burt, who looked defeated, "you need to take Mom upstairs to bed, bring her a cup of tea, and let her rest, okay? And stay by the phone."

Burt nodded. "Okay, honey. Bye. Be safe."

Charlotte drove Jake the ten minutes through the Landfall community, out to the highway, over the creek bridge, and along to the street to the little bungalow he and Liv had bought last year. The fresh coat of yellow paint was obnoxiously cheerful in the May sunshine.

"You'll be okay," Charlotte laid a sisterly hand on his arm. "We'll find her. Like they said, it hasn't even been twenty-four hours yet." Her voice wavered on the last part — for the first time, she looked unsure.

Jake bit his lip thoughtfully, finally nodding. "Thanks Char." He climbed out, his long legs always awkward in Charlotte's little car, and walked along the front path.

He'd half-expected to find Liv's scratched, bruised, naked body slumped on the front stoop, having made an epic journey all the way home only to find herself unable to get inside. She could have died overnight on the doorstep because he'd been lying in comfort in the Graingers' green guest room, knocked out on sleeping pills to ease *his* pain, *his* suffering.

But their stoop was empty. As was the house.

All the warmth and beauty Liv had breathed into creating their home, with its soft white couch, taupe pillows, barnwood feature wall above the small fireplace, rustic dining table, and mismatched chairs — all of it seemed cold and lifeless now. Without Liv.

Where *was* she?

He was fairly sure the police wouldn't find her in the forest. The ring had been by the water — she must have gone into the lake. Would the divers find her beautiful body, bloated and white, in its depths?

Jake's body buckled at the thought. He doubled over, collapsing to his knees on the refinished oak floors that he and Liv had spent so much time on. Palms on wood, he retched, over and over again, throwing up nothing but green tea and stomach acid, until his body finally gave up and he slumped, exhausted, to the floor.

CHAPTER 8: OLIVIA

June 6

It's been three days since I last saw Mom, and four since she and Dad first came to visit me. When the two of them returned to the hospital the next day to have their cheeks swabbed for the DNA test, Mom came to spend an hour with me while Dad remained stubbornly in the cafeteria. And we just talked and talked.

After all the memories Mom and I shared, many of my biggest childhood moments up until I was twelve, I'm pretty sure I've convinced her that I'm me, even without the DNA results. And if I can convince Mom, it's only a matter of time until she can convince Dad.

But there's also Charlotte. Mom said she was not buying my story — 'not for a single second.' Charlotte's probably going to be even tougher to persuade than Dad. I don't blame her. She'd barely remember me. She was six when I was twelve. She would've grown up as an only child, pretty much.

I also told Mom a lot about what happened to me since — after I didn't die, in my version of reality. Growing up in our huge old house as a teenager, going to Rocky Point High, and then to design school in Wilmington because I didn't want to be far from home. All about my interior design business, how I helped her decorate the house at Landfall where she and Dad had retired to, after selling the big house. And about me and Jake, how we went from childhood friends to sweethearts, prom king and queen, and eventually live-in partners, and, finally, an engaged couple.

She <u>believed</u> me.

She even called me Livvie.

The name came out, and she started at the sound of it. But I knew, then, that she believed me.

I'll have to let her work on Dad. I'll have to work on Charlotte. Assuming the DNA test comes back as a match, that is. If not, I'm on my own again. And, I guess, totally delusional.

As for Jake — I've no idea what I'll say to him.

If I'll even get to see him.

I set my journal and pen on the shady bench that has become a favored spot, away from the bustle of the hospital corridors. Something tugs at me, breaking my concentration. The sound of my name, being carried off in the breeze.

"Olivia."

I turn, searching for it.

Detective Adam Banks is striding toward me. "I found you," he says with a somewhat breathless smile, his brown eyes crinkling at the corners. "I was looking everywhere. Gary is, too. Searching for you deep in the bowels of the hospital. I'll probably never see him again." He laughs, taking out his phone. "Let me text him."

I wait, eyebrows raised, until the detective slips his phone into his pocket. "What's up that you needed to send out a search party?"

"Mr. and Mrs. Grainger came to visit. They're waiting in the Lighthouse Café. The lab sent me the result of the DNA swab comparison."

"Really? That was faster than I thought." My pulse quickens. "Well?"

He gestures for me to follow him. "I want to tell you all together."

We hurry toward the hospital entrance, stepping aside as a stressed-looking group of first responders rush past us with two gurneys.

"The Lighthouse Café, huh?" I reply as we resume our quick pace down the corridor, hoping my casual tone will disguise the nerves that have my stomach churning. "What a luxury. I haven't eaten anything but tiny trays of hospital food for nine days. I have to warn you, I have no money. I hope someone else is paying."

Detective Banks chuckles, squeezing past a gaggle of student doctors. "I'm sure one of us can stand you a coffee and a pastry."

A pastry. Even with my guts flipping, that sounds amazing.

We enter the glass-lined café space, where Mom and Dad are waiting at a table, speaking in low, anxious tones. I've seen them huddle like that a thousand times — usually trying to hide some kind of disagreement in a public space.

They don't greet me as I sit, although Mom half-smiles, her lips slightly open. I can tell she wants to say "Hi, Livvie" or "Hi, honey," but she won't — not in front of Dad. Not until we know which way these results have gone.

I pull in my chair and say "Hi" almost under my breath, then take a sip of water from the glass waiting for me.

"Hi," Mom replies, after an awkward pause.

Dad looks only at Detective Banks. "You wanted us together for this, detective. Let's get to it."

Detective Banks has barely pulled in his own chair. He opens his mouth to speak when a server comes up to us.

"What can I get you fine folks?"

Detective Banks smiles at me. "Order what you like. It's on me."

I give him a grateful look. "A latte and a cinnamon roll, if you have them."

Detective Banks grins, keeping his eyes on me. "Make it two."

"English Breakfast tea," Mom says.

Dad shakes his head — nothing. Too stubborn to even enjoy his usual Americano in my presence.

"Let's have it," he presses as the server departs. "What are the results?"

Detective Banks places his hands on the table, a show of authority. He looks at each of us in turn. "The DNA strands were compared in the lab and, while there's never a 100% guarantee, this is as close as you'd get. A 99.9% chance that Olivia really is . . . Olivia. She is definitely your daughter."

He pulls out a printed piece of paper, a test tube logo on the letterhead, and hands it to Dad.

I blow out a steady stream of air I hadn't realized I was holding in. I reach across the table for Mom's hand, and she grasps mine, her eyes shining.

"I knew it. I *knew* you were my Livvie, the moment I laid eyes on you. Praise Jesus. It's a miracle."

I pull my gaze from her tear-brimmed eyes toward Dad, who is staring at the printed results. A crease deepens between his bushy eyebrows. "It's just not possible. It can't be."

"It is, Dad. It is."

I stretch my other arm toward him, but the table is too long. He'd have to reach out to touch my hand, and he doesn't. My arm rests foolishly between the table's vase and the salt and pepper shakers.

We sit for a moment, in silence, Detective Banks making a study of my outstretched arm. I pull it in as our drinks and pastries arrive, glad of the interruption.

Detective Banks stirs an unreasonable quantity of sugar into his latte.

"It's up to you all where you want to go from here. Obviously, there's no precedent for any of this, so it's hard for us to offer guidance. But right now, Olivia is too healthy to be taking up a bed here, and she doesn't have any insurance to pay the hospital bill." He taps his spoon against the side of his mug. "She also doesn't have any money, any bank accounts, or source of income. So, she will need your help.

And since we've established she is, in fact, your daughter . . ." He trails off, sipping his coffee. He's obviously hoping Mom or Dad will make a suggestion.

"She'll come stay with us," Mom replies firmly, as if there's no question. "Of course, she'll come home with us. And we'll take care of the hospital bill."

"Tilly." Dad's voice is a warning.

"Burt, she's our *daughter*. We have to look after her. You heard Detective Banks. She has nothing, not even any way of earning money, of paying for food or shelter. And she can't stay here forever. It'd only be until she's on her feet. She could stay in the pool house, if you're not comfortable—"

"We'll discuss this at home. We're leaving now." Dad's jaw has hardened again.

Mom knows better than to push him, at least in front of us. She'll have to be my advocate now.

Advocate. That word always reminds me of Jake, a legal advocate for women and children fleeing war-torn countries, desperately seeking a new life in America. My hero. If only he could fight for me, here, in this world.

But I can't push the Jake issue. Not yet. I need to get my parents fully on board with my inexplicable resurrection before I try to pick up other relationships.

One step at a time.

Mom takes a hasty sip of her tea as Dad rises, evidently done with this conversation. She gives me an apologetic half-smile. "We'll speak to you very soon," she reassures me, before following him out.

I nod slowly, the latte and cinnamon roll still untouched before me. I can't quite believe the DNA results myself. And I know it's true.

I unfurl some of the sticky pastry and pull off a section, which oozes with cream cheese frosting. I savor it, slowly. It's the first delicious thing I've eaten in over a week. I'm facing my mother's empty chair, but I can feel Detective Banks' eyes on me.

"So, it's true, then," I murmur.

"Looks that way. I can't explain it any better than you can. But the test doesn't lie. At least we know you're not a scammer trying to steal a dead girl's identity."

I laugh, unexpectedly, through a mouthful of frosting. I swallow, chasing it down with my coffee. "Well, thank goodness for small blessings." I wipe the stickiness from my lips with a napkin, turning to face the detective beside me. "Mom seems much more religious than . . . before."

He pushes his lips out with a frown. "I spoke to my senior sergeant about the case. He's been on the force over 25 years and he remembers the Liv Grainger death clearly — how devastated the family was. He said that, after the funeral, he started seeing your mom at his church all the time, always desperately praying. As if that was going to bring you back. She was always alone, though. Never with your dad."

He takes a massive bite of his own sticky roll, so big it barely fits in his mouth, making me smile.

"And here you are now, eating cinnamon rolls with a dead girl," I say, quirking an eyebrow at him. "It must seem totally bizarre to you. I'm very grateful you're being so understanding." I pause. "But I'm surprised you're putting so much time into this, not off somewhere chasing down bad guys. I can't figure out why you've been so incredibly helpful, to be honest."

He sucks cream cheese off his finger, his brown eyes on mine. "Can't you?"

"We all doing okay here?" the server asks, with impeccable timing.

Detective Banks nods, the moment broken. "Just the check, thanks."

I finish my treats as he pays up. "You'll talk to my folks to see what they decide?"

He nods. "I will, but I suspect your mom will be back here in the next day or so to take you home. I'm pretty sure she's a woman who gets her own way, right?"

I laugh. "Usually. Dad gives a lot to have an easy life, as long as he gets his golf and his poker nights."

"Right. Well, ask Marcus to call me if you don't hear from your parents in the next forty-eight hours. Otherwise, I think we're probably done here. It's inexplicable, sure, but no crime has been committed. And, like you say, I've got bad guys to chase. There's no need for me to continue with your case." A small line appears above his nose at this last statement.

I rise, wiping my hands on a paper napkin, the stickiness not budging. "I guess. Well, if I don't see you again, thanks for everything. Especially for the cinnamon roll."

Detective Banks laughs and takes out his phone, no doubt to locate the still-missing Officer Phelps. "You're welcome. It was good to meet you. Liv. I hope I'll see you around."

CHAPTER 9: OLIVIA

June 8

"Look who's here to take you home."

Marcus gives me his flash of a grin and steps aside. Mom, alone, looking small, clutches her purse like someone's going to snatch it. I haven't seen or heard from her since we met in the café two days ago.

"Hi, Livvie." She's finally able to use my name without Dad around, it seems.

I drop the book I've just finished on the tray table, rising. "Mom. I'm so glad you came back. Are we really going home? Is Dad okay with this?"

Thank goodness I pushed through this morning's depression enough to get myself showered and dressed.

Mom gives me a small nod. "He will be. For now, he's agreed you can stay in the pool house. He has some terms, but I think we can work on those."

I let out a breath. "Thank you. Thank you so much." I want to hug her, but she looks so delicate and frail, despite being a fit fifty-six year old. Maybe it's too soon for hugs.

She smiles at me, casting a glance around my curtained space. "I'd ask if you're all packed up, but . . ."

I stretch out my arms. "This is it. And even these clothes don't belong to me."

I nod at Marcus, who gives me another grin. "I think you can keep the clothes," he says with a chuckle. He's looking happy for me. Not just happy, but relieved. As kind as he's been, he must surely be glad I'm now somebody else's problem.

"And the bill?" I ask him with a grimace.

"All taken care of," Marcus replies, with a tiny sideways wink at my mother.

"Thanks, Mom. Again. You're saving my life. Possibly, literally."

I give Marcus a hug, and return the borrowed book to him. "Thanks for everything — you've been great. I'd have been miserable if it weren't for you. Well, even more miserable."

He bear-squeezes me for a moment. "Good luck, Liv. I hope it all works out for you."

Mom is nervously chatty on the car ride home, spewing out the latest gossip about various relatives. Aunt Sandra and Uncle Bob are away on a Norwegian fjord cruise, and my eldest cousin Kate is pregnant. Poor Charlie is still struggling with drugs and went into rehab. All of this is true in my life, too, but I can't tell Mom we discussed it all the last time Jake and I went over for dinner less than a week ago.

One thing remains unsaid. It's clear Mom has told none of our extended family about my miraculous resurrection.

And who's going to believe it, anyways? Even my dad doesn't. I'll be stashed in the pool house like some dirty little secret, and I guarantee Mom and Dad won't be hosting their usual Fourth of July barbecue this year. I would make a pretty shocking surprise guest.

What are Dad's terms for allowing me to live at home? Will I even be allowed to show my face around town?

I don't ask Mom, though. Not yet. She's still jabbering about some second cousin of mine, the cadence of her voice picking up as we near my parents' neighborhood. She pulls in, unexpectedly, outside an AT&T store.

"We need to get you a phone," she announces, getting out of the car.

At least a prepaid cell is something that doesn't require an ID — only money. And it seems Mom is taking care of that aspect. She buys me a basic smartphone and a prepaid plan that will alert her to add money when the balance is running low.

"Thanks so much, Mom. I really appreciate it," I tell her, yet again.

I'm grateful, but . . . wow. I'm going to be forced to rely on her for *everything*, like some helpless kid. Like a twelve-year-old being given her first cellphone. Back to pre-teenage years. Living in my parent's home, eating their food, using their energy. Hoping for some kind of cash allowance so I can buy clothes and toiletries. Hoping they'll let me out. Probably having to ask permission to leave the property.

Mom's chest expands and she beams at me, my gratitude clearly affecting her. Or my helplessness. She has her little girl back.

Thing is, I'm not a little girl anymore.

"You need some clothes, while we're shopping." The cellphone store in Mayfaire is close to a Gap and several other clothing outlets. This might be my best chance to get my hands on something other than these hand-me-down jeans, parentally unapproved T-shirt, and ill-fitting ballet flats. God knows when I'll have the money to go shopping for myself.

"If you don't mind, that would be amazing," I reply. "Just some basics. Nothing from the fancy stores you like — just the Gap and Rack Room."

We spend nearly two hours shopping for jeans, two pairs of shorts, a simple jersey summer dress, three T-shirts, a couple of light sweaters and a supply of underwear, and then to Rack Room for a pair of leather sandals and some sneakers. By the time we're done, I'm almost tearful with gratitude. I'm like a bargain-priced Pretty Woman.

"I'll pay you back for all this, I swear," I tell Mom as we load the bags into the trunk of her Tesla. "When I've figured it all out and I can start earning."

Mom brushes my promise away with her manicured hand. "If I can't spend my money on my long-lost daughter, who can I spend it on? I'm just so happy to be able to do it."

She's noticeably calmer as we wind our way through the gated Landfall community, past row upon row of fancy houses. Do they even have the same house? In my world, Mom and Dad's place is on the far side by the water, close to the country club and golf course where Dad spends his time and Mom plays bridge with her girlfriends. Their house, one of the bigger homes, is on a coveted lot, backing onto the creek that divides the mainland from the long strip of barrier islands sheltering the coastline.

My stomach flips as we park outside the house I know. I get out of the car, grabbing my shopping from the trunk.

"Your father is on the links." Mom's checking her phone. "Let's get you settled in the pool house. We'll catch up with him later."

She takes me down the side of the house and through the locked gate onto the pool terrace, treating me like I've never been here before. For her, I haven't.

"Feel free to use the pool. Oh! We should've bought you a swimsuit. Well, we have some old bikinis of Charlotte's in the guest closet — you can use one of those until we get one for you."

She's clearly enjoying this. Dressing me up like a doll.

"Thanks." It's all I've been able to say all day.

Mom points past the lawned area beyond the pool to where the land drops into mudflats, and their ultra-long dock reaches its wooden arm into the creek, Dad's prized boat gleaming white at the end.

"That's our dock, you can take a walk out there. The view is lovely from the boat house."

I know, Mom. I've been here hundreds of times since you guys moved here four years ago. Jake and I have driven that boat up and down the creek more times than I can count.

She unlocks the pool house, a space I've never stayed in since I've always lived close by. It's a large studio with a lofty vaulted ceiling and French doors to the side of the pool terrace. There's a modern queen bed, dressed in highly questionable floral linens I've never seen before, plus a sitting area with a tufted armchair, a tiny wall of kitchenette, and a small table with two chairs. The far side of the space is taken up by the closed-in bathroom and walk-in closet. Even a pool house needs a walk-in closet, according to my mother. The main room doesn't look as nice as it does in my version, with its pale-blue bamboo bedlinens and navy chaise lounge, but compared with the hospital — indeed, compared with a lot of people's homes — this is heaven.

I drop the shopping onto the bed. "This will be great. I'll be very comfortable."

It's true, but it's also notable that I haven't been accommodated in one of the four luxurious guest bedrooms in the main house. Maybe there's still a residual fear — from Dad, probably — that I'm a scammer on a long con, after all. If they let me sleep in the main house, I might sneak into the safe, and hack their computers and bank accounts.

Better not tell them I already know the safe's combination number, and that it's behind the framed Picasso sketch, and that it guards Mom's wedding diamonds and her grandmother's sapphire necklace.

"I'll leave you to get settled." Mom's looking around as if there's something she needs to do. "Do you want to join us on the terrace for dinner? Your dad will be home in an hour. We'll eat at six."

"Sounds great. Thank you so much." There it is again. That gratitude.

Mom lifts two keys off her keychain, handing them to me. "The back gate, and these doors." She's not giving me a key to the main house, though. It's obvious Dad doesn't want me there. "See you at six. At least you now have some fresh clothes to change into, right?"

I'm clearly expected to discard the faded Whitesnake T-shirt if I'm going to sit down to an alfresco dinner with my parents on the terrace.

"Right. I'll wear that jersey dress. It's such a warm evening."

Mom nods her approval, then leaves me alone in the cool room.

The wide-bladed ceiling fan emits a gentle hum and I sink onto the soft bed beneath it, marveling in my turn of fortune. Doesn't seem like I'll be a panhandler on the streets, at least.

Still, I may have to live in this pool house for the rest of my life, if I can't get proper ID and a Social Security number so I can work or get benefits. Or until I'm written back into Mom and Dad's will.

Charlotte won't like that.

She won't like any of it.

But right now, this is a hell of a lot better than the uncertainty of the past couple of weeks.

Baby steps.

I drift into unconsciousness, waking an hour later to the scrape of chairs. I peek through the closed drapes over the French doors, to see Mom setting a third place at the outdoor dining table.

I shower quickly, thankful I washed my hair this morning, since there is no shampoo in the pool house bathroom and I have none of my own. Another thing to buy. And make-up — I don't own a scrap of make-up. I find an old can of spray deodorant for men and use it sparingly, not wanting to go overboard on the musky scent. Maybe Charlotte has left some toiletries in the house that I can use.

I throw on the new underwear and the short gray jersey dress, adding the tan leather sandals. Mom's no longer outside, but the table is set, and it's nearly six.

I hesitate on the back terrace by the half-open bifold glass doors. I can hear Mom and Dad inside, talking in low voices. They're out of sight, probably at the kitchen island. From where I stand, the open living area is visible, furnished with a completely different couch and color scheme to the one I'm used to. Instead of the beachy blues and grays that

Mom and I chose so carefully — well, mostly *I* chose — it's now decorated in deep reds with splashes of orange. The huge couch is brown leather — the last thing you'd choose for a North Carolina coastal home. It's hideous. But then, in this world, I wasn't around to decorate the interior. And Mom's taste has never been the best.

I step closer to the doors to get a better look at the gaudy painting above the fireplace. Mom and Dad's voices are now audible. Dad doesn't sound happy.

"—how much did the two of you spend on clothes?"

Mom's voice is small. "Just over four hundred dollars, I guess. I know, Burt. I know. But that's how much it costs to buy even the most basic of wardrobes. And she had nothing. Only those awful hospital castoffs. And it's not like we don't have the money. I'd have gladly taken her to some nicer stores, too, but she insisted on going to the Gap and the discount shoe place. So she's not trying to get anything out of us."

A pause. I can just imagine Dad's expression.

"I bought her a prepaid cell, too. Don't look at me like . . . *No*. Uh-uh." Another heavy silence. "Liv needs a phone, Burt. Yes, *Liv*. And I may have to buy her more essentials. She doesn't have any money, Burt, not a dime. And she's our daugh—"

"Tilly, what do you think is going to happen? How's this meant to work?" I can hear the misery in Dad's voice. I want to go to him. Hug him. But I can only imagine how that would go down.

"We're going to feed and clothe her the rest of her life? Let her live in the pool house indefinitely? She's a grown woman, but she won't be able to get a job, Tilly. She . . . she doesn't *exist* as a person, in the eyes of the law. And we . . . we don't know her. She's a stranger."

A clatter of dishes. "She's our *daughter*, Burt. And as for a job, plenty of people come here and get jobs paid under the table. And as for how this will work . . . right now, my love, we're going to sit down and have a meal with our daughter.

We'll figure the rest out as we go . . ." Mom's voice is rising. "Oh Burt. Just don't — *don't* you take away my joy at having her back."

"We don't know who she is, Til. Not really." Dad's voice is barely audible now.

"That's something else we'll figure out as we go. Now, excuse me, I need to get the salad finished."

I step backwards, deliberately scraping a chair against the stone pavers, making myself heard, as if I just arrived at the table. Dad comes out onto the terrace and stops as he sees me, his expression hard to read. "Oh. You're here already."

I smile at him, sitting in my usual spot, since Mom and Dad like the seats with the best view of the creek. "I was invited to join you for dinner at six. I hope that's okay with you."

Dad stretches out his mouth — a nervous habit of his. "Fine."

"Can I help Mom with dinner?"

"She's fine. It's all done."

In my old world, he'd chastise me for not jumping up and helping Mom, but it seems I'm to be treated like a guest. Or he's not quite ready for me to step foot inside the house.

I don't blame him. We're in a crazy, impossible, unknown situation. I'd probably do the same, as I'm just like him. Mom's always telling me that. If anything, I'm slightly judging her for being ready to accept, so easily, that I'm back from the dead. The idea is preposterous. I'm not even sure what to believe and I know I'm me.

As Mom finishes dinner in the kitchen, I search for something to say that won't offend Dad. I want to tell him about my recent creek run in his boat with Jake, but that wouldn't go down well. Everything I come up with is a memory that isn't true for him. So, do I compliment him on the boat or the house, like I've never been there before? That would be a lie — and worse, it would suggest my own story about being alive all this time is made up.

Instead, we sit in tense silence as Mom brings out a platter of grilled salmon, a bowl of potato salad, and a crisp green salad with cherry tomatoes and avocado pieces. Her go-to favorites for a summer meal on the terrace. Dad opens a bottle of New Zealand Sauvignon Blanc.

"Do you drink?" he asks, filling his own and Mom's glasses.

"Uh, yes," I reply. After all the bottles of wine we've shared, it's incredible to me he doesn't know this. "In fact, that's a favorite. One of Charlotte's, too, right?" After a second, he gives a curt nod of acknowledgment and pours me a glass.

I take a sip, the wine tart, chilled, familiar. "Speaking of Charlotte, does she know I'm here? I'd love to see her. But I understand if she's freaked out and doesn't want to see me."

Dad says nothing, digging into his salmon.

Mom clears her throat. "She knows. I called her this morning to tell her we'd be bringing you home. But . . . it's too soon, for her. She's very concerned about all of it. As you can imagine. We showed her the DNA results, but she's not convinced, said you could've bribed someone at the lab, or something. So, it might be a while before you see her. And she's very busy, of course, with Taylor, and her shifts at the store."

I furrow my brow as I finish my mouthful. "Taylor?"

"Yes, she's a handful. We love having her here while Charlotte's at the store, but it's a lot."

I shake my head. "Sorry. Who is Taylor?"

Dad looks up for the first time since starting his meal, and Mom puts down her wine glass.

"Honey," she says. "Taylor is Charlotte's daughter. Our granddaughter. Your niece. She just turned four."

What?

"Wait a minute." Dad's tone is dark. He puts down his fork. "You want us to believe you've somehow been alive this whole time, that in your version of events you see us regularly, and you're engaged to Jake Johnson, and we have dinner every week. And yet somehow, *somehow*, you don't know your own niece?" His voice is rising. "Bit of a hole in your story, don't you think?"

"I . . . I can't explain it," I stammer. "In my version of events, Charlotte is single and doesn't have any kids. I mean, she's only twenty-two. Wait . . . who's the father? Are they together?"

Mom purses her lips. "Craig Phillips, that quarterback from her year in high school. She's never had a relationship with him — it was a one-night stand at a party, she said. She was determined to keep the baby, even though it cost her a place on a fashion degree. Now, we sometimes look after Taylor while Charlotte works at Zara downtown. She rents a one-bedroom in the historic district."

"Huh. That's funny. In my version, she earned that fashion degree, but still came back here and works at Zara, and lives downtown. Guess the degree didn't make much difference."

I take a bite of salmon, stunned. *Wow*. A four-year-old. My niece. I have a niece.

"Hold up," I add, glancing up. "Her daughter just turned four, you said? She'd have been conceived around . . . early fall, five years back. Man." I shake my head. "I *remember* a house party around then, at Stacey's. Charlotte was still living in the big house with you, and I was in that rented loft downtown, where Jake would stay when he was home from law school. Charlotte would've been seventeen, about to go into her senior year at high school, I guess. And I was twenty-three."

I frown, trying to recall that night. "It was Labor Day weekend, that's right. Stacey's place was miles out of town, and Charlotte had persuaded Jake and I to come pick her up and bring her back to yours, as we'd already all planned to stay the weekend at the house for Labor Day. I remember, because when we got to the party, it was totally out of control — Stacey's parents' house was trashed."

It's all rushing back to me now — I haven't thought about that night in years. I put down my wine glass. "When we went in to find Charlotte, I saw her going upstairs with Craig Phillips. She was totally wasted, probably drinking for the first time, and didn't seem like she was making good choices. She had a huge crush on Craig — all the girls did — but Jake and I followed her upstairs and persuaded her to come home. We drove out to the old house and snuck her in without waking you." I shake my head. "If we hadn't been there that night, it could've turned out very differently."

Mom nods. "I remember that Labor Day weekend, too. Charlotte was supposed to come home after a party, but she ended up staying out all night. She didn't return our calls and didn't turn up until later the next afternoon." Mom turns to Dad. "She was in a state, totally hungover — do you remember, Burt? — and we grounded her for two weeks. I always figured that party was where she got pregnant."

I sip my wine. "Yep. I guess in my version of events, I was there to prevent it. So, for me, Taylor was never conceived—"

"That's enough." Dad's voice has a bitter tone I don't recognize. "That's *enough*. You're still a stranger in our home, and you're talking about underage drinking, intoxicated one-night stands, and that our darling granddaughter should never have existed? Enough. No, Til—" he holds up a hand as Mom starts to object. "That's it." He rises, his plate of half-finished dinner in one hand, wine in the other. "I'll be in my study."

I open my mouth to speak as Dad pushes past the bifold doors into the house. "I'm so sorry."

But he's already gone.

"I'm so sorry," I repeat to Mom. "I didn't mean that Taylor shouldn't exist. I was only trying to explain why I don't know her, why she doesn't exist in *my* world. It's not a hole in my story." I grip the table, the aroma from my barely-touched plate of salmon making me feel nauseated. "I'm telling you both the truth, I swear."

Mom forces out a thin smile. She rises, pulling together the dishes. "I believe you. Your father will come around."

"And Charlotte?"

Mom's eyes meet mine. She says nothing.

CHAPTER 10: JAKE

June 3-4

Jake scrambled through the forest, its branches clawing at him. "Liv!" The undergrowth grew thicker, harsher, more combative. He fought his way out into the clearing, increasing his stride, picking up pace toward the quarry cliff, leaping out into the void like an Olympic long-jumper, one leg ahead of him. Time stopped, Jake suspended between height and depth, air and water, life and death. Then he plummeted. The quarry stretched out infinitely below him, a black hole in the universe, sucking him under for eternity.

Something pulled him back. An insistent thrum of sound waves, enough for him to catch onto. A familiar melody.

His phone.

Jake twisted himself out of the dream, out of the tangled bamboo sheets now soaked in sweat. He grabbed at the vibrating, chiming cellphone on the nightstand.

"Uh, hello?"

Sunlight streamed through the ineffective muslin curtains Liv had picked out.

What time was it?

"Mr. Johnson, it's Detective Adam Banks. I didn't wake you, did I?"

"No," Jake lied, checking the phone's screen for the time. 10.43 a.m. Crap.

He sat up, swinging his bare legs off the side of the bed, running his hand through his hair, across his growing stubble. Liv would disapprove.

"Do you have news?"

It was like Groundhog Day. This was the sixth consecutive day Detective Banks had called and Jake had asked this very same question, his voice becoming more despondent each day.

"One key update," Detective Banks replied. "The dredging of the quarry lake finished last night. There's nothing but a couple of car tires and such. No bodies. Your fiancée wasn't . . . in the water."

Thank Christ. Jake blew out his cheeks. "That's amazing news, isn't it? Means she's out there somewhere. Alive."

"Well," Detective Banks said slowly, "it means her body isn't in the forest or in the lake. Not necessarily anything else. If she were alive and well, she'd surely be home by now. Increasingly it's looking like there are other factors involved. Possibly foul play."

"'Foul play'? What does that mean? I was there with her. I'd have seen if someone else was there."

"It's just a theory we've been exploring," Detective Banks replied. "When we conducted the searches, we also noted any other findings that might suggest a third person was around. We've interviewed the hiker who found you and called 911, Kirk Evans, to see if he was with anybody else, or had seen anyone around, but he says no. At this stage, we have no reason to suspect Mr. Evans was involved any further than helping you look for Ms. Grainger. But we have to take all the possibilities into consideration."

He paused, clearing his throat. "That's why we feel it's time to hold a press conference. It's been a week, and as you know there's been some local media coverage of the search—"

Of course Jake was aware. He'd been reading all the local news websites, which had gotten wind of the police search of the forest and lake.

"—make sure the wider public knows, take it national. I know there've already been a lot of social media posts from her friends that have been reposted and that's gaining traction. We can capitalize on that attention by holding a media conference, getting not just Olivia's face but also yours and the Graingers' in the news. We need to do that as early as possible — tomorrow morning, if you're up to it."

Jake sighed. As a lawyer, he'd sat in on press conferences for some higher-profile advocacy cases, but it was different being on the other side. "What would I have to do?"

"As her fiancé, you'd be best suited, we think, to make a public statement — a plea for anybody with information, no matter how small, to come forward. You could talk about how you were celebrating your engagement anniversary, the wedding."

"What about Liv's parents?"

"We're not sure Mrs. Grainger would be up to it, and Mr. Grainger is a little more . . . closed-off in his communication. You're articulate, and ideal for the task. You're photogenic, and we'd have a big picture of Olivia on a stand next to you, and . . . well, she's very memorable."

Beautiful, he means.

What happens if you're not?

"We want to tug at people's heartstrings, motivate them to want to help," the detective adds. "Do you think you could do it? I could have one of our team come over later and help you craft a statement."

Jesus. Speaking in front of TV cameras and microphones about losing Liv, begging the public for help finding her. How would he do that without losing his shit completely?

"I'm not sure I'd be any better than Tilly — I've been as much as a wreck as she has," Jake protested. "Just because I'm a guy doesn't mean I haven't been crying myself to sleep every night."

74

"To be honest, that's not a bad thing. The public responds very positively to an emotional man, especially one in love. Even better if he's good-looking. Some tears might help your case, so don't worry about it."

Wow. Way to exploit a family's grief over their missing loved one.

With Jake remaining silent, the detective added, "So, can I send our public relations consultant Sandra over to your place today? Around three p.m.? Maybe you could jot down some thoughts beforehand, and she'll help you put them into a statement."

"Uh. I guess. Sure."

Anything to help find Liv. If there was even the slightest chance someone had seen her, or if she was out there somewhere in hiding, and saw the news, saw how much Jake and her family wanted her home . . . Yes, he'd do anything.

* * *

Jake settled himself at the long desk beside Tilly, Burt on her other side, and Charlotte at the end. Jake's seat was in the middle of the stage, with a lectern on the far side and a large Wilmington PD emblem on the backdrop between them. Below it, on an easel, stood a giant foamboard print of Liv, the headshot taken for her website a couple of years back, the one where she looked like a model. She'd hated it. At this magnification, the gold flecks in her hazel-colored, slightly catlike eyes were clearly visible, her skin was luminous, and you could see the natural bronze highlights in her chestnut hair. Jake had to turn away, or he might just fling himself at the photo in front of all these people.

A cluster of large black microphones had been placed on the desk before him, each with a collar bearing the name of some TV or radio news channel. At least a dozen camera crews were jostling for position at the front, while journalists and TV reporters waited behind them with dictaphones, pens, microphones poised. Sweat dripped down his back. He hoped his face wasn't too shiny.

Two oversized studio lights, one each side of the low stage, were turned on with an audible clang, their brightness making Jake blink. He screwed up his face. His palm dampened the single-page printout anchored beneath his hands, slightly blurring the text.

Great.

Beside Jake, Liv's mother emitted a tiny whimper while Burt put his arm around his wife's shoulders. At least they didn't have to say anything — just sit there and look heartbroken. It was all on Jake now.

Again, the weight of that gnawed at him. What if he didn't get it right? Wasn't good-looking enough to gain Liv enough attention? Wasn't forlorn enough? Was *too* forlorn? What if whatever he said, or didn't say, was the difference between Liv coming back or not?

Detective Banks stepped up to the lectern, looking clean cut and sharp in a pressed uniform. It struck Jake the man was also pretty telegenic. There was a low buzz of voices before the room fell silent. A few stragglers slipped into seats. Cameras were steadied, their tiny red lights blinking.

Jake's stomach twisted itself into a knot; suddenly he was nauseous. It really wouldn't be a good look if he threw up over the desk.

"Thank you for being here." Detective Banks scanned the cameras with a grim half-smile. He'd clearly done this before.

"Olivia Grainger, a twenty-eight-year-old interior designer from Wilmington, was reported missing eight days ago. Wilmington PD has been conducting an extensive search of the area from which Ms. Grainger disappeared. We can now report that the forest search and the dredging of the former McMahon Quarry lake has resulted in no findings, and Wilmington PD is continuing its investigation into this very troubling missing-person case. Today we'd like to share a statement from Ms. Grainger's fiancé, Jake Johnson, a lawyer with Refuge Advocacy International, who's here supported by Mr. and Mrs. Grainger, Olivia's parents."

Detective Banks stepped down. Was it weird he'd mentioned Jake's job? As if that somehow made him a more credible figure?

The bank of cameras, a multi-headed technological beast finding its prey, slid its many eyes to Jake. He swallowed, his mouth desert-like in its dryness. He opened it: nothing came out.

Shit.

Taking a sip of water from the glass beside him, he felt the liquid coat his throat. He swallowed. *Better.*

When he lifted the sheet of paper, the typed words blurred as his hand trembled violently.

"My—my name is Jake Johnson. On the afternoon of May 27, 2022, at around 2 p.m., Olivia Grainger, my fiancée, disappeared while we were picnicking at the former McMahon Quarry lake. We are planning to get married in August this year, and we had been celebrating the one-year anniversary of our engagement.

"I was packing up our belongings and Liv said she was going to take a short walk along the quarry ridge. When I looked up, she had disappeared. I searched for her but—" He took in a shuddering, deep breath. Tilly laid her hand on his on the table, squeezing slightly, smiling her encouragement. He turned his hand, linking his fingers through hers.

"—I couldn't find her anywhere. She just disappeared, and we haven't seen her since." He took a deep breath. "Liv had nothing with her. No cellphone, no keys, no money. Nothing. I don't believe she would have left me voluntarily, yet I have no idea what happened or where she went.

"Liv's mother Tilly, father Burt, sister Charlotte, and myself," he glanced to his left, "beg any members of the public who may have seen Liv, or have any information as to her whereabouts, to please come forward."

He looked directly at the bank of cameras. "Any information you may have, no matter how trivial, could be helpful." Out of the corner of his eye, he caught Tilly wiping away tears. Burt put his arm around her, his other about

Charlotte's. They were all now linked as one unit. Detective Banks nodded approvingly.

"We miss and love Liv so much, and we just want to have her home. Liv and I have known each other all our lives. We're childhood sweethearts — we were even prom king and queen." Jake grimaced self-consciously at that bit, which Sandra had insisted on including. "We're each other's person. We're due to be married soon and are looking forward to spending our lives together. Our future together. Please, help Liv return to us. If you can help in any way, please call the police tipline number at the bottom of the screens. Thank you."

Jake blew out a breath. Thank Christ. He'd managed to get through it without breaking down. Then he stopped, a final thing occurring to him, and turned back to the cameras. "Liv, if you're watching. I love you. We all do. Come back to us."

The room was silent. Detective Banks coughed expertly at the podium, and the cameras shifted back to him. "I will now take any questions from the media."

A barrage of voices. Jake started in his chair, almost deafened by the sound. Tilly patted his arm. He looked at her, at the tears rimming her immaculately made-up eyelids. Why wasn't he crying too? Would that look bad? He turned away from Liv's mom, back to the cameras, ashamed.

"Yes, first question. Fox News," Detective Banks pointed at a reporter near the front, a short woman in a blue power suit.

"Is it true Olivia Grainger was naked when she disappeared?"

Jake closed his eyes.

"Yes, that is correct," Detective Banks confirmed in a toneless voice. "Ms. Grainger had been swimming in the lake immediately before her disappearance, and Mr. Johnson found her clothes and belongings, her purse with her phone, car and house keys, identification and credit card, all still at the picnic site. Next question—"

Another buzz of voices.

"—CBS, go ahead."

"Is the Wilmington PD suspecting abduction?"

"We're investigating all and any possibilities at the moment. The fact that Ms. Grainger's body hasn't been found at the site or in the lake—" Tilly let out a mewl of distress at this "—suggests she either left of her own accord, or there was another person involved . . . Go ahead, ABC."

"What about the hiker?" A male reporter checked his notes. "Kirk Evans. He told the media he'd found Mr. Johnson in distress, while looking for Ms. Grainger at the site? Is Mr. Evans under any suspicion in this case?"

"Not at this time," Detective Banks replied. "That said, we're pursuing all possible leads, and Mr. Evans has been helpful and co-operative with our investigation. Last question — NBC, please."

A tall woman with brown hair stepped into the light. Jake's heart skipped. The reporter was beautiful, effortlessly glamorous, just like Liv. But with a much harder expression. She lifted her puffy mike toward the podium and parted her red-painted lips.

"In the case of missing persons, it has historically tended to be the person closest to the victim who is responsible. Is Jake Johnson a suspect in this case?" The reporter's eyes flicked directly to Jake and back to the lectern.

Beside him, Tilly gasped and squeezed his arm. A low murmur flitted around the room. The cameras slid back to Jake, staring him down even as Detective Banks spoke.

"No, Mr. Johnson is not a suspect at this time," the detective replied firmly. Jake fought hard not to squirm, aware that every eye in the room was now on him. "Wilmington PD is, of course, pursuing every avenue in this case, but we have had no cause for suspicion about Mr. Johnson or any of Ms. Grainger's closest friends or family. That's all for today, thank you for coming out."

Detective Banks ignored the cacophony of voices objecting to this sudden closure of the conference, shuffling some papers, eyes down. He stepped over to Jake, putting a hand on his shoulder, and leaning down, said in a low voice, "Time to go."

Jake pushed back his chair and shuffled off the stage into a side room, not even checking to see if the Graingers were behind him. What that last reporter had said — that had always been his fear. That *he* might be a suspect. That everyone would think that he could've done something to Liv, and be lying about all this.

His legs shook and he collapsed down on a plastic chair beside a water cooler. Liv's family entered the room, as if in slow motion, barely walking. Tilly's skin was a strange color, tan foundation mixed with a sickly pale-yellow base. Charlotte and Burt's faces were grim, stony. All three stared across the room at Jake, as if seeing him for the first time. As if looking at him in a new light.

Charlotte broke the spell, rushing over to sit beside Jake.

"Jake. We know you didn't do anything, okay? We know it wasn't you. Don't listen to those reporters."

He nodded, putting his head in his hands. His whole body was shuddering now.

"Hey, hey. *Don't.* You did great, and it'll work. They'll find her." Charlotte's voice was lower than usual, soothing. Like Liv's.

He swiped at his damp face. He hadn't realized he was crying.

The PR officer, Sandra, made her way over and crouched in front of him. "That went well — you did a good job with the statement. Now, is somebody driving you home?"

"I'm taking him," Charlotte replied, not waiting for Jake to respond.

Jake wiped his face again, and met Sandra's gaze. "I didn't cry," he sniffed. "I was too emotionless. They think it's me."

Sandra patted his knee. "No. No. They had to ask that: it's an obvious question. And don't worry, you looked plenty distressed, believe me. It went as well as it could have. You go home. Get a good night's rest, okay?" She patted him again, then rose, turning to Liv's parents, who were standing motionless, just watching.

"I'm taking you home." Charlotte pulled Jake to his feet. "Dad's got Mom. Hang on, I'll just say goodbye." Jake watched as Charlotte hugged her parents, unable to cross the room to do the same. Despite Charlotte's reassuring words, he didn't know how he'd be received.

Charlotte guided Jake out of the room, along the corridor to a back exit. Outside was the rear parking lot where they were parked, away from the cameras. She drove efficiently to the exit where the car was buzzed out of the side gate.

Jake had half-expected a crowd of reporters to swarm the car, but there was nobody there, just a few TV crews on the sidewalk, packing up into vans.

"See?" Charlotte shrugged. "Nobody cares about us. They just *had* to ask those questions."

Jake nodded, although he remained silent.

They drove wordlessly until Charlotte drew up outside Jake and Liv's little yellow house. She looked at it for a moment, then said, "Have a good rest, Jake. I'll call you later."

"Thanks."

Jake let himself inside, collapsing on the soft couch. But he was dirty — he was sullying the white linen covers. Dirty with sweat from the TV lights, from tears, from the grime of suspicion. Dirty from the dark look that the last reporter had given him. That Burt Grainger had thrown him.

It was you.

You did it.

It's always the husband or boyfriend.

Jake's skin crawled. He surged up off the couch, slipping out of the sports jacket, blue shirt, and dark jeans Sandra had carefully curated for the press conference. Stepping into the gleaming white bathroom, he turned on the rainhead in the walk-in shower and, out of habit, threw his underwear in the wooden laundry box. He caught himself in the oversized, wood-framed mirror, illuminated by the industrial-style light above it. He barely recognized himself. He looked like a man possessed, haunted, his face drawn, too thin.

Jake stepped under the shower, standing for an age beneath the steaming hot water, letting it drip down his face, into every crevice, his nose and eyes. Washing him clean. He wanted to drown in it.

There was so much space in this glass-encased shower. Liv had insisted on it. They'd often showered together. She'd distract him from washing, pushing her wet body up behind his, rubbing against him, her skin slippery, warm, erotic. He'd step too far under the rainhead's wide torrent, making him splutter. He'd kiss her, laughing, streams of water and the tendrils of Liv's long, wet hair getting in their mouths. He'd guide her back against the herringbone marble tile, lifting her leg onto the little bench, holding her arms above her head, pushing himself into her, making her cry out. She was loud when they were at home.

Jake closed his eyes, allowing a tiny half-smile at the memory. The first smile in more than a week — since Liv had last touched him, at the lake. She could almost be here with him now. These rivulets of water could be the gentle touch of her fingertips down his body, caressing his back, his butt, his chest, his rapidly thickening penis. He held himself in his right hand, not too hard, as if it was her gentle grip. He leaned with his left hand high above his head against the tile, feeling Liv beneath him, imagining her long legs wrapped around him. He pumped rapidly until he came with a soft yell, collapsing against the hard, tiled wall.

Empty. Alone.

CHAPTER 11: OLIVIA

June 11

I adjust the seat on Mom's buttermilk-yellow cruiser bicycle in my parents' garage, raising it to accommodate my longer legs. I've got at least seven inches on Mom. It's somewhat of a mystery why she has this particular bike, since in my world I'd helped her pick out this model to cruise around her gated community and visit friends. I guess she chose it for herself anyways.

Mom watches me, an eyebrow raised. "Are you sure you want it that high?"

"I'm sure. You don't mind me borrowing it?"

"Well, honey, you don't have a driver's license, so it's this or walking. And you can't get to many places on your feet around here."

It's true. It's a twenty-minute bike ride from here to Wrightsville Beach, today's destination, and an hour's ride to the city's historic downtown. Mom wouldn't hesitate to give me cash for transit, but there are no direct buses from outside the gates to either of those places, plus it's probably a half-hour walk to the community's entrance alone. Without this bike, I'd be marooned at the house.

This is my first taste of freedom in two weeks.

"And Dad's on board with me showing my face in public? I don't want to upset him any more than I already have." I drop into the front basket a beach bag containing a hat, water, sunscreen, one of Mom's recent book club reads, and the bagged lunch Mom was thrilled to make for me.

Mom smiles patiently, even though I've already asked her this question. "He gets it. I explained there's little risk in you being out in public. Nobody will recognize you as an adult. As long as you don't start telling people you're Olivia Grainger come back to life, we'll be fine."

Although that stings a little, I smile back, putting on a round bike helmet with a flower design. "I won't. Thanks, Mom. I'll be back for dinner later."

I push off, out of the open garage door, and snake my way through the well-tended streets of Landfall. My parents' house is about as far away from the gated entrance as you can get, and it's a ten-minute ride to the barriers that lead out to the main road. From here, it's a straight shot along the River-to-the-Sea bikeway, over the bridge onto Harbor Island, and over South Banks Channel Bridge out to Wrightsville Beach. The salt air fills my lungs and I find myself briefly grinning as I pick up speed on my descent from the second bridge, passing a group of surfers outside the wings joint, the wind cooling my skin in the summer heat. It's 11.30 a.m. and a scorching day.

I stop at the beach entrance at the end of Stone Street, and lock up at a rack that's already jammed with bikes. The condos to one side have awesome water views from balconies decorated with bright patio furniture, and there's a gorgeous pale-blue beach house on the other side. It would be wonderful to live here — albeit a little busy with all the tourists and beachgoers.

I sling my bag over my shoulder and step out onto the sand. As it's Saturday, the beach is full of families having fun, the sand littered with vividly colored umbrellas, blankets, folding chairs, and plastic buckets. The warm air buzzes with the sounds of summer — children laughing, music blaring from portable speakers, a parent shouting at unruly teenagers hanging out in the water, the high pitch of a little girl's squeal, all regularly punctuated by the crash of ocean on shore.

I hold my mom's wide-brimmed straw hat on my head as a breeze lifts it slightly, and step my way north along the hot sand, thankful for my new sandals. Further away from the Stone Street beach entrance, the family groups start to thin out and my pulse slows. I've never been a fan of big crowds.

That's not the only reason I headed in this direction, though. I know where I'm going, even if I don't want to acknowledge it to myself.

I stroll along the beach and spot them, out in the wide band of rippling, azure water.

This is where the best surfers hang out.

The shore along Wrightsville Beach is shallow, Jake has told me many times, so they have to paddle far into the ocean to catch the big swells. I've sat here a few times, reading, or sketching a design concept, occasionally looking up to catch him ride a crest in the distance. I can only tell it's him by the orange shorts I bought him, and if he wears something differ-ent, he's much harder to spot among the group of weekend surfers. And during the week, I never have time to join him here, I'm always so busy with work.

If only I could fix that now. Take the time to be together, to let him teach me to surf. I miss him so much. What's he doing in our reality — assuming that world still exists? Is he looking for me, missing me? I'm overwhelmed with need for him. To see him, touch him, kiss him.

I drop down onto the sand at the exact spot where I last sat happily watching him, which was only a couple of weeks ago. And a whole universe away. On this version of this beach, I have never been here before. And I'm miserable.

I lift off my jersey dress, exposing my borrowed black bikini from Charlotte's stash in the guest bedroom. Rubbing a fresh application of sunscreen onto my skin, my gaze fol-lows the tiny humans on their surfboards.

How did I get here? Is this world an entirely different physical plane than the one where I watched Jake surf? A brand-new parallel universe that was created when my life path split when I died — or didn't die — at the quarry sixteen years ago?

I was never great at science, but my favorite teacher at high school was the physics teacher. Mr. Green spoke of the infinite universe, and how its infinity means there is an infinite chance of an infinite number of worlds exactly like our own, as well as infinitely varying worlds in all the infinite possible ways they could vary. It blew my mind as a fourteen-year-old who had never thought much about anywhere outside North Carolina. It sparked my interest in the solar system and what lies beyond.

But I always figured that those mirror universes, if they existed at all, would be impossible distances from our own. When I entered this realm, I didn't *travel* anywhere. I was right there at the quarry lake.

Mr. Green put me onto reading the *His Dark Materials* trilogy, which remain my favorite books. In Philip Pullman's stories, the universes are not vastly distant, but instead folded in on each other, just a hand's reach away. All that's required to step through is finding and opening a door between worlds.

The quarry lake. That's where I supposedly died as a child — but in my world, Jake saved me. It's clearly no coincidence that in that exact place, I fell, and woke up in this alternate world.

That's my door. A tear in the fabric of the universe. A hole I fell through.

Maybe it's a door only for *me*, because my life path split there sixteen years ago. Maybe all worlds are full of holes between alternate realities, which vary from person to person, all depending on their life choices and decisions, big and small.

Infinite possible worlds, infinite outcomes.

I smile at myself, glad nobody is privy to my preposterous internal ramblings. They'd think I was crazy.

Not Jake, though. Jake would appreciate the theory, and he's always loved the idea of infinite universes. But I can't explain this to Dad, or even Mom.

For Mom, my resurrection is simply a God-given miracle, and that's that. No alternate timelines or parallel universes involved. That would go against her new-found religious beliefs.

And Dad, well, he doesn't believe any of it.

I've caught him staring at me several times over the three days since I moved into the pool house. Like he can't believe I'm here. He's trying to reconcile this incredulity with the undeniable fact of my physical presence. Of our shared DNA.

Last night at dinner, as Mom and I talked about more shared childhood memories, Dad listened hard, nodding almost imperceptibly.

A camping trip when I was eleven and poor Charlotte, only five, was stung by poison ivy, her arm swelling to epic proportions.

The pair of kittens we adopted when I was eight, only one surviving — which became our long-time cat, Tabasco.

The swallow's nest in the attic in our big old house that three-year-old Charlotte came across and wanted to keep, and was inconsolable when Dad got rid of it.

I watch as a group of surfers lying flat on their boards paddle their way gradually toward the beach. They're beautiful, tanned, toned. Three guys and a girl. As they approach the shallow shore and stand, lifting their boards under their arms to wade the last section, the fairest-haired guy breaks from the group, waving farewell. He heads in my direction, still a way off, as his friends head north toward the pier. His coloring and physique are just like Jake's. Still, it's not surprising I'd think of him, considering where I'm sitting. Everything here reminds me of him.

The fair guy gets closer, pushing his hand through his wet hair, the gesture familiar, his arm obscuring his features. My heart begins to race.

No.

He walks right toward me, as he drops his hand, hitching the board further up under his arm.

Oh my God.

It *is* Jake.

My heart beats so fast it feels like it might explode. My guts churn, bringing me dangerously close to vomiting on the sand.

He's only about thirty feet from me now.

What should I do?

I can't say anything to him, I'm supposed to be dead . . . Yet I can't pass up this opportunity. He knows I exist, and that I was at the hospital asking for him. Even if he doesn't believe me.

Maybe he'll believe it, if he sees me.

This could be my only chance.

He is steps away, and I'm still staring right at him. He gives me a polite, unrecognizing smile, squinting in the sun. It breaks my heart. I guess I thought he'd know me. Regardless of what world we were in.

"Jake."

He stops, holding his hand against his forehead to shade his eyes, staring at me. I can almost see his mind whirring, trying to work out if he knows me.

"Uh, hi. I'm sorry. Do I know you?"

I scramble to my feet, brushing sand from the back of my thighs. I blow out a sharp breath. Now or never, Liv.

"Yes. Yes, well . . . I mean—I'm Liv," I blurt out in a rush. "Livvie. Livvie Grainger."

Jake freezes, then slowly steps back. He drops his surfboard with uncharacteristic carelessness onto the sand. He opens his mouth, closes it, opens it again. It's clear that the man I love, have loved all of my life, doesn't know me.

It takes him several seconds to speak.

"You — you're the woman. The one the police told me about? Claiming to be Livvie Grainger?"

I nod, pressing my lips together. "That's me."

He narrows his eyes, obscuring the ocean-blue irises I've studied countless times. I know every shade of blue in those eyes, every gray fleck, the bright streak of turquoise in his left eye.

"What do you want? Why are you pretending to be her?" His voice is low and harsh.

I step toward him, hands out. "I'm not pretending. I'm really her, Jake. I'm really me. I know it's been a long time, for you, but . . . don't you recognize me?" I take another step. "I can tell you everything only the real Liv Grainger would know, all about the times we spent at the quarry lake, the day we found it — well, your dog, Ginny, found it and we followed. Look, here's my scar." I sweep my hair from my face to show him the mark on my eyebrow. "That's from when you chased me around your parents' coffee table and I fell into it, and your Dad had to take me to ER because there was so much blood. Remember? I can tell you hundreds more things. It's *me*, Jake, I swear."

He shakes his head, frowning. "It's impossible. You can't be Liv. I watched her die when we were twelve years old. I couldn't save her. I saw her body on the rocks below. It broke me. You *can't* be her." He's furious. "You're just a woman who looks like she would look now, and you're using that fact to . . . to scam us."

"I get it, Jake. I know this sounds insane." I run my hand through my hair, unsure how to go on. "But, for me, you *did* save me that day. I slipped, but you caught me. I lived, and we grew up together, and fell in love." He throws me an incredulous look. His mouth now firm, a tiny pulse beating at his jaw. I soldier on, determined to get this out.

"There are two versions of events and, somehow, they got mixed up. So, I'm here now, in the wrong version. In my world, you and I are engaged, Jake. We're going to be married in August. I know it sounds crazy—"

"It doesn't *sound* crazy. It *is* crazy. You're delusional." Jake picks up his surfboard, backing away from me. "I don't know what you want, but don't come near me again, you hear? Stay away. I mean it."

He strides off down the beach, his back and shoulder muscles flexing as he carries his surfboard, his skin lightly tanned and gleaming. He's still the most beautiful man I've ever seen.

He doesn't believe me. Doesn't know me. But he's here, and I've spoken to him.

And two things are clear.

I love him.

And he despises me.

CHAPTER 12: OLIVIA

June 16

I blow-dry my hair in the pool house bathroom, and dress for the evening in the white shorts and blue-and-white-striped T-shirt Mom bought me. All my new clothes are lightweight summer wear and, as usual for North Carolina, the late spring weather has been consistently warm. Summer officially begins next week. If I'm still here in the fall, I'll need a whole new cold-weather wardrobe. But it's hard to imagine that. I have the strong sense that all this is temporary — that it will all somehow come to a head. For now, I'm on an enforced vacation from my regular life.

In many ways, it really is like a vacation. I'm living in a gorgeous pool house by the creek. I've been cycling daily these past five days — "exploring," as Mom calls it. As if I don't already know this area intimately.

Three days ago, emboldened by the new-found freedom the bike has given me, I rode over to the house Jake and I'd bought and fixed up last year, curious to see what it looked like in this reality. To see who was living there. I pulled my bike onto the path leading to the bungalow's bright blue door, which I'd repainted a soft gray-green, and knocked.

A middle-aged woman, about Mom's age and dressed in capri pants and a twin set, opened the door. "Hello?"

"Hi. Uh, I'm Olivia. I'm sorry to disturb you . . . I used to live here. I was riding by," I gesture to my bike, "and I guess I was curious to see what had become of the place. I hope you don't mind."

She beamed at me. "Not at all, honey. Are you the daughter of the Diazes?"

The people who sold it to us last year. I smiled in return, wishing I didn't have to lie to this sweet lady. "No, from before that. Way back."

The look she gave me was assessing, taking in my age, my clothes, and the likelihood of me being a threat. Apparently I passed the test. "Well, come on in, honey, if you'd like to have a quick look around. I don't mind at all." She stood aside to let me through. "We haven't done much. We've only been here a year."

The interior was the same as the Diazes had left it when Jake and I moved in — the reception room was now furnished with a beige velvet couch and armchair. The fireplace still had its tile surround and brass plate trim, which I'd replaced.

She led me into the kitchen, talking away. The wall was still closed in, and the tan wooden cabinets, which for us had ended up in a skip, were still there. Along the corridor, the floral wallpaper we had stripped off was still above the bed in the primary bedroom, and the bathroom still had its avocado suite. The new owners had done nothing with the place.

Jake and I had never lived here in this world, that's for sure.

"Was this your room as a child?" the woman asked as I stuck my head into the small second bedroom. I nearly replied no, then stopped myself. The Diazes had been there fifteen years before putting it on the market, so nothing else would make sense. I had nodded, struggling to lie outright to this kind woman. I thanked her quickly, made my excuses when she offered me some lemonade, and left, ashamed at myself.

Is this what my life would be now? Half-truths and lies to make my existence make sense to others?

In the pool house, I slick on the lip gloss Mom has given me, wishing I had even a little jewelry to dress up this outfit. My left hand feels naked without my engagement ring, and I've developed a nervous habit of digging my thumbnail into the base of my ring finger, just to feel something there.

Aside from sandwiches on the beach, this will be my first meal out since arriving in this world. My stomach flips, more from nerves than hunger. I don't know what I'm walking into tonight.

With Dad begrudgingly coming around, Mom's been working on Charlotte this week. Telling her all about me, my 'miraculous' story, and how I know everything about our shared history before I was twelve, and even some common elements after that, such as that party at Stacey's. Then, yesterday, Mom told me Charlotte agreed to have dinner tonight.

Even if Mom can't see it, it's clear to me why Charlotte was so easily persuaded. It's because of what I told our parents about my version of Stacey's party, and how Jake and I had prevented her one-night stand with Craig Phillips. Knowing Charlotte, she'll have some questions for me. And she won't go easy.

But I want to see my sister, so badly. So I'll take it. All of it. And she's bringing Taylor, the little girl I can't wait to meet.

I lock up the pool house and stick my head through the bifold doors into the great room. Mom spots me immediately. "You ready, honey?"

With Mom chattering nervously the entire 10 minutes of our journey, we drive along the sweeping, manicured roads of the Landfall community, out to the main road, and across the two island bridges out to Wrightsville Beach. The Beach House Bar and Grill sits at the head of the pier, overlooking the wide stretches of sand to each side. The patio is already jammed, and we are led to a rustic table painted in a distressed blue at a cool spot inside, next to the row of open French doors. Fishing nets and huge glass jars hang from the vaulted ceiling, strung with tiny white fairy lights. There's a giant blackboard at the far end, which has today's specials chalked onto it. Nothing has changed here, which is comforting.

I let Mom and Dad take the seats facing the open doors looking out over the water, while I sit across from them, facing the restaurant entrance. This way, I can see when Charlotte arrives.

We've only just started scanning the single-sheet menu when I spot my sister pushing through the door, a little girl holding her hand. Charlotte looks great in a red sundress and sneakers, her chestnut-brown hair in a messy bun. Her pretty daughter barely comes up to Charlotte's upper thigh, even though my sister is short like Mom. Taylor's hair is chestnut brown like mine and Charlotte's, pulled into cute bunches and swept off her forehead with a yellow clip.

Charlotte speaks to the hostess and spots me, but then immediately turns back to the front desk. She avoids eye contact as she makes her way through the tables, leading a reluctant-looking Taylor. She's saying something to her daughter, a warning of some kind.

"Honey, there you are." Mom gives Taylor a hug off the side of her seat, "Hi, baby girl." Taylor hugs her back, all the while eyeing me suspiciously. She sticks a thumb in her mouth, defensively. I smile.

"Hi, Mom. Hey, Dad," Charlotte says, ignoring me. "Taylor, take that chair and I'll sit at the end." Charlotte clearly isn't keen to sit next to me, placing her daughter as a barrier between us.

But Taylor doesn't budge, shaking her head with a deep frown. She looks up at her mother, who leans down. "I don't want to sit next to her," she says in a stage whisper, loud enough for us all to hear.

An awkward moment of silence is unexpectedly resolved by my father. "Sugar plum, how about I go sit over there?

You sit next to Meemaw, and Mommy can sit at the end next to you? Is that best?"

Taylor nods, sucking furiously on her thumb, creating a slurping sound.

"Quit that." My sister pulls the offending thumb out of her daughter's mouth. "Sit up here. No thumbs at dinner, remember?"

Charlotte takes the seat at the head of the table, the furthest possible spot from me, while Dad sits beside me. At least he's warming up. Charlotte, on the other hand, looks like she's going to take a lot of coaxing.

"Thanks for coming," I tell my sister. "I'm really glad you're here."

She picks up the menu, still not looking at me.

"And Taylor," I turn to my niece, "it's great to meet you. I'm your Auntie Liv. Or Auntie Livvie, if you like."

The child screws up her nose. "Mommy says I don't have an auntie, not really. She says you're not supposed to be here."

I twist my mouth, nodding. It's a reasonable point. "I know, it's super-confusing. We're all confused about it. But maybe we can all figure it out together and get to know each other. Deal?" I smile at her, since she doesn't reply. "I like your yellow barette."

Taylor sneers, smelling my desperation. Across the table, Mom nods at me, encouraging. *Keep going, you'll get there.*

Dad orders for us — his favorite task, in both worlds, even though we're all highly capable of ordering our own food. It gives him purpose. He requests the lobster and crab feast, a pricey bottle of Chablis, and a gourmet mac 'n' cheese for Taylor. He's overcompensating with food for the awkwardness of the situation. At least he's trying.

Charlotte still isn't acknowledging me, and Mom is forced to fill the silence with inane small talk about her latest book club read. When the wine arrives, Dad makes a big production of pouring small amounts into the large glasses, swirling his around excessively, sticking his nose in, and exclaiming delight at the bouquet. It's the kind of performance that would usually have me and Charlotte rolling our eyes at each other, but she's studiously ignoring me, while giving Mom one-word answers, and focusing on Taylor's juice box. I stay silent, sipping my wine. It's insanely delicious. At least I'm getting something positive out of this.

Our meals arrive, brought to our table by our young server, along with a glamorous, gray-haired woman I know well. She doesn't recognize me. Mom jumps up and greets her with enthusiasm. "Juliette! What a treat to be served by you personally. I didn't even know you'd be in the restaurant tonight."

Mom told me earlier today her friend, Juliette, a woman she met at the Landfall ladies' book club a few years ago, was the owner of this restaurant. I already knew that, of course, having met Juliette several times at Mom and Dad's parties. Plus when we've eaten here, many times over the past few years, Juliette has sometimes stopped to chat with us, or just to me and Jake, on our date nights.

"I've been trying to be more hands-off, but I had to help with serving tonight," Juliette replies, still hugging Mom. "We're desperately short-staffed. In fact, if you know someone in need of work, we'll take anybody at this point." She releases my mother and throws me a curious look. "Burt, Charlotte, it's great to see you. Charlotte, I know you're busy at Zara and with little Taylor here, but if any of your friends are looking for serving gigs for the summer . . ."

My sister gives Juliette a half-smile, while blowing on some pasta for Taylor. "I'll ask around."

Juliette glances at me again, clearly waiting for an introduction.

Mom's eyes widen in panic. "Oh, erm, Juliette, this is Olivia. A . . . a distant cousin, staying with us for the summer," she blurts. Thankfully, Juliette is focused on smiling at me, and doesn't notice the red flush creeping up Mom's neck.

"Well, this food looks wonderful," Mom adds, glancing at me apologetically as she takes her seat. "We'd better dig in. Thanks so much, Juliette. We won't keep you from your customers."

Juliette raises an eyebrow, quickly covering up her surprise at Mom's uncharacteristic abruptness with a smile. "Of course. Enjoy." She drifts off to speak to another table of customers.

We busy ourselves with cracking open lobster and crab. I have to hand it to Dad — he sure knows which dishes require utter concentration, and not much conversation.

"Maybe Juliette would hire you, Livvie?" Mom says as she digs out a crab claw.

Charlotte scoffs, despite the suggestion being directed at me. "She doesn't have a Social Security number, Mom," my sister says, as if I'm not sitting right here. "She can't get a job. Ever."

I was about to make the same point. "Charlotte's right, Mom. I'd love to start earning, and I did some part-time serving while I was at design school, so I've got some experience. But I can't see Juliette willing to hire anyone under the table, even if she's desperate."

Mom pulls out a whole claw of unbroken crabmeat, triumphant. "Leave her to me. She already thinks you're a relative. She'll help me out if I ask her for a favor."

Charlotte puts down her fork with a clatter. "And *why* wouldn't your so-called relative have any ID or Social Security number, Mom? She's obviously not an illegal immigrant. It makes no sense—"

"Charlotte, that's enough." Dad's voice is quiet but firm.

Wow. Dad is defending Mom but, by extension — me.

Little Taylor's brown eyes are wide, trying to figure out what we're arguing about. "I'm done." She pushes her cheesy dish away. Charlotte digs out a pink-covered tablet from a purse I don't recognize and sets her daughter up with purple headphones and a videogame. It's only when Taylor can't hear our discussion and is fully engrossed that my sister speaks to me, at last.

"Okay, then." There's a chill in her voice I've never heard before. "Let's get down to it. You say you're my sister

— the sister I barely remember because she *died* when I was six. And Mom says you know all the stuff that only Livvie would know. But I know con artists do their research and can be very clever . . ." She narrows her eyes and sits forward in her chair, already poised to eviscerate whatever I'm about to say. Mom and Dad both seem to hold their breath, each staring at their plates. "So my question is, can you prove it?"

I answer slowly, carefully. "I know it sounds impossible. I know it *is* impossible. But this is what has happened. As for proof, I think I've done all I can. Mom and I have been over so many details, so many memories of our shared history, she now believes me. I'm happy to do the same with you — I'd love to have the chance. And there's the DNA test that proves I'm Mom and Dad's daughter—"

"That's just words on a piece of paper," she interjects. "You could've faked that. Bribed the lab."

What is this? *CSI*? I shrug. "I guess that's possible, if I were very smart and resourceful. I'm neither. And I didn't. I don't have the money. The results are real. *I'm* real."

Oh, how I want Charlotte to believe it. Even though I'm not entirely sure *I* believe that last part.

My sister glances at Taylor. Her daughter is deep into her bouncing bunnies game.

"What I want to know is, how did you know about Craig Philips?" she hisses. "I never told Mom and Dad about that night at Stacey's. But you knew. How does that work? You were *dead*. You were never at that party."

I take a fortifying glug of my wine before answering. "Exactly. How *do* I know about it? How could I possibly know, if there isn't a version of events where I *wasn't* dead. Where I *was* at that party. Where I saw you with Craig? Where Jake and I stopped you going upstairs with him. You were drunk, and we wanted you to realize you weren't making a good choice. You agreed, in the end, and let us take you home."

My sister's frown deepens. "What? You stopped me? But . . . but Craig is Taylor's father. That," she glances at Taylor

98

again, "*poor choice*, as you call it, that was the night I conceived my daughter."

I suck in a breath. This might not go down well. "I know that. But in my version of events, you don't have a daughter. You really want to be a mom, but no, Taylor doesn't exist in my reality."

Charlotte pushes her plate away. Her face is pale. "Let me get this straight. Not only are you not supposed to be here, but now you're saying my daughter should never have existed? Because *you've* decided my drunken one-night stand with Craig shouldn't have happened?"

Mom visibly balks at this, and lowers a trembling hand onto the table.

"I have only a hazy memory of that night," Charlotte continues, "and sure, there was some regret when I woke up the next day and Craig was gone — and later, when I discovered I was pregnant. But what matters is that I got my baby girl out of it. I wouldn't change that for a second."

She leans forward, her lip curled, eyes meaner than I've ever seen them.

"As for Jake Johnson, who you claim to have been in a relationship with all these years, well, let me tell you something. He doesn't even *know* you. He thinks you're a crazy woman."

She points her finger at me. "I know you accosted him on the beach the other day, telling him you and he are in love, and that you're supposed to be getting married. And the reason I know that is because his *girlfriend* is one of my best friends, and he told her all about you going nuts at him on the beach."

Girlfriend? Jake has a *girlfriend*?

Charlotte smirks at my expression. "He's been with Savannah for three years, and she's beautiful and amazing, and he loves her. She's about to move into his condo, and she's convinced he's going to propose on her birthday. So, no, honey, he ain't about to leave his incredible model girlfriend for some *psycho* woman who claims to be a dead girl."

She may as well have just slapped me across the face. I grip the table, unable to look at her.

Jake has a long-term girlfriend.

Charlotte stands up, her chair scraping across the floor, as she reaches over and pulls her daughter up from her chair. Mom half-rises, but Dad pulls her back, shaking his head. Charlotte drags the headphones off Taylor's head, packing them away with the iPad.

"Thanks for dinner, Dad." Charlotte's voice is hard, as she zips up the purse, hauling it over one shoulder. "Sorry, but we're done here. Tay, say bye to Pappy and Meemaw."

The little girl's eyes are wide. "Bye," she says in a tiny voice.

Charlotte drags her daughter away between the tables, before my parents can react. She wrenches open the door with such force that it slams shut behind them. I'm aware of other diners staring at us, whispering. Mom looks miserable. Dad, resigned.

Yep.

That could have gone better.

CHAPTER 13: JAKE

June 16

Sunlight poured through Jake's bedroom window, making him squint. What had possessed Liv to choose white muslin to cover an east-facing window? He had asked her this once, around March, when they'd finally finished the room and the morning light was brighter than it had been all winter. "The better to see your naked body when I wake up each morning," had been her reply.

How he wished he could see her body, naked or otherwise, in this light now.

It was 9.45 a.m. on a Wednesday and he hadn't been to work in almost three weeks. David, his boss and good friend, had been generous and understanding. "Liv is family to us — you both are. Take all the time you need, and come back when you're ready. If you want to do a little work from home to distract yourself, let me know, but there's no need if your head isn't in the right space. Whatever works for you."

Jake had thanked him, unsure whether 'all the time you need' really meant multiple weeks off. After a month, he'd probably be pushing it — and if he didn't restart at least some work, they might need to hire someone else. David had passed off two of Jake's refugee cases to a colleague, who was already overworked. But Jake wasn't ready to go back. Perhaps he could get away with another week?

He rolled over, his body aching with tension after another night of bad dreams and restlessness. His phone was already buzzing with activity. He'd never had so many people get in touch with him as he had since the press conference, which had been all over the local and national news, and endlessly replayed in online video clips. Even this morning, two weeks after the conference, he had eleven new messages on Facebook, mostly from old friends reaching out.

Dude, just saw you on the news, it was on my Facebook feed.

I had no idea about Liv, man, I'm so sorry.

Let us know if there's anything we can do.

Take care and I hope she gets home soon.

The most recent Messenger text was from Charlotte.

Latest news piece. Thought you should see it:

She'd added a preview link to a CNN online story, dated today, and headlined:

IS LIV ALIVE? NAKED BRIDE-TO-BE STILL MISSING AFTER THREE WEEKS.

Jake clicked on it, his guts churning. It was standard fare, the main image being of Liv's widely circulated professional headshot, with a video clip of Jake's media statement embedded about halfway down. The reporter, who'd been leaving Jake daily voicemails for the past two weeks along with everyone else, had evidently given up and interviewed a former police psychologist for the piece. Some 'expert pro-filer' with an Opinion.

> *. . . Jackson Bates, whose résumé spans thirty years of psychological profiling for police departments up and down the Eastern Seaboard, told CNN the truth often lies closer to home.*
>
> *"Nine times out of ten it's a close friend or family member, often the spouse or partner, who is responsible in these cases," Bates said in a phone interview.*
>
> *"In the case of Olivia Grainger, where extensive ground searches have been undertaken with no results, the likelihood is high that somebody removed her, or her body, from the scene. We do know only her fiancé and an unrelated bystander were in the vicinity at the time of her disappearance, so suspicion will naturally fall on her fiancé in the first instance.*
>
> *"Did they have a fight, perhaps — some kind of argument that went too far? Was there a physical altercation that led to a fall over the cliff? These are the questions the police should be asking."*
>
> *Bates added it was also possible the victim was not a victim at all, but a runaway bride. However, he observed Ms. Grainger took with her no possessions that would facilitate her escape, and was not even clothed at the time of her disappearance, making this a far less likely scenario.*

Who the fuck did this guy think he was, accusing Jake?

He was a total stranger who didn't know a damn thing about Liv, or him, or any of it. Some retired douchebag looking for another moment in the spotlight, not caring who he hurt to get it.

Jake should sue the bastard for libel. CNN too.

Okay, it wasn't strictly libelous. It was all fair comment in the eyes of the law.

Fuckers.

Jake clicked through to CNN's Facebook feed, where the headline and its photo were in prime spot at the top of the widely followed page, Liv's gorgeous eyes smiling out at him. It had only been posted a couple of hours ago, and there were already hundreds of emoji reactions and 112 comments.

Shit. The story was really getting a lot of attention. But that was good, too. Liv was still front and center in people's minds, which would help if anyone learned anything about where she was.

He clicked through to the comments and reactions. Mostly sad-face emojis, dozens of "care" huggy-hearts. Several wow faces, and at least twenty likes.

Jesus. Who "likes" a story about a missing woman? *Morons.*

Also, seven angry faces. Why? Angry at who? The profiler, maybe, throwing accusations around?

Jake allowed his gaze to slide down the page to the comments, inwardly bracing, his lips screwed up as he read the first.

Aww, her poor fiancé, looks so sad. :'(Hope his pretty lady comes home unhurt. He cute tho. ;) If she doesn't show up, I'll marry him. :D

That wasn't so bad. At least there was a compliment in there.

The comment had thirty-seven replies, plus a bunch of laughter faces and two angry faces.

Hun, if u marry him, u end up dead in a ditch just like her. It's always the husband or boyfriend, listen to the expert!

Did you even watch that video? Dude looked totes shady reading statement, I didn't think he looked that sad, more like no emotion, don't trust him. That sweet little momma next to him crying, THAT was sad! Such a shame for the family, daughter probably long dead at this point.

*I know, super hot rite??! That's what I was thinking as well. :D
Nevermind ur GF, come 2 mama!! Hahaha!*

WTF, was probably him who done it!! You dumb, girl.

Fuck.

Everyone thought it was him.

That he'd . . . what? Murdered her?

Pushed her off the cliff, killing her, moving her body in their car, then going back to the quarry, and acting like she was missing when a hiker showed up?

Lying about it, to everybody?

How would he ever be able to prove that he hadn't?

Jake threw his phone down onto the comforter and rolled into a fetal position, the bedding bunched up beside him. He hugged it, as he'd been doing for weeks, imagining Liv's body under the sheets. But that side of the bed no longer smelled of her. It reeked of his own night sweats, the acrid odor of his despair. The bedding hadn't been washed in nearly a month. His parents had visited him daily in the first couple of weeks since Liv's disappearance, but he hadn't let his mom wash the bedlinens. They'd still retained a trace of Liv's coconut-tropical scent.

Jake rose and stripped the bed, throwing it all into the tiny laundry room. He'd do it later. Right now, he needed to try to ease his mind, and there was only one thing in the world that helped him when he was troubled. Mid-morning on a Wednesday would be perfect, too — the breakers would be clear of the weekend and early morning surfers he usually hung with.

Jake dressed in his surf shorts, T-shirt, and flip-flops and headed out to the garage, where he strapped his favorite board to the roof of the Audi. He drove the ten minutes to the pier at Wrightsville Beach, parking near a fancy ocean-front condo building, next to a bike stand. It was 10.30 a.m. and already hot, but there was a stiff breeze that meant the swell would be good. He grabbed a bottle of sunscreen from the glove compartment, locked the car, and pulled the board off the roof. He stepped through the beach access toward Surf's Up, the little surf shop next to the concrete steps that led up to the Beach House, one of their favorite date night restaurants.

"Hey, Randy." As he pushed through the door, the bell rang cheerfully.

"Jake, dude, so good to see you." Randy paused in his task of hanging up shorts. "Saw you on the news, man. Wasn't sure I'd see you any time soon. So bummed to hear what's been going on — your Liv is a rare jewel. Any updates?"

"No, but thanks, man. Needed to get out on the board. Try to clear my head."

"Of course, dude. Totally get it. Lemme know if I can help at all."

Jake gave him a half-smile.

So many people wanted to help. Nobody could.

He made his way through to the small bank of lockers and stripped off his T-shirt, applying coconut sunscreen liberally over his limbs and torso. He dropped three quarters into the lock to secure his belongings, slipping the locker key around his wrist on its tight band.

"All set. Thanks, man." He waved to Randy, picked up his board, and wove his way out through the racks of wetsuits.

"Take it easy, Jake. Have a good one."

The beach was quiet, with just a few tourist families around — typical for a weekday morning before the summer season fully kicked off in late June. Jake tramped through the toasty sand and into the cool ocean. The water hadn't really been warm enough in May to surf without his short wetsuit, but it had been over three weeks since he'd last been out. Surely the water would be getting tolerable this close to the equinox?

Not that he really cared about getting cold. More than anything, he wanted to feel something, anything, other than the weight of Liv's absence bearing down on his chest.

The tide was out, and he paddled for an age to get to a point where there were some decent swells to ride. He slipped into his natural rhythm: wait, paddle hard, ride the swell toward the shore, paddle back, wait.

His course was unobstructed today since he was the only one out in this spot. The solitude suited him, though. He didn't need to face a bunch of surfers who kinda knew him, who'd seen him around with Liv on the beach, and who now probably had Things To Say about the situation and their faces being all over the news.

Why couldn't people fuck off and mind their business?

Jake lay on his stomach on his board, snorting out a sudden laugh at himself for being mad at a bunch of surfers who were nowhere near him, not bugging him at all. He wasn't mad at them, not really. He was angry at the toxic commenters on Facebook, the lazy, clichéd, 'it's always the boyfriend' armchair psychologists. And he was furious at the 'expert profiler' who publicly claimed he had Jake all figured out as a murderous, duplicitous psychopath.

Jake paddled hard, catching another swell, a sweeter ride this time, letting it take him north toward the shore. It waned and he flopped back into the water, floating a while, his board bobbing nearby. The sun dried his face, leaving salt crystals on his skin. It was past noon, he'd been out here over an hour, and he was thirsty.

Reluctantly, he paddled back to shore and dragged himself out of the water, carrying his board down the beach, the southerly sun dazzling his eyes. Every footstep took him closer to the reality of his situation, the nightmare of his current truth. He could hardly bear to go back once again to his beautiful, empty home. A home that was so full of Liv, in every fixture, every finishing, yet so empty of her presence.

Maybe he'd grab some lunch, rehydrate, then head back out onto the water. Maybe he should just surf all day. Who would stop him? He didn't have anyone to go home to.

As he approached the pier, a woman caught his attention. Chestnut hair, red summer dress. She was obscured by a slim blonde woman, but something about the brunette was so similar to Liv, Jake found himself running across the sand without even realizing.

The women's backs were to him as they climbed the steps to the pier restaurant. As he got closer he realized his mistake. No, not Liv. This woman was shorter, a little wider in the hips. Hair just like hers, though. She turned and smiled at her friend.

Charlotte.

Of course. She'd told him she had today off work.

"Hey. Char!" he called.

Charlotte turned, eyebrows raised, then recognized him and waved. He waved back. He approached her at a slow jog as she retraced her steps down to the beach.

"Jake, hey. I didn't expect to see you out here. We were just going to grab some lunch at the Beach House." She glanced at the board he carried. "You've been surfing?"

He wiped a lock of wet hair from his eyes. Did it look bad that he'd been out? Like he was enjoying himself? Like he wasn't devastated about Liv?

"I needed to get out of my head, I can't stand being at home without her." He smirked humorlessly. "Didn't work, though."

Charlotte nodded, her gaze drifting over Jake's upright surfboard. "Right. Sorry." The woman she was with had also made her way back down the steps. "Oh, this is my friend Savannah. Have you guys met before? Maybe at my twenty-first party?"

Charlotte gestured to the tall, slim blonde, with ultra-long hair, wearing the kind of tasseled floor-length dress Liv would describe as 'boho'. The girl looked like a willow tree, graceful and floaty. She was vaguely familiar.

"Oh, hey, yeah, I think maybe. I'm Jake, Charlotte's soon-to-be brother-in-law . . ." He trailed off. What was he to the Graingers if Liv was no longer around to connect them?

"Hi." Savannah gave a tiny wave of her bangled hand, even though Jake stood less than two feet away. "I think we met at that party, yeah. I met Liv too. Charlie told me all about what's happening right now, I'm so sorry for what y'all are going through. I was hoping to cheer Charlie up with lunch today."

Charlie? Nobody called her that.

"Yeah, it's rough on all of us," he replied.

"You wanna join us?" Charlotte asked, not looking entirely like she wanted him to say yes. Probably because she needed as much of an escape as Jake did, and if he had lunch with them, the conversation would be about nothing but Liv and the police investigation.

"Please do," added the friend, with more enthusiasm. "You'd be very welcome. It's the least I can do, considering everything that's happening."

Jake half-smiled at her. She seemed nice. "Thanks, but I'll leave you ladies to it. I need to go check my phone." He turned to Charlotte. "I read that link you sent me earlier, the CNN report."

Charlotte grimaced. "It was a bit brutal, I know. That so-called expert. But I figured you'd better see it sooner than later."

"Yeah, I read the comments too. And there's probably hundreds more since then."

Charlotte shook her chestnut head. "Don't read them. They know nothing. Social media brings out the worst in everyone. Right, Sav? Savannah is a social media influencer. She knows all about this."

An influencer? That was a real job? Jake quirked an eyebrow at the blonde woman.

Savannah smiled at him, showing white teeth with a characterful gap in the front. "It's so true, unfortunately. So many haters out there. But you should know there are many more people who care." She placed a small, manicured hand on his salt-encrusted arm. "Most people just want to see Liv home, safe and well."

Her eyes were a vivid blue, an August sky, even brighter than his own. Colored contacts for her Instagram, or genuine?

109

"Thanks. I appreciate that." He began backing away. "You both have a good lunch. Char, I'll speak to you soon."

"See you, Jake."

Jake returned to the surf shop, Randy nowhere in sight, probably fixing himself lunch out back. He retrieved his belongings from the locker and checked his cell while hauling on the green T-shirt. Along with various new texts, a couple of WhatsApps, and several Facebook messages, he had three missed calls and a new voicemail, all from Detective Banks.

Shit. Maybe there was some news.

He punched in his voicemail code, slipping on his flip-flops.

"Mr. Johnson, this is Detective Adam Banks of the Wilmington PD. We stopped by your house to see you this morning, but you weren't home, and we need to speak with you. We'll stop by again at 1 p.m. today. It's currently 11.20 a.m. Please call me back if you won't be home so we can arrange a different time."

Fuck. Something was definitely up.

And was it Jake's imagination, or had Detective Banks' voice taken on a grim tone he hadn't used before?

He'd have to get home right away. Maybe this was the day the police told him Liv's body had been found? Or maybe it was better news?

Jake raced to his car and headed home. He showered, changed, and chugged a pint of water. He hadn't eaten anything today, but his stomach was in knots.

At exactly 1 p.m., there was a firm knock on the door. When Jake opened it, Detective Banks and Officer Phelps were standing on his porch, just as expected. But they hadn't come alone.

Five, maybe six officers were talking to each other, leaning on the hoods of their vehicles. One was drinking out of a flask.

What the hell?

"Uh, hi?"

Detective Banks moved into sight, blocking his view momentarily. "Mr. Johnson, thanks for making yourself available. May we come in?"

Jake glanced over the man's shoulder. "Sure." He stood aside to let the two men enter, Detective Banks stopping by the white couch, his young trainee hovering near the door.

"What's going on?" Jake asked.

Detective Banks took a deep breath. "I'm sorry I couldn't explain in my message. There's been no further developments with regard to Olivia's whereabouts, so let me first put your mind at ease about that. This isn't bad news. But that means we do need to take our investigation to the next level, which is a process of elimination for any and all related parties and potential witnesses.

"To that end, we've secured several search warrants, both physical and forensic, for your home and vehicle, and the same for the hiker you met, Kirk Evans. You saw my team outside." He gestured through the window at them.

"Essentially this will involve officers searching your house and car for any evidence, with our forensics team searching for any trace elements that may be of concern. I also have a warrant to take your smartphone, tablet, laptop, and any other similar items of interest. We'll conduct a forensic search before we return them to you." He held out two official-looking printouts, taking an almost-apologetic step toward Jake.

"The truth is, if you had nothing to do with Liv's disappearance, which I believe you don't, there's no need to be concerned. This will help eliminate you from our inquiries, okay? But we have to do this due diligence. I'm sure you understand."

Jake took the sheets of paper and sat down in the gray armchair to read the words, but they slipped through his head in no particular order.

Official.

Warrant.

Search.

Court.

He'd seen many warrants during his legal training, and these looked standard. But he wasn't in the headspace to be an impartial judge.

Should he call a lawyer?

"Okay," he said, slowly. "I get why you couldn't tell me this in advance. It's not something you can warn a person about. But I have nothing to hide." He looked up at each of the cops in turn. The young one looked as overwhelmed as ever. "Do your worst. Do you need me to leave?"

Detective Banks gave him a grateful, close-lipped smile. "No, you're good. Hang out on the couch, drink coffee, read a book. Move seats if anybody asks you to."

He held out his hand to Jake. He was wearing Nitrile gloves. When had he put those on? "Your phone?"

Jake slipped it out of his pocket, unlocked the screen, and handed it over. "It's been blowing up ever since the press conference," he said. "Everyone I ever met seems to want a piece of this."

Detective Banks nodded sympathetically. "It's to be expected." He gave his young colleague a look and Officer Phelps opened the front door. Moments later, the other cops entered the room, taking it over, making the usually airy space seem tiny.

A woman in a dark suit, surely uncomfortable on this hot day, took Jake's phone from Detective Banks. She typed something into it, presumably to stop it locking again, and placed it in the gray plastic box she carried.

Detective Banks gave Jake another apologetic smile, before moving away.

"Make yourself comfortable, Jake. This could take a while."

CHAPTER 14: OLIVIA

June 22

I change positions on a rattan lounger by the pool, trying to keep all my exposed skin under the shade of the turquoise umbrella. I've left the sunscreen inside the pool house and I'm too lazy to get it.

I've been very lazy this last week.

Unmotivated.

Sluggish.

Ever since Charlotte told me about Jake's gorgeous girlfriend.

Savannah.

Ugh.

I flip over the page of Mom's book club novel, a literary fiction title that's a bit heavy for me. Not exactly a summer beach read.

The door slips open behind me, and Mom steps out.

"Honey? You've got a visitor."

I sit upright, blinking in the bright sun. There's a man standing behind her.

Jake?

Mom steps aside as I shade my eyes. Detective Banks. I try to hide my disappointment. Of course it's not Jake. It was foolish to think otherwise.

He's out of uniform, in a gray T-shirt with aviator shades hooked over the neck, navy shorts, and flip-flops. His sturdy, muscled arms and legs are exposed, and covered in dark hair. There's no doubt he's good-looking, if a little stocky and swarthy for my usual tastes.

"Oh. Hey. What are you doing here?" I'm wearing only a black bikini top and white shorts. Detective Banks will have to take me as I am.

"Hi, Olivia," he replies, not answering my question.

"Do you both want sweet tea? Or I could make you some lunch?" Mom asks, evidently thrilled I have a handsome male visitor.

Of course she's excited.

It would be ideal for Mom and Dad, wouldn't it? Some knight in shining armor — or uniform — to rescue and take care of me. Happy ever after, with no inconvenience to them.

"Sweet tea would be great, thank you, ma'am."

Mom practically melts at the 'ma'am' and scurries inside.

The police detective sits on the low chair beside me as I raise the back of my lounger.

"I didn't expect to see you again," I tell him, recalling our last conversation.

He nods. "I know. I was just . . . concerned about you, I guess. I didn't know whether calling your parents would be a good idea, but I wanted to know how you were getting along with them, considering . . . everything. I was in your neighborhood and figured I'd stop by." He looks around to see if Mom's about. "I'd hoped you might be here alone, and I could check on you without your folks realizing."

"Well," I laugh, "you showed up at my parents' front door, and they're here, so they definitely realize. But that's okay. We're getting on fine."

He grins, looking relieved, his smile wide and relaxed. He really is good-looking.

"Mom's been great," I add, "and Dad's definitely softening up. I think he was in a fight with himself about how to treat me, and the side that loves having his daughter back won out. My sister is another matter — she'll take some convincing."

Mom arrives with a tray bearing a pitcher of iced tea and two glasses. Evidently, she plans to leave us to catch up. "Let me know if you get hungry," she says sweetly to Detective Banks, before departing.

"Thanks, Mom!" I call after her. I turn to him, quirking an eyebrow. "She seems excited to see you, detective."

He smiles again. "Well, that's sweet. But it wasn't your mom I came to see. And please, call me Adam. I'm not the detective on your case anymore, just a concerned person — a friend, I hope."

I pour the tea, ice cubes clinking into the tall glasses. "Thank you. Adam. It's good to have a friend."

Adam looks out over the pool toward the creek. "Is that your dock? It's about the longest I've ever seen."

I laugh. "I know, isn't it ridiculous. There's a lot of marshy mudflats to get over before the water is deep enough for the boat." I hesitate. "You wanna take a walk along it?"

He nods, picking up both our drinks as I scramble off the lounger. His gaze travels momentarily across my body before he resumes eye contact and passes me my glass. "Lead the way."

We stroll across the lawn and step down onto the wooden jetty. The mudflats glisten in the early afternoon sun. I pause for a second, laying my hand on Adam's firm, tan arm, the hair soft on my palm. I lift it again, and point. "Look, there."

A heron dips its beak between the rushes, seeking its silvery prey.

Adam smiles, his gaze sweeping across the creek toward Parmele Island. He breathes in the salty scent of the creek. "It's really beautiful. So peaceful."

We amble along the jetty. "Do you have any plans now?" he asks, his eyes still on the landscape. "Figured out anything for the future? Or are you taking it day by day?"

I fall into step beside him. My legs are as long as his, and our pace matches exactly.

"Day by day, mostly. Not much else I can do. I haven't been able to figure out anything in terms of ID and Social Security. I can't get a passport, which would normally be the first step. I mean, Mom has my birth certificate, so I've thought about applying with that. She even still has my expired passport from when I was a kid. But she also has my death certificate, which is on record."

I shrug, trying not to look too disheartened. "I'm a non-person. And we have no desire for further investigations that I know won't help. Last night, Dad was talking about how looking into what really happened could potentially involve digging up my childhood grave, and Mom just about lost her mind at that idea. So, it looks like I'll stay a non-person for the foreseeable future, which leaves me kinda stuck." I blow out a breath and focus on the swaying grasses. I don't want to get tearful in front of this guy.

"You're not a non-person. You're *definitely* real." He nudges me sideways, making my step falter. "See?"

I smile, recovering my balance. "Physically real, sure. Just not in the eyes of the law. And, I guess, you're the law, so . . ." He chuckles at that.

We've reached the end of the dock, which is wide and covered by a sturdy roof. Half of it is taken up by the boat lift that has Dad's prized possession raised out of the water from a hoist hanging from the rafters.

We sit in the shade of the roof, our legs hanging off the side, my bare feet brushing some of the taller grasses reaching for the jetty.

"I mean, it's great living here," I continue. "Obviously. It's a wonderful place, and I love Mom and Dad, even if Dad's hesitant about me. But Mom treats me like . . . It's not only like she has her daughter back, but also like she has her *twelve-year-old* daughter back." I scoop my hair up from my neck and take a breath. "I'm totally dependent on them for food, clothes, a roof over my head, anything else I need.

116

My only freedom is the bike I'm riding around on, and even that's borrowed. I have to find a way to be financially independent, somehow. I'm starting a serving job next week, which Mom landed as a favor from a friend who owns the place. But it's only for the summer, as it's all cash—" I stop abruptly.

Crap. Adam is a police detective, and my new job is illegal.

I turn to him with a grimace. "Any chance you didn't hear that?"

He waves it away, his gaze on a group of squawking seagulls fighting over something in the water. "I'll look the other way. Got bigger criminal fish to fry than someone with no options taking job under the table."

I smile. "Thanks. I appreciate that. It's temporary, anyways."

"Right."

We sit in silence for a few moments, drinking our sweet tea. The heron we spotted earlier swoops before us, scattering the unruly gulls. It lands in the reedy shallows beside our dock, eager to land the spoils of the seagulls' squabble.

"Herons always look like they're from another time, to me," I say to Adam. "Pterodactyls."

He smiles, watching it. "Right? Prehistoric." He heaves another breath, parting his lips as if he has something else to say, but stops. Maybe he's thought better of it.

"I guess I'd better head out." He swings his legs up and rises, helping me to my feet and picking up our drained glasses. "I have a racquetball game with a buddy to get to." I follow him down the dock, wondering what he was going to say, before I catch him up.

We walk slowly back along the dock, the boards creaking beneath us. "Well, thanks for coming to check on me," I tell him as we cross the lawn. Mom is on the terrace, clearing away the half-drunk pitcher of tea. She's watching us, clearly analyzing our body language for any hopeful signs of intimacy.

"No problem. It was my pleasure," Adam replies, his voice soft. He touches my arm lightly. "Hey, I'm glad you've found a source of income, even if it's something I shouldn't know about. Might help you feel a bit more independent, right? Then maybe the rest will fall into place."

I have doubts about that, but he's being sweet. "Hope so."

We approach Mom, who is beaming, the pitcher suspended in her grasp. "How are you guys doing?"

"Fine, thanks, Mom."

Adam reaches out, smiling charmingly as he shakes Mom's free hand. "Thanks for the tea, Mrs. Grainger. I have to get going, but I'll see you again soon."

"You're welcome, detective. Come back any time."

She's positively cooing at him. I snort and Mom shoots me a wide-eyed look as if to say, *what?* Before I can say anything, she turns and disappears through the doors into the house.

"I really appreciate you taking the time today, Adam. It was kind of you. I don't really have any friends, so . . . you know. Thanks."

He nods. "Happy to." He heads for the side gate, hand on top as he pauses. "If you need someone to talk to, you—"

"—know where to find you," I finish for him. "Thanks. I may just take you up on that."

Adam flashes another warm smile. "I hope so. See you around, then. Don't be a stranger." He lets himself out of the side gate.

Don't be a stranger.

But that's what I am. Isn't it?

CHAPTER 15: OLIVIA

June 27

"Order slips go up here, and yell 'ORDER, TABLE FIVE or whatever — just to make sure the kitchen knows, okay?"

I nod.

"Then Carlos or whoever's in the kitchen will ring the bell when the order's up. And don't leave plates under the lights for more than three minutes. Got it?"

I nod again, wiping sweaty palms on my new Beach House apron. "Got it."

"And Hayley took you through the point-of-sale protocols already?"

"Yes. I think I'm good. I can give it a shot. I'm bound to come up with questions as I go, but I'll ask."

Juliette gives me a reassuring shoulder pat. "Absolutely. Ask Hayley or Kevin. Deborah's fairly new. She only started last week, so maybe don't bug her." She gives me an assessing look. "I'll be in the office doing the books, if there's an emergency. But I'm sure you'll do fine. Better to start you this weekend than next, considering how busy it will be for Fourth of July. We get a lot of tourists coming to Wilmington for the holiday."

"I'm sure you do."

I'm lying to this lovely woman, by omission. Of course I know about the tourists, I've lived in the area my whole life. But Mom told her I was a relative from out of town who needed a job and somehow didn't have a Social Security number. I have no idea how Mom got Juliette to trust that I wasn't some criminal on the run or something, but she did. And Juliette has been unfathomably accommodating, agreeing to pay me a lower-than-usual hourly rate, in return for it being cash only, at least until Labor Day weekend. I'm determined to make myself indispensable to Juliette in that time — it's not like there are many other places, if any, that will give me an under-the-table job without asking questions.

I slip between tables to where the platinum-blonde Hayley and a tall, skinny, Black man in his mid-twenties, presumably Kevin, are talking. I wait for a pause in the younger servers' conversation.

"You think it'll get busy tonight?" I ask them with my friendliest smile.

Hayley shrugs coolly as Kevin turns to me with a slight sneer. "Olivia, right?" His tone is icy.

"That's me. Liv," I tell him, showing him my new name badge. "You're Kevin? Nice to meet you."

"Sure." He turns back to Hayley, his back toward me, and resumes their conversation.

Wow. A warm welcome.

I move away, busying myself by grabbing an order pad and pen. A fourth server is putting on her apron by the bar. Behind me, Hayley and Kevin snicker unkindly.

Are they laughing at me?

The other woman, who's maybe in her mid-fifties, her hair a fiery red fading to grayish-brown at the roots, steps over. "I'm so glad not to be the new girl anymore!" she exclaims with a crooked grin. "I'm Deb. I've only been here a week. What's your name?" She squints at my name badge, fumbling for the reading glasses around her neck.

"Hi, Deb. I'm Liv. Great to meet you. I hope you've gotten the hang of this, because I may have questions."

She waves away my concerns. "Of course, sugar, ask me anything. It's a piece of cake. I've been a waitress for thirty years, and it ain't no different here 'n anywhere else. Where did you work before?"

Crap. I should've thought through a convincing back story that doesn't clash with what Mom told Juliette.

"Uh, just little coffee shops, mostly. Not any big restaurants like this." That's true, at least. I did work at two popular downtown coffee shops while at design school.

"Nice! Anywhere I'd know?"

"Probably not," I lie.

Deb nods, still smiling, waiting for a further explanation about where I've worked or where I'm from.

I smile back, unable to offer her more. The restaurant door opens and Hayley scurries to the front desk. "Guess we'd better get started," I say. "I'll grab you if I need help?"

"Don't hesitate. Good luck." Deb pats me on the arm reassuringly.

At least she's friendly, and Juliette is, too. It'd be nice if the younger servers were more welcoming, as I don't have any friends here. Another major problem in this new reality.

Aside from Jake, I have a small but tight friendship circle in the world I left behind. Jake's brother Ed and his wife Annabelle, my fabulous best friend Nicole, whom I met in design school, and Sara, my oldest friend from high school and her partner, Ben. We all hung out as a group, meeting up weekly.

Now there's nobody.

I created fake Instagram and Facebook profiles a few days ago, after my visit from Adam Banks reminded me how few friends I have in this world. Not to try to befriend any of them again, but simply to be able to see where they all are now. After all, I had been the one to encourage the self-doubting Nic into realizing her dream of launching a size-inclusive fashion line when we were in our early twenties. Would she have done that anyways, without me telling her how amazing and talented she was? It seems not. I looked up her company website and her label's Insta handle, and I couldn't find either. Nic's personal Instagram feed was there, but from the captions it looks like she's now a buyer for a retail clothing chain.

And what about Jake's brother? I swear if I hadn't helped him create his Match.com profile, four years ago, pushing him to go out on real dates, he might never have met Annabelle. And, true enough, when I checked, stalking his Facebook page, there are photos of him with a dark-haired woman I don't recognize. Guess he's with someone else in this world.

Like Jake.

It both horrifies and somewhat thrills me that I've had such an effect on these people's lives. These people who, in this alternate timeline, don't even know I exist.

Shaking my head, I force my thoughts to the present, focusing on my new job as the restaurant fills up with noisy tourists and locals. I smile my way through various mistakes, occasionally grabbing Deb for advice or help, even though Hayley and Kevin are far more knowledgeable about this restaurant's protocols. They've been nothing but frosty to me, so I'm not about to give them the satisfaction.

The work is fun, though, and I soon pick it up. The customers are largely friendly and happy, exuding their good vacation vibes, and through their chatter making me a part of their beach experience. The tips are generous and, the more I smile, the bigger they seem to get.

I kinda like it here. And Deb is fun and kind. I could imagine becoming friends with her, grabbing drinks after work, even if she is more Mom's age. Maybe I can make it work here, in this life. Make some new friends, earn enough to rent a small studio somewhere. Maybe Juliette will keep me on after Labor Day, if I reassure her that I'll stick around, unlike her more transient summer workers. Maybe. Or am I being delusional?

Halfway through my six-hour shift, around 8.30 p.m., most of the customers in my section are eating happily and one of my tables has just been cleared. As I grab a few minutes behind the bar to hydrate and rest for a moment, Kevin and Hayley's laughter peals out loudly from the front desk. I glance across. They're talking with a tall, golden-haired couple who've just walked in, and they are evidently on friendly terms with the newcomers.

Kevin moves aside as Hayley leads the couple over to my section, the only free table, and I nearly drop my water bottle.

Jake.

Of course Jake would come in on the first day of my new job.

Looking handsome in a white linen shirt and blue jeans.

Holding the hand of some willowy blonde in her early twenties.

Oh, Christ, is that *Savannah*?

It has to be. She's gorgeous. The model girlfriend Charlotte told me about.

Hayley sits them at my free table, handing them each a menu. She chats with them again for a moment, laughing at some unknown joke. The blonde is laughing with Hayley, but Jake is grim-faced, staring at his menu. As Hayley leaves them, the blonde says something to Jake. He shakes his head.

This is the point I'm supposed to go over to my new customers with glasses of ice water and introduce myself as their server, asking if they want drinks to start.

I can't do it.

I grab Deb's arm as she returns with some dirty plates. "Deb. I need help. Please, switch tables with me. You take the new couple, they're bordering your section anyways, and I'll do your family with the bratty kids."

She looks over at Jake and Savannah, a crease on her brow. "Sure, but why? Your new table looks way better than my family."

I grimace. "It's my ex and his new girlfriend. It's super awkward, I can't do it."

Deb smiles at me kindly, patting my arm. "Say no more. I got you."

"You're a lifesaver. You can have all the tips from the family table, too."

Deb sashays between the tables to look after Jake and Savannah, all smiles and welcomes, while I turn to her family table with three under-tens. The kids are making a spectacular mess on the floor with their fries, but it's totally worth having to clear that up if it means not facing Jake and his girlfriend.

"How are we doing over here? Need more ketchup?" I ask the family, half-watching Deb in my section.

Jake's gaze flicks from his menu up to Deb, then over to me. He doesn't seem surprised to see me. I flush and turn back to the parents, who are barking requests for ice cream sundaes and more drinks.

"You got it," I tell them, trying to muster a dazzling smile that's more for Jake's benefit than theirs.

Kevin is at the kitchen counter as I put in the order. "Swapped tables with Deb, I see?" he comments with a curl of his lip.

Why is this guy being so mean?

"Yeah, I wanted to take the family off her hands, she's got a busier section than me," I lie.

"Oh, is that right? Not because you didn't want to serve Jake and Savannah?"

I frown at him.

How could he possibly have figured out I know Jake?

"Hayley is Savannah's cousin," he continues, answering my unasked question. "Hayley heard *all* about this woman called Olivia who's been claiming to be Jake's long-dead childhood friend and how they're supposed to get married, and some such bullshit. We've been talking about it for weeks. Didn't take us three minutes to figure out it was you when you showed up today. I'm not wrong, am I?" He sneers at me.

I catch my breath, taking a moment to respond. So that's why he and Hayley are being so mean. "My personal life is none of your business," I tell him, giving my tone a chilliness that matches his. "Excuse me."

I turn back to my order, my pulse racing. That's what Kevin and Hayley were laughing about with Savannah at the door.

Me — the weird woman who thinks she's a dead girl.

Yet Jake hadn't been laughing.

I grab my family's fresh drinks from the bar, glancing over to Jake's table. Savannah is talking about something, her manicured hands gesturing, her gaze on the water view outside.

Jake's eyes are on me.

I turn back, serving the family, then checking on my other tables, studiously avoiding looking over to Jake and Savannah for the next hour. After they've paid up, Jake quickly disappears outside while Savannah talks with Hayley for a few minutes at the door. Occasionally, they glance over at me as I clear the last of my tables, bringing empty glasses back to the bar.

Hayley and Savannah part but, instead of leaving, Savannah steps over to where I'm stacking glasses. She stops a few feet from me.

"Hi. I'm Savannah."

I freeze, a glass in each hand, my eyes wide as I turn to her.

"You're Olivia, right?" she continues. "Look, I don't want to be a bitch here, I really don't. But I know you approached my boyfriend a couple weeks ago with some story about how you're his childhood sweetheart and you and he are supposed to be engaged, or something. I honestly have no idea what that's about, but I just want to make something clear to you." She pauses to look me straight in the eye. "Jake and I are together, and we're happy, okay? So I figure . . . you should probably stay away from both of us. And we won't come eat here again. We wouldn't have even come tonight if we'd known you were working here, as it's super awkward. Cool?"

I nod, dumbly. She's actually being relatively nice.

"Great," she says. "You take it easy. And watch out for Hayley. She's my cousin, but she can be kind of a mean girl."

Savannah turns and glides elegantly out of the restaurant, Hayley watching us from afar.

I give Hayley a brilliant smile, and turn back to my task.

I want to cry.

125

CHAPTER 16: JAKE

June 27

One month gone.

This was not a milestone Jake had ever expected to mark. He opened his laptop, which he'd only gotten back from the cops a few days ago, on the desk in Liv's little office. It comforted him, sitting in this room, even if her Ikea office chair was a bit small for his lanky frame. Here he could be surrounded by her swatches, tile samples, and interior renderings pinned to a corkboard. He could see her creative mind at work. It brought him closer to her.

Liv often seemed close to him. As if she were right there, just out of reach. Behind an invisible curtain, perhaps.

He typed an email to his boss.

Hey David, hope you and Andi are good.

    I wanted to check in with you, as it's been a month. I know Steve has been covering my caseload and I'm very grateful, but guessing that's not sustainable for much longer. Maybe we should grab a coffee to talk about me coming back, but maybe working from home some of the time?

    I'm free tomorrow or whenever works for you.

Cheers,
Jake

He hit send and flicked to another browser tab to check on today's media. No new stories about Liv, but a host of new comments on the most recent flurry of reports about the searches at his and Kirk's homes. He skipped past them. He knew better by now than to go down that rabbit hole of assumptions and incriminations.

Jake turned back to his email inbox, as if willing it to produce new messages. He hadn't heard from Kirk since he reached out to him three days ago. It had turned out Kirk was a friend of Bill Waterton, a buddy of Jake's father, whom Jake had met a few times. Bill had called Jake's father to mention the connection, as Bill had been in a running group with Kirk for years.

"The group you were thinking about joining a while back?" Jake's mom asked when Ted Johnson brought the topic up with Jake over dinner.

"That's the one," Ted had replied. "Only I decided against it, as I was playing so much golf with Burt Grainger. Figured that was enough exercise." He patted his growing belly and laughed. "Maybe should've joined, huh?"

Jake had gotten Kirk's email address from Bill, in the hope of both sharing the trauma of being investigated and apologizing for dragging him into all this. The poor guy just happened to be in the wrong place at the wrong time, and now his home and devices were being searched, and he was probably suffering accusations, too. Nowhere near as many as Jake was getting, but still.

However, Kirk hadn't replied to the email. He might be mad at Jake for getting him involved. He might think it wasn't a good idea for them to talk ahead of what could end up as a criminal case.

Or, Kirk might not have replied because he was guilty. He might've come across Liv in the woods, murdered her, dragged her into his car, and disposed of her body. Or Liv might be tied up in Kirk's basement right now. No, not his basement — his house had been searched. Some secret location, then, where she was being kept alive but slowly tortured for Kirk's amusement.

That would be a good reason not to reply to Jake's email.

As if mocking him, Jake's inbox popped up a new message. He huffed a mirthless laugh at himself. That could be Kirk now, apologizing for not getting back sooner, checking Jake was okay.

But it was David.

Hey Jake, great to hear from you.

It's so good to read you're beginning to feel up to coming back to work. That tells me you're feeling less overwhelmed with the situation, which is great news.

However, I think it's not a good idea from our standpoint to have you working on the cases right now, given everything that's happening. This is a tough pill to swallow, as I hope you know that you have all our support, but we have to consider the optics of the situation. You're currently a very public face, and any Google search of your name is pulling up a whole bunch of stories and suggestions that we at RAI believe aren't true, but our clients don't know that.

As you will understand, when our clients are in such a vulnerable position, especially the women and families fleeing persecution, it doesn't look good to assign counsel whose name is even remotely linked to allegations of a possible domestic crime.

It sucks, it's totally unfair, but that's the way it is right now. Hopefully that changes very soon.

I hope you understand that we'll need to continue your leave — which will remain fully paid, with all benefits in place — until this situation is resolved one way or the other.

Don't worry about Steve and the caseload, we've got a few new summer interns doing the grunt work, so he's managing okay, and we've promoted Frannie.

*You focus on taking care of yourself, your family, and
the Graingers, and please know our hearts are with you all
in this terrible time.*

*I'd be happy to go for coffee sometime later in the week
to talk further if you'd like to do that.*

Sorry, and take care,
David

Shit.

Those bastards in the press, and all those basement-dwelling, underachieving social media commenters, were now costing him his job. A job he loved.

What was he going to do now? What if Liv never showed up? David wouldn't put him on fully paid leave forever.

And what the hell had David meant by "until the situation is resolved one way or the other"? Did David believe there could be a version of resolution that involved Jake's guilt? Surely his friend could expect only one possible resolution — Jake's name being cleared of all suspicion. Whether or not Liv was found.

Jake slammed his laptop shut. He couldn't respond to that right now. Anyways, it was nearly 2 p.m. and Detective Banks was stopping by. With more questions, no doubt. Or maybe the police had news. Maybe they'd found something at Kirk's place. Detective Banks had confirmed the results of their searches on Jake's home, car, and devices hadn't shown anything, but he hadn't shared the outcome of Kirk's search.

Jake tidied the living space, clearing away three empty pizza boxes and a couple of beer cans. He was no good at keeping things tidy without Liv around. What was the point? Unless he had visitors, nobody would see it.

He loaded the dishwasher, imagining himself in the future, sitting on the couch. A gray, middle-aged man, thick around the middle like his father, unemployed, spending his days watching Breaking Bad reruns and drinking IPA from the can, surrounded by trash. A male, twenty-first-century Miss Havisham, in his case still mourning his lost bride.

Yeah, he probably needed to nip that one in the bud.

A knock on the door heralded Detective Banks and Officer Phelps on the doorstep. No team behind them this time, thankfully.

"Come in." Jake stepped back, hand outstretched and the two men walked by. "Take a seat. Can I get you guys anything to drink?"

"No thanks, we're good," Detective Banks replied, as Officer Phelps opened his mouth to respond. The young trainee closed his mouth again, evidently thinking better of contradicting his boss.

They sat in the armchairs, Jake taking his usual spot on the couch. The corner where Liv could put her feet on his lap while they watched a movie, his big thumb pads rubbing her soft soles, soothing those high arches. Jake's lap was too light without the weight of her legs — he was unanchored. He might float right up into the little vault of the ceiling they'd uncovered.

"What can I do for you guys?" he asked. "You said you had questions."

Detective Banks gave Jake his usual sympathetic half-smile, which Jake had figured out was a well-practiced expression for victims' families. Or maybe for suspects the police detective wanted to keep on side. Perhaps both.

"Just a few clarifications," Detective Banks corrected. "I understand you've recently been in contact with Kirk Evans?"

"Uh, yeah. That is, after I got my devices back, I sent him an email to see if he was okay after, you know, all the searches. And to apologize for all of this. I feel bad, dragging a bystander into this mess. Assuming he is just a bystander." He raised an eyebrow, continuing after the policeman said nothing. "Anyways, he didn't reply."

Detective Banks pulled the sides of his mouth down. "And how did you get his email address? You previously said you didn't know Mr. Evans."

Was this starting to look bad?

"I didn't — I don't know him. A friend of my dad's, Bill Waterton, contacted Dad when he read about Liv. Turns out Bill is buddies with Kir — Mr. Evans. They're in a running club together. I'd been meaning to try to contact Mr. Evans, so I asked Bill for his email address." Jake paused. "How did you know I emailed him? It was after the forensic search."

On the armchair near the window, Officer Phelps was scratching away at his notepad at a rapid pace.

Detective Banks furrowed his brow. "Mr. Evans called me after receiving your email, to ask for advice as to whether he should be in contact with you. We recommended to him not to respond, considering this is an ongoing investigation. It's better if the two key . . . parties in an investigation aren't in contact with each other. You're a lawyer, Mr. Johnson, I'm sure you can understand that."

Jake pressed his lips together. It made sense. "Yeah, you're probably right. I shouldn't have reached out to him."

Detective Banks shot his colleague a fleeting glance. "Can you tell me if you'd ever met Kirk Evans before that day at the quarry? Considering there's a connection through your father and his friend."

Jake bristled. "I've already told you, a number of times, I had never met the guy. I hardly even know Bill, and I would definitely have no reason to meet any of his running buddies. But it's a small city, we're all one or two degrees of separation from each other. Why Kirk and I should be any different . . ."

Detective Banks nodded. "That's true enough. But you keep calling him Kirk, not Mr. Evans, which seems very informal for someone you claim not to know, especially as he's your parents' age."

Jake shrugged, feeling like a petulant teenager. "I'm an informal guy. And he introduced himself as Kirk at the quarry, so that's what I call him."

"Sure, I get it," Detective Banks replied with a reassuring smile. "We just have to pursue every possible theory and eliminate those, one by one. And one is that you and Kirk already knew each other and were working together to make your story more convincing."

Jake gave a harsh laugh. "Did you read that on social media?"

"No. But I'm guessing you did."

Jake picked at a hangnail on his thumb. "I've been seeing all kinds of theories about what I, or Kirk, or both of us, might have done to Liv. I know none of them are true about me but, like I said, I never met Kirk before in my life. He might be the good guy he seems to be, or he could be a psychopathic murderer, for all I know." He stopped, looking Detective Banks directly in the eye. "Can I ask whether the searches of his home and car turned up anything suspicious? You've only told me about my searches, and I already knew those wouldn't show anything."

"We can't discuss details of an ongoing investigation," Detective Banks responded.

"Especially not with me, huh?" Jake replied, in a colder tone than he'd intended.

Detective Banks didn't answer, bestowing another expertly curated smile. He raised his eyebrows at his wide-eyed young trainee, whose pen was suspended in anticipation, and gave an almost imperceptible nod. Both men rose from their seats.

"Well, thank you, Mr. Johnson. That's all for today." He walked towards the main door, his officer following closely behind. "I'd recommend not reaching out to Mr. Evans again, as we don't yet know how all this will shake down, but if it turns into a criminal investigation . . . Well, as a lawyer, I don't need to tell you. And maybe resist reading the online comments, for your own sanity." Detective Banks held out his hand for Jake to shake. "We'll be in contact again with any further questions or information."

Jake shook the man's hand and opened the front door. "I know I had nothing to do with Liv's disappearance, and you guys have found no reason to suspect otherwise. But I feel like I'm on trial by social media, and the jury is against me. Am I going to need to retain my own counsel?"

Detective Banks patted Jake on his arm, then stepped outside. The younger officer nodded at Jake, walking past them toward where their vehicle was parked.

"You're the lawyer here, Mr. Johnson," Detective Banks replied, his voice low. "You need to do what you think is in your best interest. But you know what can happen when any suspect lawyers up. It can have a very detrimental effect, in terms of public perception. If you have nothing to hide, you might be better off trusting in the system. But it's up to you."

Well, that was a non-answer. Jake blew out his cheeks. "Maybe you guys could make some announcement that nothing was found during my searches that was suspicious? The last thing everybody read in the news was that my home and devices were being searched, which cast me in a suspicious light, and nothing's been reported since. I'm trying to do damage control here. My boss has placed me on indefinite leave because of what this might look like."

"We can't do that, Jake. I'm sorry. Even though the searches turned up nothing, it doesn't entirely clear you, and it won't look good if we make an announcement suggesting your innocence if that later turns out to be off the mark. We still have a ways to go here."

Jake scrunched up his face. "Won't look good for the Wilmington PD, you mean," he added, his tone bitter.

Detective Banks didn't respond. "Hang tight, Jake. We'll be in touch." He stepped off the tiny porch toward the car and his waiting trainee.

Jake closed the door and leaned back against it.

Christ. This was getting worse. He really might need his own lawyer.

Who would he call on for that? His close friends from law school weren't a good idea — too much of a conflict of interest. If he asked his dad for a recommendation, Ted would most likely suggest . . . well, Bill Waterton, but Bill was Kirk's friend, so he was out. Maybe David would have a suggestion. Not that Jake wanted to ask his boss, who was already showing signs of suspicion, for advice on hiring a criminal lawyer.

He couldn't think about that now. He was exhausted, both from what had felt like an interrogation and from very little sleep last night. More terrible dreams of drowning in the quarry lake, Liv's hair always slipping from his grasp.

Jake stepped into their bedroom and collapsed on the downy king-size bed. His duvet was bunched up like a body, the way it always was these days. It was too hot to pull it over him at night, and he needed something to hug. He clutched it now, as if it were Liv in his arms. He pressed his mouth against the soft bamboo cover, and pushed his pelvis against the bulk. Her scent filled his senses. She was right there. Of course it was only the fabric conditioner, mixed with traces of the coconut sunscreen they both used. But it smelled so good. Like home. Like love.

He squeezed tighter, his face buried in what he imagined to be her neck, his tears drawn into the fabric, into her skin.

He would sleep here a while, just like this, holding her.

CHAPTER 17: OLIVIA

July 4

I climb into the back seat of my parents' car, a child again.

"It only takes twenty minutes to drive downtown, but parking will probably be a nightmare," Mom says, getting into the passenger seat, tucking her new floral sundress under her.

"I'll drop you ladies off on the boardwalk while I find a spot." Dad's voice is gruff as he pulls into the street.

Mom claps her hands excitedly, overcompensating. "Oh, it'll be so fun to see the fireworks. We haven't done that in years, have we, Burt?" He says nothing as she turns her head back toward me. "We usually have a Fourth of July party in the backyard, and your father sets off fireworks from the end of the dock. And before we moved to Landfall, we would have parties at our big old house, with fireworks from the next field."

I know, Mom. I've been at every one of your summer parties since I was a child, and Jake's been helping Dad set off the fireworks for ten years.

I smile at her, saying nothing.

"But it's good to have a change," she adds. "And no mess to clear up after!" She laughs, a little forced.

The community's luxurious homes and generous front gardens glide past us as Dad cruises the smooth, curved road to the gates.

"Charlotte's still meeting us there, with Taylor?" I ask Mom.

"Yes. It'll be a big crowd, so we'll meet her at six by the information point and then grab a spot in Riverfront Park. Burt, I'll come get you at the information point after we're settled."

"Fine," Dad grunts.

He remains quiet on the drive to downtown Wilmington as Mom rambles nervously about her upcoming charity fundraising dinner. She's probably worried about me and Charlotte tonight, after what happened at dinner the last time.

She's not the only one who's nervous.

I pick at a tab of plastic on the cooler containing our picnic on the back seat beside me. Is Charlotte even going to be civil to me? Maybe the crowds, the side entertainment, and the fireworks will be enough to distract from our issues. Little Taylor will no doubt need a lot of attention in order not to have a total meltdown that far past her bedtime.

Dad drops us off as close as he can get to the heaving streets that have been closed off for pedestrians, while he heads off to find parking. I lug the heavy cooler with me, as Mom walks in front, carrying two picnic blankets through the crowds to the information desk on the riverwalk. Charlotte is already there, in a wide-brimmed hat and cute gingham playsuit, holding onto little Taylor, who is tugging at her hand, eager to visit the cotton candy machine. It must be a nightmare to keep hold of a kid in an environment like this.

"Hey, honey . . . hi, Tay!" Mom squeals, overdoing the enthusiasm as she hugs them. I know she only saw them a few days ago.

"Hi, Charlotte," I say, when Mom is done fussing.

My sister looks at me. "Hi." Her face is expressionless. An improvement on last time, anyways.

136

I crouch down by Taylor. "Hey there. Remember me?"

Taylor ignores me, pulling at her mother's hand again. "*Now* can we go to the cotton candy, Momma?"

"Oh, alright, Tay. Don't pull me, okay?"

We make our way over to the stall, adorned in Stars 'n' Stripes, and displaying cotton candy in all colors of the rainbow.

"This reminds me of when we were kids," I tell Charlotte, persisting despite her chilliness. "We were at the state fair when we were . . . I dunno, I guess you were maybe five? I would've been around eleven. I was supposed to be old enough to mind you for a minute. We were at the coconut shy, and Jake and some other kids from school were playing, I got distracted. I turned around and you were gone, and I was terrified. I couldn't tell Mom or Dad I'd lost you, so Jake and I hunted for you, me in tears the whole time. Eventually, we went to the first aid desk and found you, totally happy, sitting on the counter with a huge puff of pink cotton candy somebody had given you. I never did tell Mom and Dad I'd lost you."

"What?" Mom asks, eavesdropping as she pays for Taylor's cotton candy. "When was this?"

"Back when we were little. No harm done," I reply. "Do you remember that, Charlotte? You wanted to give me your cotton candy to cheer me up, I was crying so hard. You were totally chill, having a lovely time with the nice people who were looking after you, but I was a mess, so you ended up comforting *me*. You were such a generous kid."

My sister hands Taylor the cloud of pale pink sugar, twisting her mouth. She nods, just once. "Yeah. That's an early memory of mine. Not of you crying, but the kind people who gave me cotton candy and looked after me, after I wandered over to the stall. You were busy with the big boys. I didn't think you'd miss me."

I smile at her. "Well, I did miss you."

A familiar crease appears above her nose, but she turns away. "Let's find a spot to have a picnic, or Taylor will eat nothing but sugar." The comment is aimed mostly at Mom, but it's sort of to me, as well.

Progress, maybe?

We settle between several large families in the park, spreading out our blankets and food. Mom fetches Dad from the information kiosk while Charlotte focuses on feeding her daughter. I watch them, as I munch silently on a sandwich. Okay, so Charlotte isn't exactly being friendly, but at least this time she's not overtly hostile. Maybe Mom had a talk with her when they saw each other earlier this week. Charlotte can be gruff like Dad, but she'd do anything for Mom, and if Mom asked her to accept me, she'd try.

Taylor eats a couple of sandwich triangles and some carrots and hummus, followed by strawberry yogurt, and then she's done. Instantly, buoyed by the combined sugar content of yogurt and cotton candy, she's desperate to run around and explore. There's a host of game stalls and food trucks lining the park, and the live country band has started on the stage at the other end. They'll play for a couple of hours until it's time for the fireworks.

Poor Charlotte hasn't eaten yet, and looks exhausted. She's already done an eight-hour shift at Zara today, and even now she can't relax with Taylor trying to drag her to her feet. I pour Charlotte a plastic cup of the wine I smuggled in a steel water bottle.

"Drink this, it's rosé. And eat something. Let me take Taylor for an hour." She looks like she's going to protest. "Come on," I coax. "What can happen? We'll play whack-a-mole, get Taylor's face painted, listen to the band. And you can chill out here, just relax. Okay?" I get to my feet, not intending to give her a chance to refuse. At least now I have a week of restaurant earnings in my wallet so I can pay for this stuff.

"Momma, I want to go with *yoo-oo-uu*," Taylor whines, tugging at her mother again.

Charlotte winces. Then, tempted by the wine, she gives in to my suggestion. "Okay. I'm trusting you," she murmurs for my ears alone.

She raises her voice to her daughter. "Honey, go with your Auntie Livvie. I haven't eaten my dinner yet, and she'll

138

be able to take you to all the fun stuff that I'm too tired to do. Okay? You go have a fun time, and come back and tell me all about it."

Auntie Livvie. She didn't make eye contact, but she referred to me as *Auntie Livvie.*

A major breakthrough.

I hold out my hand to my little niece. "Come, it'll be great. Which first, whack-a-mole or face painting? We could do your face like a butterfly. You like butterflies, don't you?"

Taylor nods, her pout diminishing. "Pink and yellow?" she asks in a small voice, brown eyes wide.

"Absolutely, pink and yellow. And maybe with some swirly patterns." I keep my hand outstretched and this time, she takes it. Without another word to Charlotte, who is digging into the picnic cooler, we stroll over to the face painting station and get in line.

"Hi Taylor," a mom calls from in front of us, her hand on the shoulder of a small boy. "Archie, say hi to Taylor." The boy smiles, not removing his thumb from his mouth. "Who's this? Where's your Momma?" the woman adds, narrowing her eyes at me.

"My Auntie Livvie," Taylor replies, still holding my hand. She points over to our blankets. "Momma is there with Meemaw and Pappy."

The woman nods, not breaking her gaze from mine. "I'm Blair, I know Charlotte and Taylor from playgroup." She holds out her hand. "I had no idea Charlotte had a sister. Auntie . . . Livvie, was it?"

"Just a term of affection," I reply, confident that Taylor wouldn't understand my response. "Olivia, or just Liv. Friend of the family's. Good to meet you. And this is Archie?"

"Yes." Blair seems satisfied with my explanation. "We're going to have his face painted like Spiderman, aren't we, Archie? He's obsessed," she adds, in a confidential tone. "It's Spiderman everything. He wanted to wear the entire costume tonight, but that thing is so hot and synthetic, especially on a warm night like this, I had to tell him it was in the laundry otherwise he'd have been complaining all evening. Kids, huh? You got any of your own?"

I shake my head as little Archie is called to have his face painted. "It's nice to get moments like this with other people's, and then get to give them back when they get over-tired," I reply with a smile. "It'll be a late night for this one tonight." I nod my head at Taylor, whose face is alight with excitement.

The other face-painting artists calls us over. "Nice to meet you, Blair."

Taylor and I bond over butterflies, whack-a-mole, and silly dancing to the funk band for over an hour. Eventually I bring her back to our picnic spot, where Mom, Dad, and Charlotte are relaxing. I even get a slight, but discernible, smile of gratitude from my sister.

"Thanks," she mutters, looking away again.

"No problem. We had super fun, didn't we, Taylor?"

"Yes." The child slumps into her mother with her thumb in her mouth. It's past eight and, as I predicted, the kid is fading.

I'm about to sit down and finish the wine, when a tap on my shoulder stops me. Adam Banks is standing before me, his smile dazzling. He's even more tan than the last time I saw him a couple of weeks ago at the house, and his white T-shirt shows off his color.

"Hey, Liv, good to run into you," he says. "Hi, Mrs. Grainger. Mr. Grainger."

"Hello, detective," my mother coos, as Dad nods a greeting.

"Good to see you too," I tell him. "I'm surprised you spotted me in this crowd."

He laughs, looking at Taylor, who is drifting into a nap on her mother's lap. "I was watching the band and I couldn't miss you and that little girl. A pair of crazies doing the most insane dance moves ever."

I chuckle. "My niece requires very silly entertainment. You wanna head over to the band again for a while? I think they're playing another half-hour or so." Truth is, I don't want to subject him to the interrogation I can see Mom's waiting to start.

Adam nods, waving farewell to my parents. Even as we leave, I can see Mom leaning in to tell Dad something, no doubt about her transparent hopes for me getting involved with Detective Banks.

"You doing okay?" Adam asks as we weave through the crowd toward the people dancing near the stage.

"Pretty good, I guess. Definitely progressing with my family. Tonight is the first time I've been able to bond with my niece, or be on civil terms with my sister. So that's a big step."

He stops behind a group of dancers, nodding his head to the beat of the funk band. Or at what I'm saying. Perhaps both.

"And the job I'm not supposed to know about? That going well?" He has to raise his voice over the music.

"Yeah, it's fun. I got lucky and drew the long straw to get tonight's dinner shift off work, otherwise I'd be there now. Keeps me busy, gives me something to do, and the tips are really good. I'm earning more than I thought I would. It almost makes me feel like I could manage, you know? Get a small place of my own, or something. But I guess that's a pipe dream. It's probably not sustainable, working like this."

Adam pushes out his generous lips as he considers this. "Probably not. Not without a Social Security number, not paying your taxes . . . It'd catch up with you, even if generous folk like me look away. You won't get this kind of preferential treatment from other authorities."

He grins, turning to me, but the smile fades. "I've done as much research as I can on what happens to John or Jane Does without any ID. It's generally . . . not a good outcome. I don't know how I can help you any further. I feel totally useless." He screws up his nose. "I hate it. I'm not used to being unable to help. I took this job so I could help people, and I do, every day. But with you . . . I've got nothing."

I put my hand on his arm. "It's not your job to take care of me. You did your part, and you really did help me. Getting me back with my family, getting the DNA tests done, everything. It's not your fault this situation is so weird and unprecedented. It's not in your control. Not in any of our control." I turn back to the band. "I just have to figure out how to live with how it is. At least now I have comfortable accommodations, and I'm earning some money. Could be a lot worse."

He nods again, but says nothing more.

We listen to the music for a while, occasionally commenting on the song being played, or pointing out an eccentric dancer. As the band moves into a final slower number, I wonder if Adam will ask me to dance, but he doesn't. Couples move before us in a sultry two-step, and it's a little awkward to be watching but not joining in. I'm somewhat relieved when the band stops, and the crowd applauds.

"I better get back to my family for the fireworks," I tell Adam. "You care to join us?"

He smiles. "No, I'm with buddies, I shouldn't desert them all night. One of them is my ride home, and I'll never find them when everyone's leaving. But I'd love to check in with you again. Do you have a cellphone now?"

"Oh. Yeah, sure." I give him my number and he taps it into his own phone. "So, yeah," I add awkwardly, "keep in touch. Have a great night."

He smiles at me. "I'll text you. Goodnight, Liv."

I join my family just as they're rising to gather the picnic items. The crowd has intensified ahead of the fireworks. Little Taylor is asleep in Charlotte's arms, her head lolling on her shoulder. I smile at them, and my sister gives me an involuntary smile back, then quickly turns away.

"Have fun with Detective Banks?" Mom asks, pointedly.

"Sure, he's a nice guy," I say, packing up some trash.

"You going to see him again?" She folds up a blanket, trying to act all casual.

I sigh, closing the cooler. "Maybe, Mom. I don't know. Look, the fireworks are starting."

As the spectacular colors explode against the darkening sky, Mom's question repeats in my head. What will I do if

Adam texts and wants to meet up? He's showing clear interest, researching options for me, taking my number. Coming round to the house when he's not on my case anymore, and he's off duty.

But I don't think I can return his interest, no matter how keen Mom is, or how convenient it would be to get involved with a man who's as good-looking and kind as he is, and who could take care of me.

I don't want to be taken care of. By anyone. I need to be my own woman. Independent. Free.

And there's the small matter of the man I'm in love with.

Jake Johnson.

CHAPTER 18: OLIVIA

July 15

"Bye, Juliette. Have a good dinner shift."

Deb holds the restaurant door open for me as our boss waves back. She's managed to hire a couple more servers, both fun and friendly, since we got slammed on the holiday weekend. That means that Hayley and Kevin are outnumbered by people who like me. Plus, I sometimes get to do only the lunch shift. A win–win.

"You riding your bike?" Deb jangles her car keys as we step down to beach level. "I can give you a ride home if not."

"Thanks, but yes, I'm on my bike. And I think I'll stay on the beach a while. It's so beautiful today and I've got my new book. You get home to Frank."

Deb waves farewell as she heads for the parking lot, and I step out onto the sand. It's just past 5 p.m. and the sun is still high. The air out here feels almost as hot as the Beach House kitchen, with its sizzling pans and deep-fat friers. But I've always loved the heat.

I plop cross-legged onto the sand and rub sunscreen into my skin. It's the same brand as the one I've always used

— was using at the quarry lake the last time I saw Jake. *My Jake*, the real one. He was rubbing it into my back just before I fell over the cliff. The tropical coconut scent of the lotion reminds me of him, of our summers together. So many summers. I never got sick of him. Nor that smell.

I pull out my journal and pen, along with the novel Mom discarded after she was done with her latest book club. Since she's lived at Landfall and joined the ladies book group, she's bought a hot new title every month, so her bookshelves are now crammed with great reads. In my old reality, I often borrow Mom's new books once she's done with them, and I've picked up that habit here. Guess some things are the same in both worlds.

I've started writing a list of elements in my life that are the same, and those that are different, to see how I've affected things. I open my journal to the page I've dog-eared for the purpose.

Different than my old life
- *I'm a non-person who died aged 12, no ID or Social Security, no design business, etc. etc.*
- *Jake and all my friends don't know me*
- *Mom and Dad's home décor, terrible and for sure not done by me :O*
- *Mom now religious, believes I'm a miracle*
- *Charlotte has a daughter, Taylor (!!) b/c Jake and I weren't at party to stop her one-night stand with Craig Phillips*
- *Jake doesn't work at Refuge Advocacy Int'l — instead some private law firm*
- *Jake has a girlfriend, Savannah, and lives in a condo at the beach*
- *Jake and I never bought our place together, new family now lives there*
- *Nicole doesn't have her own fashion line, instead works as a buyer*
- *Jake's brother Ed never met Annabelle on Match*

Same as old life
- *Mom and Dad live in same house at Landfall, moved there from our old house in same year*
- *Parents' hobbies (book club, bridge, fundraising, golf, poker)*
- *Mom's yellow bike (selected without my influence, even tho I showed it to her in my version)*
- *Charlotte still works at Zara, even tho her path was different, and lives downtown*
- *Jake is still a lawyer*
- *Jake surfs*
- *Jake still prioritized a home near the beach over being close to downtown office*
- *Sara and Ben still married and have same kids*
- *Other friends' lives seem unaffected in major ways*

There must surely be countless more items to add to this list, tiny ways I affected people's lives — or failed to — since I was twelve. But it's impossible to know what they all are.

And it's surprising how many things are the same. I always thought my high-school friend Sara would never have got together with her now-husband Ben if I hadn't steered her toward him at prom. But it seems they found their own way, without my involvement.

I met Sara when I was fourteen, and Nicole when I was nineteen — yet in this reality, my two closest girlfriends haven't even heard of me. They're not even friends with each other in this world, as I introduced them. In my world, we've hung out as a trio since our early twenties.

I jot this additional thought down in my 'Different' column and turn to my Liane Moriarty novel. But it's hard to focus while I'm obsessing over the minutiae of my parallel realities. My gaze slides up to the blue horizon. This section of beach is a little further north than where Jake surfs, but there are a couple of figures far out in the swell.

I lie back on the warm sand, closing my eyes, slowing my breathing. I've been attempting moments of mindfulness to quiet my ever-racing thoughts. Doing my utmost to live in the present and embrace my blessings.

Warm sun on my skin. Soft sand at my back. A gentle breeze caressing me. The crash of the ocean on the shore. My body, young and vital.

The skin on my thighs cools as a shadow passes over them. I open my eyes, squinting into the sun. A tall person, silhouetted against the bright light, is standing directly over me.

"Hey," a low voice says.

Jake.

I start upright into his shadow, looking up at him. He's in red shorts and a blue T-shirt. Same simple dress sense as ever. I make a mental note for my list.

"Uh, hey," I reply. "I . . . wasn't expecting to see you."

Jake gestures over his shoulder toward a waterfront condo complex. "That's my building," he says. "I was on my deck and spotted you on the beach. Figured maybe we could talk. If that's okay with you."

I raise my eyebrows. "Sure. Of course. Uh . . . wanna sit?"

He drops down beside me, mirroring my crossed legs. He stares out at the water, which is softening to a deep corn-flower blue in the late sun.

"I hope Savannah didn't offend you the other night, after we had dinner at the restaurant." His words are slower than usual. "I couldn't stop her from talking to you, so I was a coward and waited outside."

I let out a small laugh. "No. She was fine. Told me to stay away, but she was surprisingly sweet about it. She seems like a nice person."

He nods. "Yeah, she's great." He turns his head to look directly at me, his eyes clear, blue. "We're very happy. Been together three years. I'm planning on proposing next month, on her birthday."

I manage to force a smile, even though my stomach is churning. "How did you guys meet? She seems . . . young."

"She's twenty-five, only three years younger. We met at a charity event my law firm was sponsoring when I was a new associate there. She'd been hired to do the event's social media. Savannah is a social media influencer and model, and does PR work on a freelance basis."

"Right." I draw a face in the sand, but can't bring myself to give it a smile. I flick it out of existence.

Jake watches my finger. "I've been thinking a lot about you. Everything you told me. If you're really Livvie Grainger, back from the dead. It feels like . . . I dunno. It's really freaky. Like you're here to give me some kind of closure about that day, the day you died, when we were kids. I totally blamed myself for your death. I've been living with the guilt for sixteen years."

I examine his face. It looks sadder than I've ever seen it.

"Jake. We were stupid kids at a quarry and nobody knew we were there. You have nothing to feel guilty about." I hesitate. "How did it happen? If you don't mind talking about it." I have little memory of that day, apart from what my Jake has told me when reminding me of his heroics.

Jake meets my gaze, nodding slowly. "I'd done a big running jump into the water, and I ran back up to the top of the cliff. You were on the edge, trying to figure out whether you could do it too. You turned to me and slipped on the scree and went kinda slowly over the edge. I grabbed for you, had a grip of your wrists, but my hands were still wet and greasy from sunscreen. I couldn't hold on. You slipped through my fingers, right down onto the rocks that you'd just been figuring out how to clear. Your body was just . . . broken."

His voice catches. "I totally freaked, of course. Ran down, and tried to pick you up, but I couldn't. I stayed on the rocks with you for . . . I don't know how long, just crying and holding you. My old lab Ginny was there, going nuts. Eventually I had to leave you. Ginny wouldn't run home with me. She stood guard over you the whole time until I came back with my folks." He rubs the back of his hand against his eye. "It was the worst day imaginable. Your poor parents . . ." He trails off, screwing up his nose, blowing out a hard breath.

I raise both eyebrows. "Jesus. That must've been horrific. But . . . it wasn't your fault, you know. It really wasn't." I put a hand over his. "And look. I'm here now. There's a world in which you saved me that day. For me, it was different. You grabbed me, and I was fine. I barely even remember the incident, although you've reminded me about saving my life often enough." I emit a quiet chuckle. "It's kind of annoying, actually."

Jake manages a half-smile. "It's so wild. You died that day, but here I am, talking to you on the beach. And I *know* it's you." He studies my face. "I knew the moment you came up to me last month. You're unmistakable. I always knew you'd turn out to be . . . you know. Beautiful. I didn't even need to see that little scar to know it was you. Your face, your voice, everything. Older, but the same. So, yeah, I'm sitting here talking to a dead girl." He's sifting sand through his fingers. "If you didn't have a job at the Beach House, if Kevin and Hayley hadn't been bad-mouthing you, and if Savannah hadn't approached you, I'd think you were a figment of my imagination." His gaze wanders away. "Or a ghost. You always believed in ghosts when we were little."

I laugh, nudging him slightly, the way Adam had with me on the dock. "I'm real. Corporeally speaking. Not in the eyes of the U.S. government, but that's another issue."

"Yeah, I can guess. But I want to hear more about your version of our lives. You said . . . we're together?"

I nod, my smile fading. "In my . . . timeline, I guess, you and I were never with anyone else. We first kissed at the lake when we were fourteen, lost our virginity to each other a few years after that, also at the quarry. Prom king and queen our high-school senior year. You went off to Princeton and I stayed here to go to school for interior design. Mom and Dad helped me rent a loft downtown, which you moved into after law school. I started my business, which has been doing well, and that allowed you to go into legal advocacy for refugees, instead of having to earn top dollar at a private practice. Which I guess is what you do now."

Jake nods thoughtfully. "Yeah. It's okay. Refugee advocacy would've been great, though. But I was able to buy my condo a couple of years ago, and having this much access to the beach is amazing." He lifts his chin backward, toward the building behind us. "Savannah gets a lot of free swag but she doesn't have a big income, so she's probably gonna move in soon." He says the last part quietly, almost as an apology. "In your version, you and I live together?"

"We bought a little fixer-upper not far from here, by Bradley Creek, a year ago. I redesigned the interiors myself and it's really sweet. And . . ." I blow out a breath, "in my version, we're getting married next month. August 20th."

Jake frowns. "That's Savannah's birthday."

The day he's planning to propose to her.

"Huh." Not much more I can say.

Jake narrows his eyes as he watches two surfers bring their boards to the shore. "And in your version, we're happy, right? You and me? We love each other?"

I follow his gaze. "Very happy. Never loved anyone else. We're kind of fundamental to each other. Like we *are* each other, you know? I mean I've had some issues with that, with the wedding approaching so fast. Fears about how we've never known anything else, so how can we be sure? But I never for a moment stopped loving you." My voice cracks, my sinuses filling up. "Since I've been here, and I no longer have you, I realized just how much. How incredibly lucky I was. How I should never have taken you for granted."

He doesn't look at me, but places his sand-crusted hand close to mine. "I can see how it would've happened that way between us. If you'd lived. Even at twelve years old, I already adored you. I didn't recognize it as love, at that point, but I did think we'd be together always."

I nod. "You told me the same thing, the day we first had sex. You'd just turned seventeen, I was still sixteen. That was the first time you said you loved me, too. I told you it had been different for me. When I was twelve, you were just my best friend who happened to be a boy. Then I hit thirteen and puberty, and all these feelings gradually formed, and I developed a crush on you that I couldn't handle. I was in total agony until you kissed me in the lake when we were fourteen." I smile, pushing away a tear that has slipped down my cheek. "We never stopped kissing, after that."

Jake smiles. "It's amazing we made it another, what, two, two-and-a-half years before we slept together? I remember being a very horny teenager."

I chuckle through my tears. "I know. I remember. Lots of quarry pool erections."

Jake laughs, turning his handsome face to me. A phone dings a dual-tone bell I don't recognize. His expression changes, a flash of darkness passing across his eyes, and he pulls his hand away from mine. He checks his cell, pursing his lips.

"Savannah. I'm picking her up in an hour, and I have to change first."

"I need to get home anyways," I tell him, hiding my disappointment. "My folks will be serving dinner soon, and I need the free food."

He nods, rising to his feet. The sadness is back.

"Thanks for talking to me, Liv. I needed to hear this stuff."

I stand, brushing sand from my shorts. "I don't know that it helped you get any closure." I stare into his beautiful face. "I don't want to complicate things for you, I swear."

"It's okay. I mean, of course it's ridiculously complicated and messed up, but it's not your fault. None of this is even remotely explainable. I just have to figure out how to accept there's a version of life where you didn't die, where I was able to save you. Maybe if I can do that, I'll feel more . . . I dunno. Settled."

"I hope so." I turn away, my heart breaking, not wanting to let the man I love go. "Take care, Jake."

"You too, Liv. See you around."

He heads off in the direction of his building and I wander down the sand toward my bike.

As I pass into shadow under the pier, out of Jake's view, I stop behind a barnacle-crusted pillar, finally able to let out the sobs I've been holding in.

CHAPTER 19: JAKE

July 4

Jake cursed under his breath at the turgid stream of Fourth of July traffic. Why had he thought meeting his brother at the fireworks would be a good idea?

He had to go all the way up to Market Street before he found a parking spot. After reversing into a space, he paused to put his sunglasses on and pull his ball cap down so his face was barely visible. He hadn't been out in public much, except to the beach, and he didn't want strangers recognizing him from the news. It could turn nasty.

Jake strode the twenty minutes back to the historic downtown district, making his way to the park near the river-walk where the Fourth of July festival was. He wove through the crowds, trying to locate the spot where his brother had texted to say they were sitting, near the side of the stage.

Ed called out to him, getting up to greet Jake as he walked towards them. They hugged, slapping each other on the back before stepping back.

"Sorry I'm late, man," Jake said. "Traffic was a nightmare. Hey, Annabelle." His sister-in-law was looking good, as usual. Her glossy red hair, which was loose around her shoulders, complemented the green, strappy sundress she wore. Stocky Ed, on the other hand, was balding rapidly and looking more and more like their short mother as he aged. Jake thanked the universe for the millionth time for making him favor his tall father.

"No problem, take a seat." Ed gestured to the plaid blanket laid out on the grass. "You hungry? Annie brought enough food for six people, God knows why." Annabelle only smiled in response.

Jake sat down, cross-legged, across from Annabelle. "Great, I'm starving. I've barely eaten all day." He leaned forward to take a thick slice of quiche from a Tupperware container. "Man, it's busy this year."

"I'm just so happy you came out," Annabelle's pretty face held an expression of affectionate concern. "How are you holding up?"

Ah, *that* phrase. It was the line he'd heard more than any other over the past five weeks. If he had a dollar . . .

Jake gave the usual close-lipped, subdued smile and nod, which seemed effective in pacifying friends and family. "I'm hanging in there. It's rough, obviously. Comes in waves. Sometimes I'm doing okay, I can get out of bed, go for a surf, do my laundry. Others, not so much." He shrugged. "The better days are getting more frequent. And I need to get out more, not just surfing but with other people. Do stuff like this." He forced himself to take a big bite of quiche.

"Good for you," his sister-in-law replied with a soft smile. "I can't imagine how hard it must be for you. I mean, it's been tough enough on us. We love Liv like a sister, you know that. Ed and I wouldn't even be together if it weren't for her. We really miss her, Jake."

Jake nodded, swallowing his food along with the lump forming in his throat. "I know. Mom and Dad are really upset, too. And so many people have been reaching out to me, asking if they can help. It's kinda great knowing how many people care so much about her."

Ed placed his hand on Jake's shoulder, squeezing it lightly. "Totally, man. She's the best. And all the rest of that stuff — the comments, the people who don't know her, or you — just ignore them. They're small-minded pricks with nothing better to do than make up dumb theories and state them like fact."

Jake let out a breath. "It's hard. We've no idea what happened to Liv, and yet I'm on trial by social media, and everyone seems to be finding me guilty. I had to ask Detective Banks last week if I needed my own lawyer."

Ed's eyebrows raised. "What did he say?"

Jake took a sip of water as he looked at his brother. "That as a lawyer myself, I was better placed to judge that, and it was up to me. But also, that lawyering up can look defensive, and I'm already under public scrutiny. He suggested maybe I would be better off trusting in the process. I mean, that's kinda comforting in itself. I'm pretty sure he believes me. Which I really need. Not everybody does." His mouth twisted wryly. "I've been indefinitely benched from work. David says the optics aren't good."

"That sucks, man. I'm sorry, I know you were hoping going back to work could distr—"

Whatever Ed was going to say next was drowned out by the noise of the crowd as the band came onto stage and began to play a cover of one of Jake's favorite tunes, 'Carolina Can'. It had been one of the songs on repeat on his iTunes playlist at Princeton, causing his New Yorker roommate to tease Jake endlessly about his country roots, but Jake didn't care. The song made him think of home. Of Liv, who'd just rented the loft in the red-brick warehouse conversion he could see the corner of right now. He could remember longing for the semester breaks, when he could stay with her there, making love on their cheap new Ikea sheets, and making plans for the future.

"I'm gonna head to the front and watch the band a while," Jake announced to Ed and Annabelle. He rose, quickly joining the small crowd at the front of the stage, where he could more clearly see the charismatic male singer, a short Black dude in an oversized cowboy hat. The song came to a close, and Jake joined the others, clapping and whistling his appreciation.

The next number was a classic foot-stomper that had everyone dancing. Jake smiled, wishing he was brave enough to dance along with them. He would have, if Liv had been there. In fact, she'd have forced him into it. He could almost see her among the crowd now, her long limbs always a little ungainly but unabashed in their joy.

A woman on the far side caught his eye. Well, her hair really. She was watching the dancers, was shorter than Liv, but had hair just like hers — the exact same shade of chestnut. He smiled. Of course. *Charlotte*. He should've guessed she'd be here tonight.

Jake waited until the song finished and pushed his way through the applauding crowd toward her. "Hey," he greeted. It was tough to smile at her, though, when they were sharing so much pain.

She turned to him, her eyebrows popping up. "Jake, hey. I didn't think I'd see you here this year."

"Just trying to get out more. I've hardly seen anybody," he replied, a touch defensively. Was five weeks of a missing fiancée too soon to be out and about? "How are you doing? It's good to see you out," he added pointedly. If she was out, why couldn't he be?

"I'm okay. Trying to get on with life as much as possible. Hey," she turned, stepping aside to reveal her companion. "You remember Savannah." It was the blonde he'd met with Charlotte at the beach a couple of weeks back.

"Yeah, right. Hi again."

Savannah smiled with a disarming sweetness. "Hey, Jake."

Her voice held that soft sing-song tone people had used when his grandmother died, when Jake was ten. "So good to see you here. I've been thinking of you and this whole situation so much—"

The band started a new number, and they moved away to hear each other more easily. They stopped next to a face-painting station, where a small boy was getting the full Spiderman treatment.

"—so awful, what people are saying online," Savannah continued. "That kind of public vilification is the last thing you need, given everything you're already going through. I'm so sorry."

Vilification? Jake hadn't thought it was as bad as that. Just some douchebags on social media spouting dumb theories.

"I can't stop myself reading the articles, but I've been trying not to read the comments," he replied honestly. "Especially not in the past couple of weeks. Ever since the cops did the searches on my home and stuff."

Savannah twisted her pretty mouth, brow furrowed. "Probably for the best. You need to focus on what's important. Finding Liv, bringing her home, right? I swear, it's so distressing. I can't stop thinking about it."

Sure, it was all about Savannah and her feelings. Typical of a woman whose job was to look gorgeous on Instagram to make it all about her.

"It's kind of you to give it so much of your attention," he replied, in a slightly chilly tone.

Savannah raised a perfect eyebrow, ever so slightly. "Of course. This is my close friend's sister we're talking about, too. I've been devastated for Charlie." She smiled at Charlotte sympathetically.

Okay. Maybe he'd misjudged her. "Thanks. It's good to have people around who care."

Charlotte, who'd been watching the little boy in the Spiderman face paint, looked at Jake. "How'd it go with the police searches? I haven't spoken to you since they took away all your devices."

What was she asking? Whether the police found anything to suggest he might have had something to do with what happened to Liv?

"Fine. Obviously nothing came up." Jake's voice was deliberately cool again. "They won't tell me the results of the searches on the hiker, that Kirk guy. They've been asking whether we knew each other before it happened. We didn't." He shot a glance at Savannah, who was listening carefully. "But I made the mistake of emailing him, just to apologize for dragging him into all this, and the cops got antsy about how I got in contact with him. He's a friend of my dad's buddy, Bill. Still, it didn't look great."

Charlotte grimaced. "I guess you have to be real careful, public perception being the way it is. That hiker's under a bunch of scrutiny. Just lay low and don't do anything until it blows over?"

Would this ever blow over? What if Liv was gone forever?

"I can't afford to put a foot wrong right now." He blew out a breath, so exhausted by these conversations about Liv, and yet she was all he could talk or think about. "Well, it was good running into you. I'm gonna head back to Ed and Annabelle."

"Say hi to them for me," Charlotte replied. "Have a good night."

"I'll call you soon, okay?" Jake smiled at her, then held his hand up to Charlotte's friend. The blonde gave him a tiny, fluttering finger-wave back.

When he arrived back at the picnic spot, his brother and Annabelle were propped on their elbows, mid-kiss. How lucky they were to have each other. Liv was responsible for that. She'd made Ed upload his profile to Match.com, vetting the women before he replied. Annabelle was the third girl Ed had gone on a date with. They'd been inseparable since. That was four years ago, and they'd been married for two.

"Get a room," Jake said as he sat down.

They broke apart. "Sorry." Ed looked anything but. Annabelle grinned, as she sat up, smoothing her hair back into place. "Where'd you get to?"

"Ran into Charlotte and a friend of hers. Charlotte says hi."

"Is she doing okay?" The concern in Annabelle's voice was clear.

Jake shrugged. "As well as any of us, I guess." He couldn't talk about it for a second longer. "You two look particularly cozy tonight."

Ed beamed, looking at his wife for confirmation. Annabelle gave him a tiny nod. "We're celebrating. I wasn't sure whether to tell you, but . . . we're pregnant." Ed's grin got even brighter, if that was possible. "Gonna be parents, God help us." He nudged Jake. "You'll be an uncle in the New Year."

Jake felt himself genuinely smiling for the first time in more than a month. "That's amazing, you guys! Congratulations. I'm so happy for you." He hugged his brother, then Annabelle.

She squeezed him back, a tear in the corner of her eye. "Thanks, Jake. It's so hard to share something so happy, with what's going on, but we hope it will help." She put a knuckle to her face, stopping the moisture from ruining her make-up. "I'm glad you think it's good to have happy news right now."

"Of course," Jake replied. "It's important that life goes on, and good things still happen. Do you know if it's a boy or a girl yet?"

"Way too early," Annabelle tipped her head to the side to rest on Ed's shoulder. He put his arm around her, pulling her close. "But we've already picked out names, and we decided not to keep those a secret. If it's a boy, we think Teddy, Jr. We need to keep the name going, right? Your dad would be disappointed otherwise. And if it's a girl, Olivia, of course. Couldn't be anything else."

Olivia? *What?*

In loving memory of her would-have-been aunt?

Jake's expression soured as he looked over at his brother, whose expression was frozen in place. Jake would expect this kind of insensitivity from Annabelle, who was sweet but a little self-centered. But from Ed?

"She's not *dead*, Annabelle. She's *missing*. Isn't it a bit early to be naming babies in her memory?"

Annabelle's face dropped. "Oh, Jake. It's not like that, I swear. Right, Ed?" She turned to her husband for help.

Ed put a hand on his brother's arm. "Of course, man. We just love the name, and your Liv is so important to us. Whether Liv is back with us by then, or not, we'd want our daughter to be named Olivia. But if it's painful for you, we won't. We've got other options that we like. We're not saying we think she's dead, man, that's not it at all."

Jake heaved in a breath. God, he was so hyper-sensitive these days. "Sure. It just feels weird, that's all. Liv's only been gone a few weeks" — he wasn't sure five weeks qualified as a few, but whatever — "and it already feels like people are moving on."

Mostly, he was scared *he* might become one of those people. There he was, going out, having fun at a Fourth of July festival, listening to country music, when Liv was God knows where, having God knows what done to her. Or rotting in a shallow grave somewhere. But he wasn't about to say as much to his brother. Instead he asked Annabelle about her new PR job and maternity leave, and she seemed grateful for the change in subject.

As the warm evening moved into twilight, the crowd thickened, and the sky cast a warm orange glow across Cape Fear River to the west. Jake, Ed, and Annabelle started to pack up their belongings to minimize the space they were taking up. Ed held his wife close to him as the red, white, and blue fireworks lit up the sky above the river, reflected brilliantly in the water.

Jake had never felt a moment of jealousy in his life. He'd never had any need to, with such a blessed existence as his and Liv's. But, as he saw his brother and sister-in-law's joy at their forthcoming baby, and as he stood surrounded by happy families, he felt it now.

CHAPTER 20: OLIVIA

July 18

I re-examine the text from Adam.

> *Hey. It's been a couple weeks and I wanted to check in. How's it going? I have today off and figured, if you're free, maybe we could grab coffee this afternoon. If busy, maybe later in the week. LMK!*

A solid text. Breezy, but to the point. I'm not working until later, 5 p.m., and it's only 11.30 a.m. now.

More than that, I desperately need a distraction. Something to get me out of my head since I had that conversation with Jake on the beach a few days ago. Previously, I could imagine that sitting on the sand, reading, and watching the ocean would be a regular part of my new life. But not if I'm going to run into Jake any moment, and reopen that wound of longing and pain. Of love for a man that I never imagined would go unrequited.

But Jake was clear. He's curious about me, yes, but he loves Savannah.

I type a reply to Adam.

*Sure, coffee would be great. Can do this afternoon, as I'm
on dinner shift tonight. Meet you somewhere around 1 p.m.?
I can ride downtown. I need the exercise! 24 South or Java
Dog?*

They're the two coffee shops I worked at back when I
was living downtown and going to design school. Not that
they would have any record of me ever being an employee in
this world. No more free pastries.

My phone dings.

*Perfect. See you at 24 South at 1 p.m.
Looking forward to it :)*

It's a full hour's ride along the River-to-the-Sea bikeway
from Mom and Dad's house to downtown, and I'll have to
be back by four, so it'll be a real workout. And I need it. Too
much of Mom's home cooking, treating me to all my favorite
childhood meals, has left me feeling flabby. And if I'm not
eating here, it's a free dinner on my break at the restaurant,
usually some delicious fried fish or a salmon burger. Just
because I'm in a parallel universe doesn't mean I shouldn't
watch what I eat.

Mom barely suppresses her glee when I tell her I'm
going for coffee with Detective Adam Banks, and is more
than happy to lend me the bike again. It's become almost
mine anyways, by default. I change into white shorts and
blue-striped T-shirt, slathering on extra sunscreen, as it's 94
degrees and I'll be riding in the midday sun.

I wind my way through the Landfall community and out
onto the main road, which links up with the River-to-the-Sea
bikeway. I ride over the bridge that traverses Bradley Creek,
near my and Jake's old home, and past Airdrie Gardens. Jake
and I used to walk to this park, after days of stripping wallpaper from our new home, for the summer concerts last year.

The sun scorches my face, and I'm glad of Mom's bike
helmet protecting my head, my eyes shielded by the cheap

sunglasses I bought with tip money. As I glide along the first stretch of the quiet roadway, the shady parkland each side brings a welcome coolness, and I reach above my head to flutter my fingers through the Spanish moss dripping from the avenue of oak trees.

Interspersed among the parkland are houses, which gradually increase in density until I finally find myself cycling through the edges of downtown. After a sweaty fifty minutes, I pass the tall spire of the First Presbyterian Church and, with some relief, swing down onto Front Street, with its palm trees and charming historic buildings. I glide past the red-brick converted warehouse where I rented my first loft, after moving out of my family's house, and pull up outside the cute 24 South cafe. Locking my bike and helmet to a traffic meter, I wipe at my forehead and push my sunglasses up onto my head, hoping this will give a much-needed lift to my damp, squished hair.

I'm five minutes early, but Adam is already drinking coffee at one of the two small outside tables on the sidewalk. He grins at me. "Hope this is okay. It's in the shade, so I figured we could be outside." He's wearing a pale gray T-shirt that's dark with moisture on the chest and under the arms, paired with navy shorts and sneakers. He looks hot . . . in every sense of the word.

I smile as I take a seat across from him, ineffectually fanning my neck with my hand. "Thanks, it's great. I'll grab a coffee in a minute. I gotta rest. That was the hottest bike ride ever."

"I'm impressed. How long did that take you? It's kinda far."

I glance at my watch. "Fifty-six minutes." He grimaces. "But it's mostly flat. And very pretty."

Adam glances over to where my bike is locked up. "You know, you're not supposed to use traffic meters as bike stands."

I raise my eyebrows with a half-laugh. "Seriously, Detective Banks? All the shit I have going on in my life and *that's* what you're busting my balls about?"

He chuckles. "I have a hard time being off duty." He gets up, grinning. "I'll grab you a coffee. What do you want?"

As Adam fetches me an iced latte, I cool off in the shade of the building. Within minutes, he returns with a tall, ombre concoction in a glass topped with a cone of whipped cream and drizzled with caramel.

So much for getting into shape.

"Good thing I have an hour's ride back," I laugh. "How many calories does two hours of cycling in hot sun use up?"

Adam joins in my laughter, his gaze clearly admiring as it sweeps across me. "You're fine." He resumes his seat, takes a sip from his own coffee. "How have you been? It's been a couple of weeks since I saw you at the Fourth of July fireworks."

I spoon a heap of whip, unashamedly, into my mouth. It dissolves deliciously on my tongue. "I'm okay, I guess. Same as before. Still a non-person, still living a temporary and unsustainable life, my future a black hole of uncertainty. But I have a lovely place to live, some nice new friends," I gesture at him, "and iced coffee with whipped cream on a hot day. So . . . it's not totally terrible."

He takes another sip of coffee. "Any other new friends?"

"Deb, at work, is a lot of fun. A lot older than me, early fifties I'd guess, and super friendly. We've hung out a couple of times after the lunch shift. She has a daughter away at school and I think she likes to mother me a bit, and she's probably picked up that something is wrong. There's a couple of sweet new young servers at the restaurant, too, but they're in their late teens and a bit too young to be real friends with."

I pause, trying to sip coffee through the hole I made in my cream without getting it on my chin. "I've kinda reconnected with Jake Johnson, too. My, uh, ex? My fiancé in another life? I don't know what to call him."

Adam places his cup carefully down on its saucer, lining up the handle with the side of the table. He looks like he's figuring out how he feels about this. "Jake's the guy you asked us to get in touch with? The one you said you were with at the quarry, the day you fell?"

"Yeah, that's him. He's a lawyer, his office is somewhere around here."

"And you've been spending time with him?"

"No, no. Not really," I shake my head. "We ran into each other at the beach. He has a waterfront condo on Wrightsville, real close to the restaurant where I work. But it's not anything. He has a long-term girlfriend, Savannah, so it's not, you know, like that. Like it was."

Adam frowns into his cappuccino, avoiding my eyes. "But *your* last memory, from before, was being engaged to him, right? Being in love with him? About to marry him? So, I'm guessing it must still be like that for you. Even if he has no memory, or knowledge, of those events."

I half-smile at him. "I've never been with anyone else. He was my world, so . . . yeah," I reply, a little sadly. "You don't just instantly get over something like that. No matter how the other person might feel."

Adam picks up his cup, narrowing his eyes at me over the rim. He cradles the cup in his hands, blowing out a breath. As if what I just told him caused him visceral pain.

"Liv, look. I guess it's pretty clear to you by now that I like you. That I'm . . . you know. Attracted to you. You're really great to talk to, and so beautiful. So goddam intriguing. I mean, you shouldn't even exist." He gives a half-laugh. "I haven't been able to stop thinking about you since we met. It's been driving me crazy."

"Adam—"

"No," he cuts in. "Let me finish. This whole deal with you is, if I can put it bluntly, totally fucked *up*. Christ, I have no idea if you're an alien from another dimension, or if you have some kind of identity disorder. Yet I'd be willing to live with all that uncertainty to be with you. To take care of you." His brown eyes rise to meet mine, his lashes long and beautiful. There's a sadness behind those eyes that I haven't seen before. "But, Liv, if you're in love with another man, and you're not into taking things further with me, that's another matter."

I put my iced coffee down on the table with a clunk, reaching for his hand over the table. I hate that I am hurting this man, who's been nothing but kind to me. But I also don't know him all that well, and he's asking a lot of me. What can I do?

"I get it," I tell him honestly. "I really like you, too, and I do want you to be in my life. You're fun to spend time with, and kind, and you make me feel safe and cared for. But you know I'm going through all this weirdness, the levels of which are unfathomable. So, I'm not sure what I have to offer. What I'm capable of offering—"

He swirls his coffee mug, saying nothing.

"—I *am* sorry. I wish it was easy. I wish it weren't the case. You're so comfortable—"

"I don't want to be the comfortable option, Liv," Adam mutters, pulling his hand away.

I shrug. "But you *are* comfortable, and that's a great thing. We've only known each other a little while, and I already feel like I trust you completely. I *know* you're a good man. And that a life with you would be a good one."

Adam drains the last of his coffee. "Yeah, it would. But I'd need to be your first choice, Liv. And you need to figure out if that's the case." He stands abruptly, scraping back his wooden chair. "Look, I'm sorry to cut our coffee short, but that's what I really wanted to say. Now it's kinda up to you."

I get up, too, reaching out to give him a slightly awkward side-hug. "I need to figure some stuff out, Adam. But please know that I want you around. I just don't yet know in what capacity, yet. If you can live with that . . ."

"I'll be waiting, Liv Grainger." Adam gives me a close-lipped smile and lifts his fingers to his temple in a tiny salute.

I smile back. "Sounds good. See you soon."

As I sit, watching Adam stride away along the characterful street in dappled sunshine, it occurs to me that it's a lot less cheerful at this table without him. It's strange that, in such a short time, he's become so important to me.

And he's definitely cute.

But he's also being pretty demanding for a guy I'm not even dating. Especially given that he knows I'm going through a lot right now.

I slurp my coffee, watching his back getting smaller and smaller.

Should I even be thinking about taking things further with Adam, when it's really Jake I want? Admittedly a Jake I'm not sure I know anymore, and a Jake who doesn't love me.

Is it better to be alone, or be with Adam?

CHAPTER 21: OLIVIA

July 22

"Liv! Call for you. In the office," Juliette hollers across the almost-empty restaurant.

I stop stacking the last of the dirty glasses onto my tray and wipe the perspiration from the back of my neck, puzzled. Who'd call me at the restaurant?

I bring the tray to the dishwasher and call, "Thanks, give me one second."

It's nearly five, the end of my shift, and there's a tiny lull in customers before happy hour and the dinner shift begins. It's been a hot and sticky afternoon, even with all the restaurant's French doors open to the ocean, and I'm desperate to get home for a shower. Not long now.

I slip into the coolness of Juliette's office, and pick up the cordless receiver from the desk stacked high with paperwork. "Hi, this is Olivia."

"Hey. Liv. It's Jake. Sorry to call you at the restaurant, but I . . . I didn't have your cell. I, uh, wanted to talk to you."

I freeze for a moment, surprised. *Jake?* My stomach does a little flutter at the sound of his low, familiar voice. What can he want?

Juliette steps into the office, giving me a sly smile as she digs around a metal cabinet for a pack of napkins. I lift a hand in acknowledgement, all my concentration on the call.

"Uh, hey, Jake. How did you know I was working?"

"Oh. I got home early from work and saw your bike in the stand near my building, so I figured—"

"Right." He knows which one my bike is. "So, what's up?"

"I — I kinda, well, wanted to talk some more. When you have time. I'm trying to process all of this, you know. You being here. I guess I wanted to spend a little more time talking, getting my head around it. It's so weird . . . I see you, and you're so real. Then I go home and it's like I've imagined you. I'm having a hard time with it, is all."

I nod, even though he can't see. "Sure. I'm just finishing up my shift but I'm free tonight? Or Sunday night, maybe. I'm pulling a double tomorrow."

"Tonight's good. There's a Friday concert at Airlie Gardens tonight, maybe we could check that out and then go for a drink? I think it's 6 to 8 p.m., ten bucks."

My insides flutter again. My Jake and I went to several of those concerts last summer, the gardens are really close to our home.

"Sounds great," I force out. "I'll meet you at the main gate at six?"

"Sure. Let me get your cell number in case we miss each other, or one of us is late."

We exchange numbers and I hang up, my pulse racing. Concert in the gardens. Drinks after.

This kinda sounds like a date . . .

What would Savannah make of her boyfriend taking me out on a Friday night?

It's a fairly safe bet, though, that nobody will be at the concert who would recognize us. The jazz, folk, and blues music draws a much older and less trendy crowd than the kind of circles Savannah hangs in. It's much more likely we'd run into some of Mom's bridge or book club friends. But they don't know me in this world.

Anyways, right now, my main concern is how to ride the twenty minutes to my folks' house, shower, change, and ride the twenty minutes to the gardens, all in just over an hour. I grab my share of the tips, pack up my apron, and head out, bumping into Deb at the door as she arrives for her dinner shift.

"Hey girl," she laughs. "Where you going in such a hurry? Hot date?"

I walk backward out of the door. "Kinda. Gotta run. Have a good shift."

"The cute police detective, is it?" Deb calls.

"Nope. Tell you 'bout it tomorrow."

"Oh, Lord, is it that hot blond ex of yours?" she shouts.

I laugh, but don't reply, waving at her as I run down the steps to the beach level and my bike. The heat is overwhelming. If I thought inside the restaurant was hot, it's ridiculous out here. I'm not even riding yet, and my shirt is sticking to my back.

I pant my way through the humid air on the ride back to my folks' house, where I slip straight into the pool house to take a quick, blissfully cool shower, and change into the floral playsuit I splurged on last week. I slick on some red lipstick that goes great with my chestnut hair. I even manage to blow-dry it. It'll be frizzy in a half-hour, especially after another ride, but, hey.

Mom knocks on my door as I'm gathering items into my purse. "You eating dinner with us tonight, honey?"

"Can't, thanks Mom. I'm heading out to meet a friend at Airlie Gardens." I kiss her lightly on the cheek and usher her away from the door, locking up behind me.

She follows me down the path, watching as I mount the bike. "Which friend? Detective Banks?"

"No, Mom, not Adam. Just a friend. Gotta run. Have a nice evening."

I swerve out of my parents' drive, picking up speed to swoosh my way through the wide, manicured streets of Landfall, while cursing my parents for picking the house furthest from the gated entrance. I pedal harder, and make it to Airlie Gardens with three minutes to spare. Vanity has prevented me from squishing my newly washed hair with a bike helmet, but nothing can stop the frizzing effects of the sticky evening. I smooth my hair down, before wheeling the bike through the crowd.

Jake's already by the entrance pillar. He's taller than everyone else, his blond crop shining in the late sun. He watches me lock up my bike at the stand, that beautiful smile of his lighting up his face. "Hi. Glad you could make it. I have a blanket and lots of snacks."

"Great, I'm starving. I haven't eaten dinner."

"I figured."

It's so like Jake to realize I wouldn't have had time to eat between the end of my shift and getting here. Always so considerate of others' needs. Conversations with my girlfriends over the years have shown me how rare that quality is in our boyfriends.

He pays for both our tickets at the gate — "my treat, I invited you" — and we settle on a spot at the back of the crowd, where we can still talk. Jake spreads out a plaid blanket under a huge tree dripping with moss. The music hasn't started yet, and roadies are busying themselves on stage with risers, and at least a dozen music stands.

"I don't even know what tonight's concert is," I tell him. "I saw a few acts here last year. It's usually jazz, blues, or folk, right?"

Jake pulls a demi-baguette and some ham and cream cheese from his backpack. "Yeah, I think it's some jazz swing band tonight. The Big Birds Band, or something."

My hand, which is reaching for some bread, freezes mid-air.

Is he *serious*?

"The Big Buzzard Boogie Band?" I ask, slowly.

"That's it. You know them?" Jake's spreading cream cheese onto a crust of bread.

I suck in a breath. "You could say that. We — that is, you and I — saw them here last summer, about a month after

171

we got engaged. We loved them, and we chatted with them after. They're, uh, due to play at our wedding next month. In . . . my version."

"Huh. That's wild." He shakes his head. "This is nuts, Liv. I mean, the whole thing is just insane."

"I know. But I don't think *I'm* insane. It's something else, something most people would consider impossible, but is just simply beyond our comprehension. Something we can't explain. Like supernatural stuff that people believe in. Or religious faith. You know?"

Jake nods, but slowly.

On the stage, the musicians take their places. I recognize the band leader immediately. But that was in another life — he wouldn't know me here.

Jake and I don't talk much as the band plays, choosing to enjoy the music and each other's companionship, munching our way through Jake's simple picnic. Even as the sun lowers behind the treeline, the air remains close. There's little breeze to cool us and vast clouds slowly roll in, gathering above the oak tree, creamy and edged in charcoal gray as the light dims.

Jake lifts his ocean-blue eyes to the sky. "Looks like the weather's gonna break."

At that, as if to prove him correct, a low growl of thunder echoes the drum solo on the stage. As the band moves into its final upbeat number, fat raindrops give the crowd a teasing advance warning of what's to come. A couple of umbrellas go up, and several audience members lift jackets over their heads. Under the heavy oak, Jake and I are mostly sheltered, but not for long as the rain starts to pelt down. Quickly, we gather up the picnic blanket and move closer to the wide trunk, the ground shielded by the dense foliage overhead.

"That's all for tonight — you folks have a great evening and stay dry!" the band leader yells into the microphone. As if mocking him, the sky opens up, and a torrent of rain pours down on the crowd. It slips through the oak leaves, dripping intermittently onto our hair and shoulders. I'm already damp with sweat, so it barely matters at this point.

The crowd disperses rapidly while a few others join us under the shelter of the oak.

"You got an umbrella?" Jake asks.

I shake my head. "Nope, not even a jacket."

"Me neither," he replies. "Let's wait for the crowd to clear the gate, then make a break for it. We can head to the bar at the Bradley Creek marina. It's only a few minutes' ride. I rode my bike here too, as I knew you'd be riding."

Damn. I was hoping he brought his car. I laugh as a huge drip lands on my forehead, and glance down at my thin, sleeveless playsuit, the only thing I'm wearing. A bike ride will be interesting.

"We're going to get soaked, for sure. But it's quicker than walking."

We give the audience another ten minutes to clear the gates, then brace ourselves for the deluge. Jake grabs my hand as we break out into the open lawn, my thin leather sandals squelching in the grass. By the time we get through the gate to the bike stand, I'm soaked, hair plastered to my face. "I didn't even bring a helmet!" I holler at him over another crack of thunder.

"Have mine," he calls from the other end of the bike stand. But I shake my head, knowing his giant helmet will be way too big for me.

"Never mind, let's just get there!"

We ride furiously through the rain, laughing, my sopping underwear uncomfortable on the saddle. Once over the creek bridge, we're at the marina bar in a matter of minutes, Jake grabbing my wet hand again as we scurry from the bike stand and up the steps into the loud, busy room.

It's packed, as usual, at 8.30 p.m. on a Friday night, and there are no tables free. An up-tempo Luke Bryan song blares out from the sound system as Jake and I stand by the front desk, dripping onto the welcome mat. A group of old guys on a nearby table watch us, chuckling at our disheveled state. "Is it raining out there?" one of them calls. They break out laughing.

A hostess finally leads us to the last two seats squeezed together at the corner of the bar. The secluded spot is a relief, as my soaked playsuit is sticking to every part of my torso, and we turned more than a few heads as we wove through the tables.

"You drink beer?" Jake pulls his stool close enough that our knees graze.

I nod, pushing wet hair out of my eyes. "The IPA they serve here is good. You like it, too."

He raises an eyebrow at me. "I do, huh? You and I come here?"

"It's the bar closest to our place. We come in here all the time, probably every week or two. The house we bought is just around the corner, on Bradley Road. Less than a five-minute walk."

"Wow. That's wild. I've never been in here before." Jake turns to the waiting bartender, Griff, whom I know well, but, no surprise, doesn't recognize either of us. Jake orders a pitcher of the IPA.

A pitcher.

Guess he's not planning on making this a one-drink conversation.

"What's our place like?" he asks as he fills our glasses.

"It's sweet, real pretty. A bungalow on a wide lot. It was kinda shabby inside, but we renovated the whole place, and now it's gorgeous."

And it is. I poured everything into making it the perfect home for us.

"Two bedrooms and a small den, which I use as my office to run my interior design business. A good-sized living room, which we opened into the kitchen, so now it's one great room stretching from front to back. A separate garage, where you keep all your surfboards as well as your car. It's only a seven-minute drive to the beach, so it works for you."

I take a sip of my beer. "Of course, in this version of life, somebody else has bought that house. I went there a few weeks back, told them I used to live there, and they let me look around." I grimace. "It still had the eighties décor from when we bought it."

"Not a fan of the eighties style, huh?" Jake pushes a dripping lock off his forehead.

I shake my head.

He hesitates for a moment, before continuing, "There really are two different versions of this world? One where you died and one where you didn't. And you've seen both." He studies his half-filled glass. "I mean, you're right — I do like this beer, it's delicious. You *know* me. Not just from when we were kids but also as an adult. You know I have more than one surfboard."

He leans in. "Okay, tell me some things only I would know. That only Liv Grainger could also know."

I smile, shifting uncomfortably on my stool. My clothes are still damp. "Testing me, huh? Okay, that's fair."

I spend a few seconds sifting through for the right memory.

"We were with your old dog, Ginny, the day we found the quarry lake. I'm pretty sure you never told anybody else about that. We were about ten, maybe just turned eleven. We'd taken Ginny for a run on our bikes, and we were exploring the woodland at the end of the track. Ginny was off leash, and she disappeared into the trees, so we followed her and found the wire mesh fence with the unsecured section she'd gone through. We could see there was a clearing in the trees, and she was barking in the distance. We followed her and it opened up into the quarry, with the turquoise pool at the bottom. We'd never have found the place if it weren't for Ginny."

Jake looks at me, his lashes still damp, his eyes a dazzling blue despite the low light of the bar. "Do you remember Ginny's brother's name? The black lab from the same litter, who got hit by a car?"

"Oh, yeah. Rummy. That was *sad.*" It really had been. My first experience of death. "We were, what, seven? I remember being at your house, your old place by the river. We were looking for him in that huge yard. I remember Ed had let him out. Then your dad came into the house, carrying Rummy. We were all crying, even your dad. We had a funeral for him in your yard. Poor Ed never forgave himself."

Jake is gazing into his beer, playing with a trickle of condensation on his glass. "Fuck," he mutters, then looks up at me. "You're really her. I mean, I knew that. But I kept doubting myself. It's so . . . it's *impossible.*"

"I know. But like I say, it's clearly not, because here I am. It's just something we don't understand. Yet."

Jake looks dazed. "But how?"

I shrug. I've had time to think about this, and have a theory.

"I don't think there's ever just one, or even two versions of events. I think there's an infinite number. Every choice, every possible life path that anyone could go down, from major life changes to tiny decisions, all those versions of reality exist somewhere in space and time. And they're not universe-length physical distances away. They all exist right on top of each other, folded in, just out of reach. And maybe there are soft spots between them, created where those life splits happened. It took me falling off a cliff as an adult, at the exact same place where I 'died', aged twelve, to thrust me through a soft spot into this version. And here I am." I wave my hands in the air.

The corners of Jake's mouth turn down as he considers this theory. "Like the portals to another universe in *His Dark Materials*? Have you read those books?"

Exactly.

"Yes, just like that. Only without the Dust." I laugh. "We both read those books when we were around fifteen. We've been obsessed with them ever since. They've made a new TV show of it, and we've been enjoying watching that together."

Jake grins. "Yeah. I have too. Sounds like you're as much of a geek as I am."

"We made each other that way, I always figured. I'm glad you turned out like that anyways, without my influence." Another thing for my 'same' column.

Jake takes another sip. "We were always geeky kids. And even though I lost you at twelve, I think your influence stayed with me."

"No kidding. *Neverending Story* was our favorite movie when we were, like, eight, right? Later it was *Lord of the Rings*. We were always swapping fantasy and sci-fi books."

Jake gives his beer a wry smile. "We had a lot in common."

"We still do." My voice is quiet.

He frowns, watching the beads of condensation drip down his glass.

He's thinking about Savannah, I can tell. Thinking how different we are, probably. Yet how both of us suit him.

"Does she know you're with me tonight?"

Jake doesn't have to ask who I'm talking about. He shakes his head. "She's out with girlfriends downtown. I couldn't tell her. She wouldn't understand, she'd worry that maybe I wanted to get back with you."

He lifts his eyes to mine, his knee now pressed against my thigh. "That's not why I'm here. Savannah and I . . . we may not have as much in common, all that shared history, but we're happy. She's an amazing woman. Very kind and loving."

I press my lips together. "I'm sure she is. You wouldn't be with her otherwise."

He reaches forward, pouring us both a refill. "I never had girlfriends in high school. After you died, I was broken. Devastated. It took me a long time to get close to another girl. I didn't even go to prom. I didn't date anyone fully until Princeton, and those were crappy relationships with women I didn't really care for. I didn't allow myself to love anyone until my mid-twenties. Until I met Savannah. She saved me. Saved me from the grief I was still carrying over you, I realize now."

His hand rests just millimeters from mine on the bar. I suck in a breath, and move mine closer so our skin touches.

"Jake! Hey, buddy! I never see you in here." A man's voice, loud, behind us.

A muscular, gray-haired man, probably in his fifties, is pushing through a group of people. He's dressed casually, in a tank and shorts. He slaps Jake on the back. Jake's eyebrows are raised in surprise. And something else. Guilt?

"Oh, Kirk. Hey, man. Good to see you." Although Jake does not look the least bit pleased.

The man turns to me. He looks closely at my face and wet hair. "And who's this?" I'm clearly not Savannah.

"Right, yeah, this is, uh, Olivia. An old family friend."

Well, that at least is true.

Kirk examines my face, carefully, almost as if he's searching his memory. "Olivia, good to meet. . ." His eyes narrow. "Oh, I know you! I couldn't figure it out for a second. Wow. Out of context. And with your clothes on this time." He laughs. "It's a relief to see you looking so well."

Wait, what? With my clothes on?

Jake looks equally perplexed.

"Do I know you?" My voice is chilly.

"Ah, no, you wouldn't recognize me," Kirk replies easily. "You weren't conscious." At Jake's strangled noise, he adds, "I was hiking by the old quarry a couple of months ago, and my dog found you unconscious on the rocks down by the lake. Not a stitch of clothing on, and no clothes nearby. I had to carry you to my car, take you to the ER. You didn't seem to have a head injury, but you also wouldn't wake up. I waited around for a while at the hospital, but you were admitted, still unconscious when I left. I gave the nurse my name. He said he'd tell you."

"Oh my God!" I exclaim. "You're the hiker who found me! Wow. I never imagined I'd meet you. Thank you. Thank you, so much. God knows how long I'd have been out there if your dog hadn't found me. I'd have probably died." I hold out my hand and the man, Kirk, shakes it, with a warm smile.

Jake is still frowning. "You carried Liv up the quarry path, through the woods and back to your car, all while she was naked?" Jake's tone is accusatory.

It's an uncharacteristic display of possessiveness — and one that inwardly thrills me, since it means Jake at least feels *something*.

Kirk lifts his hands, palms out, in defense. "Hey, man, I covered her with my hoodie. And," he turns to me, "if it helps, that's my husband over there." He gestures with his thumb to a table where a handsome biracial guy in his forties is seated with another couple.

I laugh. "Thanks. I know you were only helping. It was above and beyond for a stranger." I gesture to the pitcher. "You want a beer?" At his nod, I pour some of the frothy IPA into Kirk's glass.

"I always wondered what happened to you. Why you were out there naked, with no belongings nearby and no car on the track," Kirk says, taking a sip.

"It's still a mystery." I glance at Jake, whose eyes are wide. "I was in hospital for a while with some memory loss. But I'm fine now."

"Honey, I'm just glad to have helped. And to see you reunited with your loved ones." Kirk gives Jake a knowing look. He finishes his beer. "I'll leave you guys to it. I'm glad you're okay, Olivia. Have a great evening." He pats Jake on the back and turns away.

"Thanks again, Kirk."

Reunited with your loved ones. If only it were that simple.

"You okay?" Jake's expression is quizzical.

"I'm fine." I take a breath. "It was good to see the man who found me and be able to thank him. How do you know Kirk?"

"He's a friend of Dad's. Part of his running club. I don't know him too well, just from a few family barbecues."

"Huh. That's weird. Ted isn't in a running club in my world. He's always playing golf with my dad." Something new for my 'different' column. "Are you worried Kirk saw you here with me?" I ask bluntly.

The little line between Jake's eyebrows, the one I've smoothed out with my thumb so many times, appears again.

"It's probably fine. He knows I'm dating Savannah, but he's only met her once. He's not even close enough to Dad to mention it, I don't think."

"Good."

But I can tell he's uncomfortable, now that he has been recognized. He glances over at Kirk's table, where both Kirk and his husband are looking at us.

Jake picks up his half glass of beer and lifts it to his lips. He finishes it in a few swallows. Pulling out his wallet, he takes out a twenty, leaving it on the check tray. "You wanna head out?"

I don't want to head out, no.

"I need to get changed so bad," he adds. "I don't seem to be getting any drier in this sweaty place."

I have no option but to agree. Even though I want to stay in this bar with Jake forever.

Or at least, for another couple of drinks.

I want so much to place my hand on his knee, laugh about something like we always do. To lean in for a kiss and run my hand through the short, damp spikes of hair above his neck. For us to stroll home to our sweet little house and make love under the new, soft, bamboo sheets I picked out just weeks ago. To wake up with him tomorrow, spooning in bed, the sun streaming onto our naked bodies through white muslin curtains. Then drive to the Beach House for a lazy brunch, and lie on the sand with a book while Jake surfs. I want to marry him, next month, in front of all our friends and family. Honeymoon with him in Cambodia, Vietnam, and Thailand. Begin the next big adventure of our lives with him. To be with him. Always.

That's what I want.

"Sure," I reply instead, finishing my own beer, determined not to let my face crumple in front of him. Sucking in a breath, I stand, my feet squelching unpleasantly in the wet leather of my sandals.

Jake pulls out his phone to send a quick text, and I have to turn away. I know who that message is going to.

I wave farewell to Kirk, who salutes back with a grin, as we head out into the night. The rain has stopped but everything is dripping, and the humidity isn't entirely gone. A strong scent of petrichor from the parking lot concrete engulfs me. It takes me back to our rainy senior prom night when Jake, in his ill-fitting tux, had told me 'petrichor' was his favorite word and I pretended I knew what it meant. I looked it up the next day.

So many memories. Memories the Jake unlocking his bike beside me will never know. This Jake never even went to prom.

It's dark enough that Jake doesn't see the tear sliding down my cheek as we ride back over the creek toward our homes. At the gate to Landfall, we stop a moment, and I wipe my face clear of moisture.

"This is me. Thanks for tonight. I'm glad we were able to do it."

Jake smiles at me under the glow of a street lamp. "Me too. It meant a lot to talk this stuff through." He pauses, pushing his lips together, and gives me a sad smile. "I'll see you soon, Liv."

He rides off, his strong physique making short work of the stretch of main road toward the bridge to the barrier islands.

Will I see him again? Or does Jake now have the closure he was looking for?

One thing is clear, though. He's not breaking up with Savannah any time soon.

CHAPTER 22: JAKE

July 22

Jake pulled into his usual parking lot, the one next to the cool blue condo building that overlooked his favorite section of beach, near the pier. He parked and beeped the Audi locked. Even though it was past seven in the evening, it was still crazy hot by the water. The freshly pressed blue cotton shirt he was wearing was already sticking to him, the shower he'd taken a half-hour ago negated.

He screwed up his face and headed for the pier steps, passing the little surf shop he frequented. There had been weeks without any new developments in Liv's case, and Jake was beyond frustrated. The police didn't seem to be doing anything. They'd found no new clues, and Detective Banks seemed to be getting tired of placating Jake whenever he called. Which was several times a week. Sometimes daily.

Maybe this dinner tonight wasn't such a great idea, he thought as he mounted the steps. But then again, he wanted to stay in close contact with Liv's family. He found it comforting, even though it was painful dealing with their obvious distress.

At the top, he pushed through the door to the Beach House Bar and Grill, pausing to take some calming breaths.

The welcoming space inside the restaurant usually soothed him, with its lofty vaulted ceilings, kitschy fishing décor, and the elegant rows of French doors to each side that led onto the pier, giving diners a great ocean view.

"Reservation?" asked a platinum blonde hostess he didn't recognize, barely looking at him.

"I'm meeting my in-laws." He read her name badge. She looked like a Hayley. "I see them over there." He gestured to a table near one of the open doors, where Tilly and Burt were waiting.

Hayley guided him over, handing Jake a menu with a disingenuous smile. "Your server will be with you soon."

"Hi Tilly." Jake gave Liv's mom a gentle kiss on the cheek. "Hey, Burt." He shook Burt's broad hand over the table and sat down opposite them. They reminded him so much of his own parents — a strapping, tall father and petite mother. Except Tilly was a lot more glamorous than his own mom. "Good to see you both."

He examined the menu, even though he already knew it backward. He could feel Liv's parents watching him, so he forced himself to look up.

Tilly smiled sadly. "We haven't seen you in weeks. How are you doing, honey?"

Jake pushed out his lips. "Not great, right now. I was feeling a little better when stuff seemed to be happening — you know, even the bad stuff, like searches and such. But this . . . this *nothingness* is driving me crazy." He took a sip from the water glass in front of him, shaking his head. He wasn't the only one going through this. "How are you guys feeling?"

"Same." Burt's voice was gruff. "Don't know what the police are doing, but it sure don't seem to be much."

Tilly reached across the table to Jake's hand. "It's so hard, for all of us." Her voice wobbled.

Oh God. Please don't let Tilly have another meltdown right here in the restaurant.

Mercifully, they were interrupted by a server stopping at their table — a middle-aged woman with a shock of red hair and a much warmer smile than the hostess who'd greeted Jake.

"I'm Deb, I'll be looking after you tonight. What can I get you fine folks?"

Jake pulled his hand from Tilly's and picked up the menu. "I'll take the Beach Burger with yam fries and a bottle of Foothills IPA. Thanks."

Burt and Tilly both ordered the fish tacos and a bottle of white wine to share, even though Burt was clearly driving the ten minutes back to their home at Landfall.

"No sweat." Deb departed with a toothy grin.

"They've got a bunch of new staff here," Jake observed. "Liv and I had dinner here in, I dunno, maybe late April, early May. I only recognize the guy behind the bar."

"We were a little early tonight, and Juliette came over to chat a while before you arrived," Tilly replied. "She had some staff leave just before summer hit, and had to hire four new servers. I guess it tends to be kind of a transitional job for most people."

Jake nodded as Deb came back with their drinks.

"Your food will be out in a while, they're just a little backed up in the kitchen," she apologized. "Friday night, you know? Enjoy those drinks."

Jake sipped his IPA, the same local beer he always ordered at the marina bar near Liv and his house. Just the taste brought a flood of memories. Liv sitting at the bar with him or at a little table in the corner, her squeezing his knee, shoving fries into her mouth, laughing.

"Honey, we wanted to check in with you, but we also figured we need to talk about some stuff." Tilly shot a sideways glance at her husband.

Now what?

Jake sat back in his chair. "What's up?"

Liv's mother took a sip of her wine, leaving a fuchsia-pink lipstick mark on the glass. She seemed to be bracing herself.

"The wedding plans, Jake. I know it was all finalized weeks ago, and we put the deposits down on the catering,

184

the jazz band, equipment hire, and so on. Obviously, there's no venue cost, with it being in our yard, but all the other expenses are a lot. It's just over four weeks away, and many of those deposits are non-refundable within twenty-eight days. So we need to decide tonight about whether we're going to keep those bookings in place."

Jake frowned, confused. "Huh? Why wouldn't we?"

"Honey," Tilly reached across the table, although Jake didn't move. He was beginning to see where this was going. "We're talking about tens of thousands of dollars. Which Burt and I have always been more than happy to pay for, you know that. But sweetie, Liv's been gone nearly two months now, and there are no leads. We can't assume she'll be back within the month. And even if we did get her back in the next few weeks, the chances of her being in a fit state to get married on August 20th, considering what she might have been through—" she stopped, drew a deep breath, and soldiered on, "—they're pretty low. So, maybe it's best to canc — *postpone*, until Liv is safe and well with us again."

They wanted to cancel the wedding. *Fuck*.

Jake closed his eyes, trying to grasp what Tilly was saying. Of course, there was an undeniable logic to it. But the idea of canceling his and Liv's wedding . . .

"I–n-no," he stuttered. "No way," he said more firmly. "I can't cancel all our plans. Liv put so much work into making everything perfect. She planned it to the last detail. And I know we don't know where she is *right now*, but that's today. We might get her back next week, or tomorrow. She might be *fine* for the wedding. I don't want to ruin it all for her, not while there's even the tiniest chance. I can't do it." He scowled. "No way."

Burt's expression, always stern, darkened further. "Jake, son, it's a lot of money. Nearly twenty thousand on deposits alone. That's money we're gonna lose if the wedding doesn't happen. And we all know the chances of it going ahead on that date are small." He held up his hand as Jake tried to interrupt. "Yeah, we may get her back in time, and we all want that, but it seems remote, given what we've been told. Let us cancel, just for now, and we'll make the exact same plans when we get Liv back. If she wants to. I mean," he blundered on, "we don't know for sure she didn't disappear voluntarily because she didn't *want* to get married, because it was all getting too much."

Burt's words were like a slap in Jake's face. The last part particularly hurt because it was something Jake had obsessed over, many times.

"Of course she wanted to get married," Jake said quietly. "She was so excited about the wedding. She didn't leave me. Not by choice."

"But Jake," Tilly's voice was soft. "She left her engagement ring. On the rocks at the quarry. It didn't fall off by itself. It fit her perfectly."

Jake had nothing left. A bead of sweat trickled down the back of his neck, further dampening his shirt. He took a swig of his beer and gazed out of the doors toward the ocean, where the low evening sun was casting long, dancing shadows on a group of people playing frisbee at the beach. He should've brought his surfboard, ditched dinner with the Graingers, and gone out on the cool water instead.

"She loves me," he muttered, more to himself than to them.

"We know, honey," Tilly replied. "Of course she does. She always has. But we have to be practical."

Jake turned back to them. "I'll pay you back for the deposits. I'll wire you twenty thousand bucks from our joint savings account as soon as I get home. I didn't ask you to pay for the wedding in the first place. Liv and I can afford it. You insisted on paying, as parents of the bride, and Liv convinced me to let you, but there was no need. I'd prefer to cover the deposits myself, then I'll have full control of it. And I'm not canceling. It would be a betrayal of Liv, our plans, our life together. Please don't make any calls to any of the suppliers, okay?"

Burt exchanged glances with Tilly. He held up his hands. "Okay, son. If that's your decision."

"It is." Jake rose, scraping his wooden chair back, swigging the last of his beer before standing up. "I'm sorry, I'm not hungry. Please excuse me, I need some air. I'll make that transfer later. Sorry about the dinner."

He didn't wait for them to say goodbye, weaving through the tables to where Deb was carrying a tall burger and two plates of fish tacos toward them. "Sorry, we need to nix the burger and yam fries," he told her, squeezing past.

"You want those to go?" she called after him, but he didn't turn. He pushed out of the doors, past the platinum blonde with her mouth agape, and ran down the pier steps onto the sand, where he bent over, hands braced on his knees.

Jesus. Even Liv's parents seemed to be giving up on her, and it hadn't even been two months.

What was the standard amount of time for declaring somebody dead after they went missing? He'd been taught it at law school. Five years, that was it. Even that seemed too soon. Jake would never give up on Liv.

Ignoring the niggling feeling that Liv's parents might have been right about some of the things they'd said, Jake strode across the sand, out of range of where the Graingers could see him from the restaurant.

The sun was lowering behind the buildings lining the shore, and the beachgoers were beginning to pack up. He followed the waterline, kicking off his sneakers, and rolling up his pant legs, allowing the few inches of ocean to rush over his feet as he walked.

They had done this a thousand times, Jake and Liv — gone for a date at the Beach House, then walked along the water's edge, kicking up saltwater and sand at each other. He'd ruined a long white dress of hers that way, but she'd still laughed.

Even before they bought the fixer-upper near the beach, when they lived in the loft downtown, a half-hour drive away, they would come out here. Liv would wait for him on the beach while he surfed on summer evenings and weekends, reading or sketching designs. She'd always insist on walking a mile or so along the beach and back after he'd packed up the surfboard on top of the car.

"You've had exercise, but I haven't," she'd say. "Humor me."

Jake would've been happy to humor Liv forever.

He wandered almost all the way down to Crystal Pier, two miles south of the fishing pier, before turning back along the sand. The sky now had a burnt umber glow, the light fading fast. The surfers were long gone and a bunch of kids were in a circle, grilling meat over a disposable foil barbecue, one of them playing guitar. The smell of their cooking made Jake's stomach growl. He should've taken Deb up on the offer of takeout. He had barely eaten all day, again.

He kicked his way through the surf, enjoying the pull of the sand beneath his feet as the ocean dragged it away. It was strangely gratifying how hard work it was compared with walking on solid ground. Like it gave him a purpose.

"*Shift your butt, slowpoke,*" he could almost hear Liv saying. "*Stop making a meal of it.*"

"*Hey, I've got sixty pounds on you, my feet sink in further.*" He'd stop in his tracks, crossing his in a pretense of petulance, and she'd walk back to him, flinging her arms around his neck.

"*Yeah, you're kind of a heifer.*"

She'd kiss him, and he'd run his hands through her hair, devouring her. One time it had been so late and dark on the beach, and their kissing had gotten so frenzied, his erection so hard, that he'd pulled her into the blackness under the fishing pier, thigh high in the water, the waves fighting against them. He'd pushed her up against one of the concrete piles and lifted her soaking dress to the waist, removing her string bikini bottoms, stuffing them in his shorts pocket. Then he'd unzipped his fly and fucked her right there against the pillar, the noise of her cries drowned out by the slap of the surf around them. He'd exploded inside her like the crash of the ocean, collapsing against her drenched body while she'd laughed breathlessly and clung to him.

That had been less than a year ago.

For a couple who'd been having sex with each other for twelve years, their lovemaking only seemed to get better, more exciting.

God, he *missed* her.

He closed his eyes and held his hand out, as if she might take it.

Yeah, there she was. Just behind him. A fraction outside of his peripheral vision.

Just out of reach.

CHAPTER 23: OLIVIA

July 30

Charlotte hands a battered, gray stuffed bunny to Taylor. "Here's Muffin. You and he will be fine with Auntie Livvie, you'll have fun, right? Remember you had fun with her at the Fourth of July festival?"

I crouch down to my niece's level. "Is his name Muffin? He's very handsome. Do you think he'd help us bake some cookies?"

Taylor sticks a thumb in her mouth and nods, just once, at the word 'cookies'. It's the first time I've been given free, unaccompanied rein inside my parents' house since I came home from hospital nearly two months ago, and I'm taking care of a four-year-old.

What could possibly go wrong?

"Thanks." Charlotte's only half-looking at me. "I appreciate you babysitting. With Mom and Dad away, I didn't know who else to ask. All my friends will be at my party."

I smile, grateful for her new-found trust in me, even if it's reluctant. And even if it means I'm not invited to my sister's birthday party. I guess that would be too much to hope for. "I'm happy to do it. My birthday gift to you. You have a great time and relax tonight. I can put her to bed in the lavender room, so just pick her up any time tomorrow."

"You'll be sleeping in the main house with her, right? Not in the pool house?"

I nod. "Of course. I have special permission from Mom and Dad to sleep in the green room tonight, so I'll be right next to her. It's all good. And I have your number in case there's an emergency. Which there won't be," I add quickly.

Charlotte gives me a thin smile. It's clear she'd prefer not to owe me any favors, but she's out of options, and I'm more than willing to watch Taylor, no strings attached. My sister steps out of the house and gets into her car, waving at her daughter beside me, before she pulls off.

"Happy birthday!" I call after her. Closing the front door, I turn to Taylor.

"Okay, kiddo. What do you want to do first?" I check the clock over the mantel. "It's 5 p.m. We have cookies to make, and I've set up an art station because I seriously need to see how amazing you are at painting. I've *heard* good things, but I need to see for myself. Then we have fish sticks and peas for dinner at six, followed by a cookie and ice cream for dessert. Then we finish with a story and bed around seven. Sound good?"

Taylor stares up at me, her brown eyes wide. It's possible she's never been given an itinerary before. Or options.

Muffin the bunny looks equally unimpressed.

I laugh. "*O–kay*. Cookies first, I think. We can paint while they're baking."

Taylor warms up to me over mixing cookie dough and adding chocolate chips, of which many are sampled. She insists on decorating each cookie with smiley faces made of M&Ms, and she's backed up by Muffin, so I'm outvoted.

We spend the twenty minutes the cookies take to bake cleaning up, and I set Taylor up at a small table with paints and a large sketchpad of Mom's.

I tie a plastic bib around her neck, even though she's already wearing a kid's apron — I don't want to incur Charlotte's wrath for Taylor ruining her clothes — before telling my little niece, "Have at it. Paint me a picture of Muffin."

She nods solemnly.

My phone dings in my pocket. My heart leaps for a moment, but when I glance at the screen, it's from Adam.

Hey. How's your Tuesday evening going? Hope you're doing well. I've been missing our talks. :)

He's sweet.

I type a reply, with half an eye on Taylor, who's digging with fervor into a pot of red acrylic paint. Thank God I spread paper over the floor first.

Fine, thanks. Babysitting my niece at my folks' house. Mom and Dad are away on golfing trip and it's my sister's birthday party tonight. It's all finger painting and cookie dough here. How's your night?

His response only takes a minute.

Saturday night off work and I'm bored. No plans and buddies all working. Any chance you need a babysitting companion? We could watch a movie or something ;)

I raise my eyebrows. He wants to come over. And that was a kinda flirty emoji. I'm surprised. After our last coffee chat, Adam had given me the distinct impression that it was up to me to contact him if I wanted to see him.

But a babysitting buddy would be good, especially after Taylor is in bed. The truth is, I'm deeply uncomfortable in this version of my parents' home, and I could use a distraction.

Sure, if you're game. I figure Taylor wouldn't like a dude she doesn't know showing up, but she'll be asleep by 7.30/8. Come round after? Bring wine, I'd better not raid my folks' pricey collection! :)

I'll be there. See you at 8.

I twist my mouth, watching Taylor. She's managed a credible red circle, admittedly rough, and two wobbly eyes. She's cute as she concentrates, head tilted to one side, tongue sticking out.

Was that a good idea, inviting Adam to the house, and telling him to bring wine? It might seem a little cozy.

Might give him the wrong idea . . .

No. He's just a friend coming round to hang out.

"That looks awesome, Tay!" I clap my hands together. "Your mom wasn't kidding about you being a great artist. How about Muffin's little nose, maybe in pink?"

The oven timer beeps and I head over to open the door. The delicious scent of fresh cookies wafts into the kitchen.

"*Cookies!*" Taylor shrieks, jumping up, knocking blue paint over the paper tablecloth.

"Hold up, kiddo. Yes, they're done, but they're still way too hot to eat. Super, dangerous hot, okay? You can have a couple after dinner. I'll cook your fish sticks now. You keep painting. How about a mouth? Poor Muffin doesn't have a mouth. How's he going to eat his cookie?"

She looks at her painting, considering. "'Kay, Auntie Livvie."

Wow. That actually worked.

My niece produces a masterpiece as I cook her fish sticks and frozen peas, ketchup on the side, which I am reliably informed is her favorite meal. She eats it happily enough, a smudge of pink paint on her otherwise flawless cheek. I lean against the counter, munching on one of the more singed fish sticks, watching this gorgeous little girl. So perfect. So amazing. A tiny person who doesn't even exist in my world.

After a well-earned dessert of soft, warm cookies and melting vanilla ice cream, I persuade Taylor upstairs to wash her face and brush her teeth, which she does ineffectually on both counts.

In the lavender room, so-called for its varying shades of purple and lilac, I tuck her into the double bed and lie down beside her, the light low. Charlotte has left a copy of *Goodnight*

Moon in her supply bag, which I read to Taylor as she snuggles beside me, thumb in mouth, Muffin tucked under her arm.

"*Goodnight, stars,*" I recite, my voice thickening. "*Goodnight, air. Goodnight, noises everywhere.*"

Is it the story or my niece's sudden affection that's bringing me close to tears?

It's hard to think of a world without her in it. This marvel of a girl.

I kiss Taylor on the forehead, as she's struggling to stay awake, and turn out the light. It's 7.40 p.m. by the time I get downstairs, and I just have time to clear up and eat a slice of toast with cheese before the doorbell rings promptly at eight.

Adam is on the doorstep, a bottle of red wine in one hand, a bunch of vivid blue hydrangea blooms in the other. He's wearing a pressed gray cotton shirt and jeans, and his dark hair is freshly washed.

He looks like he's arriving for a date.

Is this a date?

"Adam . . . Thank you. You shouldn't have."

He looks at the wine. "You told me to."

I laugh. "I meant the flowers." I take them from him. "Come in. Taylor's in bed." I glance upstairs. "She should be asleep by now."

I motion Adam into the living room while I go into the kitchen area and put the blooms in water, taking a moment to grab a corkscrew and two tall stem glasses. I walk across to sit beside him on the couch and open the wine, fumbling over the foil. There's a slight tension, an awkwardness. But maybe it's just me.

"Did you work today?" he asks.

"Yeah, the lunch shift, but I left at 4.30 p.m. so I could be here for when my sister dropped Taylor. It's so nice to have a Saturday night off, even if I'm staying home. The restaurant's so busy on Saturdays, and I've been pulling a lot of double shifts." I pour the rich, burgundy liquid into the glasses and pass one over to Adam.

"That's a lot of earnings you're . . . not paying any tax on," Adam observes with a sly smile.

I throw up a hand. "Yeah, yeah. You're not on duty tonight, Detective. Gimme a break."

He grins. "Fair enough. Cheers."

We sip our wine. The silence stretches out.

"You wanna watch a movie?" I ask brightly. "I have a couple good ones lined up on Netflix. My folks let me add my user profile to their account, which I consider a major breakthrough in our relationship."

Adam laughs. "Sure. Let's see what you got."

We settle down to watch *The Square*, which turns out to be an unsettling and brilliant Danish–English drama about an art installation and a museum curator's downfall. It's suitably engaging and unromantic, to my relief. I don't want Adam getting any ideas.

By the time the movie is done, we've finished the wine and are slouched closer to each other on the sofa, both our feet up on the ottoman.

"That was cool."

I sit up to clear away the bottle, reaching out for Adam's almost-empty wine glass, but he puts a hand on my arm.

"Liv." His voice is low, rough, as he straightens. "Come here."

Uh-oh. Guess he got the wrong idea anyways.

He's studying my face, waiting for me to lean in, inviting it. I push my lips together and give a tiny shake of my head.

"Adam. I'm sorry. I can't."

His brow furrows. "Why not? We'd be so good together."

"I know. I know. I'm just not ready. To be with another man, when I'm not over the last one."

Adam's face falls. "Your old boyfriend? Still? He's the one you want, even though he's with somebody else? Even though *I'm* the one available, the one who's here with you, right now?"

I turn away, unable to explain to him what I can't explain to myself. That I love Jake, irrespective of which reality we're in. Whether he loves me back or not.

"You've been wonderful," I tell him honestly. "I needed a friend and a confidant, which is what you've been. And I love hanging out with you. I'm very drawn to you, of course. But the truth is, I'm still in love with the man I believe I'm supposed to marry, who I promised I *would* marry, in less than a month's time. I made that pledge to him, even if it was in some other space and time, or even just in my own mentally deranged mind."

Adam lets out a sad half-chuckle at this.

"Either way," I continue, "it's my commitment, and I have to be true to that. It's the only thing that makes any sense to me."

Adam swirls the last dregs of his wine glass, but says nothing.

"I am sorry, though," I repeat. "I wish it was you. It would be so much easier."

Adam looks up at me. "I told you at the coffee shop that I'd need to be your first choice, Liv. Not what's easy." He stands, handing me the wine glass. "It's clear I'm not. And it's not your fault." He rakes his hand through his hair. "I really hope it works out for you. Whatever that looks like. But I think I'd better not see you too much from now on. For my own sake."

I nod. "I understand, Adam. I'll miss you, but I get it. Thanks for everything. You've been amazing. I hope things go great for you, too."

He gives me a twisted smile and an awkward hug, before letting himself out of the front door.

In an instant, a good, kind, loving man is gone from my life.

But I had to be honest with him, didn't I?

As sweet and caring a man as Adam Banks is, he's no Jake Johnson.

The love of my life, and the man who loves me.

Even if only in another world.

CHAPTER 24: OLIVIA

August 8

Juliette's office door is ajar, so I push it open with a quick knock. It's past eleven and she hasn't paid me for last week yet. She's at her desk on her cellphone, speaking in low tones to somebody.

"I gotta run." She hangs up quickly, a strange expression on her face. She looks up at me with a strained, closed smile that isn't like her usual warm self.

"Just came in for last week's pay. Sorry if I disturbed your conversation."

"It's fine." She digs into a desk drawer and hands me an envelope of cash. "Here you go — extra for Saturday's double shift."

I give her a sheepish smile of thanks. I'm still uncomfortable with her breaking the rules for me, and the more I come to care about her and the restaurant, the worse it gets.

Walking out into the restaurant, I fold and tuck the envelope into my shorts' back pocket. Deb is wiping down the bar counter with a tea towel while Kevin bolts the top and bottom of the row of French doors. Outside, the night is still warm. Strains of laughter and music from the beach are drifting up, gradually shut out as Kevin finishes his task.

I drop my apron in the laundry bin as Deb steps over, removing her own. "Heading out on your bike?"

"Yeah, in a while. I might walk along the ocean first, there's still a lot of people out. Care to join me?"

Deb shakes her fiery red head, as she leads the way toward the entrance. "Nah, I've done a double and I'm pooped."

She holds open the door while I step through. Deb throws a glance over her shoulder, seeming to check nobody is following us. "So, Liv, I have a question. Why does Juliette pay you in cash?"

My eyes widen in the dark as we approach the steps to the beach. "What makes you think that?"

"Oh, you know. I have eyes."

"Right."

"So, why?" she persists. "Everybody else gets a regular paycheck, even for tips."

I pull in a breath as we walk down the steps to the beach. "It's complicated, Deb. I can't really explain. I'd love to be able to, but I can't."

"Huh," she replies, an uncharacteristically cool note in her voice. "And I'm guessing, for whatever reason, you don't pay any taxes on that cash. Even though you live for free in your folks' luxury pool house."

It's a fair point.

"Believe me, Deb, the reason I'm working is because I *don't* want to live there. I'm saving all that cash to move out on my own."

We pause at the bottom of the steps, where concrete meets sand.

"You can see how it's kinda galling, though?" It's even darker in the shadow of the pier, and I can barely make out her expression. "I mean, I'm working doubles to support my husband on disability, and pay the mortgage on our crappy rancher, and you're not paying any taxes or any rent, and you just bought that cute new shirt."

It's true I'm wearing a new shirt, but it's only my third clothing purchase since Mom bought me a very basic wardrobe a couple of months ago. I bristle slightly.

"Deb, I get it, from your perspective, I really do. But there's a lot of things you don't know about me. If it weren't for my folks, I'd be living on the streets. I'd love to pay taxes and be an upstanding citizen like everybody else, but I can't. Again, for reasons I'm not able to explain to you. So please try not to judge. You don't know what it's like for me."

Deb turns toward the road, and I follow her. She's quiet for a moment, taking her keys out of her purse.

"I've tried real hard to be a friend to you, Liv, and you seem like a lovely young woman. But it's kinda tough when you tell me nothing about yourself. You know all about Frank and my kids, our nightmare vacations, my issues with my mom, everything. But it's always me doing the talking. Girl, you gotta open up if you want to make real friends. And you even turned down that police detective guy, right? So you don't even have him anymore. You're gonna end up alone at this rate." Her voice warms a little. "Take my advice, okay, hun? I'll see you Wednesday." She doesn't wait for a reply, strolling off toward her car, which she beeps open.

Dammit. I've already lost Adam as a friend and now I'm alienating Deb, too.

She's right, of course. Nobody will like me if I don't open up to them. But how can I tell anybody the truth?

I'll never be able to get close to anybody. At least, nobody but Jake, and he's with Savannah.

So, yeah. Pretty much nobody. Ever.

I glance at my bike locked to the rack, but don't move toward it. I need to take some time to think first. That stroll along the beach might help. Besides, some dude is sitting in the shadows on the wall near my bike.

I walk toward the sand, aware the tall guy by the bike stand has now jumped down onto the pavement. Is he following me?

"Liv."

I turn back, my pulse racing as Jake steps into the glow of the streetlight.

"Hey." His hands are raised. "I didn't mean to scare you."

199

I snort out a nervous laugh. "That's okay. I couldn't see who it was in the dark. What are you doing?"

"Waiting for your shift to end," he replies simply. "I wanted to see you. You wanna walk with me along the beach a while?"

"Uh, yeah. I guess. Sure." I'm suddenly nervous. What does he want?

We stroll out onto the sand, which is semi-illuminated by the pier lights and the waterfront condo complexes, but almost black near the ocean. Some teenagers with a speaker are playing rap music and laughing, and there are a few other people with dogs milling around, but most of the tourists have gone back to their hotels.

Jake leads me north, away from the pier to where it's a little quieter.

"What's up? Why were you waiting for me?" I ask finally. "I wasn't sure I'd see you again after that night in the storm. Thought maybe you'd got all the answers you needed."

"I guess not," he replies after a moment. I can't see his face clearly. "Not all the answers. The truth is, I haven't been able to stop thinking about you. About everything you said, about our life together. Your version of our lives. Your theory on life paths, and if your reality would've been the right path for my life. I guess . . . I dunno." He sighs. "I'm about to make this big life decision, and it's got me all messed up."

"Right. Savannah's birthday coming up."

"Yeah."

We walk on in silence.

"I don't know if there is a 'right' path, for anyone," I admit. "There's no right and wrong. It just is. But we can change our fate by making the best choices we know how, given the information we have available to us. If we don't like our lives, or an aspect of them, we can work hard to fix it. That's all any of us can do."

I can just about make out Jake's nod in the darkness. "I guess," he replies. "But I mean, you dying as a kid, that was plain wrong. One hundred percent God-awful. And I've felt the wrongness of that every day for the past sixteen years. I've never been right since then."

He stops. "I didn't even tell you this the other week, but it totally screwed up my relationship with my dad. He was so furious with me about your death. I think that was the main reason I felt it was my fault. He's such a man's man, you know? His position is always that the man looks after the woman, or the boy looks after the girl. He was ashamed I wasn't strong enough to pull you up. To save you. He never said as much, but I knew."

I want to reach out to him, but I stay still, listening, hearing his pain.

"I retreated into myself as a teenager, didn't do team sports, all the stuff he wanted for me. Our relationship never recovered, and I always felt . . . insufficient. To this day, we're not close."

I give in to my instincts and place my hand on Jake's arm, his skin warm beneath mine. "I'm so sorry. It's hard to hear. You and Ted are so close, such good friends, in my reality. That's awful."

He shrugs. "That's what I mean about there being a right and wrong version. In your version, I was strong enough. I pulled you up, saved you. We were prom king and queen. I was a better version of myself." His voice cracks. "I don't know how to be a good partner to Savannah if I'm always feeling like an inferior version of what I could've been. And if I'm thinking my life with a different woman could've been a better one. And now, you're here with me, on this beach, and I'm feeling nothing but uncertainty about my next choice."

I know what I want to say, but I love Jake too much to do that. He's in such pain. Instead, I step toward the darkness of the ocean. The water is black, the froth of surf briefly illuminated by the lights of the shoreline before the waves crash onto the sand. The ocean seems so much louder than usual, with the usual buzz of tourists and children's laughter now absent. I can't even make out the rap music from here. Jake joins me by the surf, the water almost reaching our toes.

A ship sparkles on the horizon. Above it, a million pin-pricks of stars are scattered across the inky sky.

"I don't think there's a choice," I say quietly, looking into the darkness. "It's not like I'm a viable option. I'm not really here. I mean, I'm here, but I shouldn't be. I'm a non-person. An anomaly. And it feels like this world is rejecting me, like a body rejects a transplanted organ. I can't work a real job. I can't be a functioning member of society. Hell, I can't even support myself." I give a shaky laugh. "I can't make new friends without having to lie about my back-ground. I have no one but my immediate family, and even those relationships are weird here. I can't get close to Dad or Charlotte, and I barely know my sweet little niece. Mom only believes all this because she's a Christian now, and I'm some kind of religious miracle to her. It's all so surface level, and strained." I can't keep the frustration out of my voice. "Yet if I move out of their pool house, I have nowhere to go, and my job at the restaurant likely won't last long enough for me to live independently. Really, I have nothing."

Jake scuffs the sand with his foot. "You have me." His voice is so quiet I can barely hear him over the ocean.

"But I don't. You're with Savannah, Jake, and you love her. You're not going to throw her over for me, and ask me to move in with you instead. We both know that's not going to happen, no matter how much I might want it to. No matter how much I love you."

Jake lifts the heel of his hand to his face, but it's a moment before I realize he's brushing a tear away. He turns to face me.

"I do love Savannah, you're right. But, Liv, I loved you first. I loved you when we were kids and, after you died, I never stopped loving you, and wishing I could change what happened. Go back and save you. And here you are, with me, right now. Saved. Alive. *Real.* And more damned beautiful and incredible than I could even have imagined. What am I supposed to do with that? Throw away this unbelievable second chance with you?" His voice breaks at this, and his shoulders heave.

I step closer and he pulls me into a hug, his hand on the back of my head, his face against my hair. His scent is so familiar, yet slightly different. His tall frame is shaking, and I soothe him, rubbing his lower back, the way he's always been soothed. The way I comforted him when Ginny died, and at his grandmother's funeral.

We hold each other a long time, the swell roaring in my ears as Jake's shuddering subsides.

Finally he pulls back, examining my face as I study his. The glow of the shoreline casts a deep shadow across his eyes and strong nose, his high cheekbones starkly outlined. A glisten in the corner of his visible eye betrays the remnant of his tears.

His jaw is set firmly, but his lips look as soft as ever.

Jake leans his face closer to mine, his gaze flitting across my features, landing like a butterfly on my mouth. He inches closer still.

Is he going to kiss me?

His brow breaks into a frown, and he gives a tiny shake of his head. He drops his forehead against mine.

"This is so fucked up."

I half-laugh, but there's sadness there, my heart breaking.

"I know. But Jake—" I pull back. "I meant what I said. I don't know what's going to happen to me, but I don't work in this world. You and I won't work in this world. I love you, you know that. And—" I stop him as he parts his lips to speak — "I know you love me, too. I know. But you don't love me the same way as I do you. No. You love me in the way you did when we were kids. You said that yourself. You've never kissed me. You've never slept with me. You've never fallen in love with me as an adult. You've never committed your life to me. All of the things we've done in my world." I place my hand lightly on his chest. "You and I don't have any of our shared history after the age of twelve that makes us . . . *us*. You have that with Savannah, though. Right?"

He nods, just once.

"You told me, last time we were together, that she saved you," I continue. "I'm glad about that. It makes me like her. I think there's probably yet another world in which I also died, but you didn't meet Savannah either, and you're alone now. And a billion other versions in which things are really terrible, or maybe even more great, and everything in between." I look out at the dark beauty of the ocean. "But I'm glad I found you in a life where you have someone who loves you, and you live on the beach, and surf every day. I know you have some issues to deal with, especially with your dad, and maybe some self-esteem stuff, but that's what therapy is for. And, in general, life is pretty good, right?"

Jake sniffs, saying nothing. His nod is almost imperceptible.

I reach up, laying my hand on his cheek. "Maybe I'm here so you can let me go, finally, and be happy. To show you my death wasn't your fault, that it was just a tiny change in circumstance that meant you were either able to pull me up the cliff, or not, that day. Nothing to do with being a better or stronger version of yourself." I smile at him. "You're already as good as any Jake in any reality. You're amazing. You can be a wonderful and loving partner. Look how much love you have in you." I lower my hand back to his heart, feeling its strong, regular rhythm.

He steps back, and rubs his face in the crook of his elbow. "You're right. I know you're right. And I can change the stuff I don't like." He laughs, his voice choking as he swears, "I fucking hate my job. And I'm gonna quit and do something like you were telling me, refugee advocacy or in-house counsel at a charity. Something like that."

I laugh too, the tension between us breaking. "Good for you. You'll love it." I heave out a breath. "Come on. Let's go back. It's getting late."

We walk back to my bike, hand in hand, saying nothing. There are no more words. He watches, as I unlock Mom's yellow cruiser, our faces lit by the street lamp.

"Will I see you again?" he blurts out, a note of panic in his voice.

I stand on my tiptoes and kiss him lightly on the cheek. "I'll be around. For a while, at least."

I smile at him as I mount my saddle, pushing off into the night before he can see my tears.

CHAPTER 25: JAKE

July 30

Jake stretched out on the wicker couch in the shade of his north-facing patio. Grief and frustration were sapping him of all energy, draining him physically and emotionally in ways he'd never have dreamed possible. He could barely muster himself to leave the house these days. Lolling on the patio sofa, trying to read, was about as much as he could manage.

Even the chic outdoor furniture set — he knew it was chic, as Liv had told him so — reminded him of her. It had been ferociously expensive, but she'd insisted on it. "I can write it off against my business taxes." That was her excuse for every overpriced home furnishing here — the industrial pendant lights above the quartz countertops, the wide-plank hardwood floors, the marble tile surround gas fireplace, and a hundred other beautiful, expensive things. She had extensively photographed and blogged about their gut-job renovation on her professional website, using the design's broad, beachy-meets-Southern appeal to pull in new clients.

"But I don't *want* strangers poring over our bedroom, admiring the bed we have sex on," he'd responded, sulkily.

She'd kissed him on the temple. "Suck it up, buttercup. If you want me to write off these expenses, this reno has to be part of my very public marketing campaign."

Liv had been right, of course, about the patio furniture being worth the investment. At least, she would have been, if she'd been around to enjoy it. She'd painted him a picture of long summer evenings with their friends and family, Burt and Jake's dad taking over the grilling on the state-of-the art gas barbecue in the corner, his mom and Tilly sharing wine on the couch, Annabelle and Ed on the wide armchairs, Jake and Liv playing with their future kids on a climbing set on the lawn. She'd sold him on that life. But it was looking less and less likely that vision would become a reality.

Not that he'd changed his mind about the wedding. Knowing it would still take place if Liv showed up was the one thing giving him comfort. Worth every cent of the twenty thousand bucks he'd given back to Burt. Never mind his and Liv's savings.

Jake frowned, ears straining. He was sure he'd heard something. There. A knock at the door. Detective Banks? He glanced at his watch. A half-hour early? Irritated, he jumped up, walking around the side of the house to intercept him.

But instead of a police car, there was a delivery van parked out front. An old guy stood on the porch, some kind of suit carrier draped on his arm. Only it was puffy, overly long, and white, bearing some kind of elaborate logo.

"Hey, man," Jake called. "Can I help you?"

The delivery guy turned. "Delivery for a . . ." he checked his tablet, "Ms. Olivia Grainger. From Bridal Wave."

Oh, Jesus.

"Uh, I'm her fiancé." Jake climbed the steps onto the little porch. "I can sign for that. She's not, uh, home."

The guy handed over the tablet and a stylus pen, and Jake scrawled an approximation of his signature in the box.

"All set." The guy handed Jake the bulky carrier. It was surprisingly heavy. "Have a good one."

Jake maneuvered his way through the front door, kicking it closed behind him. He draped the carrier over the back of the couch and turned over the paper ticket attached to the top hook.

BRIDAL WAVE
Ogden Market Place, Wilmington NC

Ms. Olivia Grainger
878 Bradley Road
Wilmington NC
Cell: 910-555-3554

One wedding dress in Caroline style/Pearl — Olivia
$5,795
One bridesmaid dress in Jane style/Aqua — Charlotte
$1,325
One bridesmaid dress in Jane style/Seafoam — Sara
$1,325
One bridesmaid dress in Jane style/Oceanic — Nicole
$1,325
PAID IN FULL
$9,770

Liv's wedding dress, and three bridesmaid dresses.
Another ten thousand bucks.
Burt and Tilly must've paid that bill months ago, yet didn't mention it at their recent dinner. Probably because the dresses were tailor-made and non-returnable anyways.
Jake ran his fingers over the white cover, tracing the words in their opulent cursive lettering. He toyed with the zip, but stopped himself. He wouldn't look. He didn't want to see the dress itself, not really. Only on Liv herself as she came down the aisle.
He brought the carrier into their bedroom and hung it on the front of the closet door. Should he call Charlotte, and

Liv's girlfriends, Sara and Nicole, to tell them their dresses had arrived?

No. They'd think he was as crazy as Tilly and Burt did. Although Charlotte already knew he wasn't canceling the wedding, from her parents, and she'd probably have let the other bridesmaids know.

He'd had multiple emails from friends and relatives about it over the past couple of weeks. Invited guests who'd previously booked travel and accommodations to be there for the wedding. They were very sorry, but given it had been two months, should they cancel their flights and hotel? Was it officially canceled? Maybe they had missed an email about it.

There had been no email about it. Not from Jake, anyways. He hadn't even responded to the direct requests for an update. They could figure it out for themselves. He had bigger things to worry about than Aunt Margie's non-refundable Airbnb.

Jake smoothed down the dress cover then stepped out into the great room. He filled the pale blue kettle in the kitchen, placed it on the stove, and dried off the coffee aeropress next to the farmhouse sink.

There were so many things he would never have picked out for himself. It would have been a plastic electric kettle, a stainless-steel sink, and a generic pod coffee machine. It was Liv who had such elevated tastes. Which had been fine with two of them earning, and her business taking off. But without her income, on the small salary he got at RAI, he wouldn't be able to keep that lifestyle going. He was barely able to afford their mortgage by himself.

If she didn't come home, he'd have to face reality and sell all this fancy stuff, and their house, too. Or, he could just quit the job he loved and go back to working in some soulless private practice for the big bucks. It's probably what he'd have done without Liv anyways. She was the one who'd always pushed him to follow his dreams.

Another knock, this one Detective Banks. Jake opened the door and led him into the living area. This time there was no wide-eyed, note-taking sidekick.

"Take a seat. I'm just making coffee. Want one? Or a tea, or water?"

Detective Banks sat in the same armchair he always seemed to take. "No thanks, I'm good."

He waited patiently while Jake finished the elaborate process of making his coffee with the aeropress.

"How are you doing?" Detective Banks asked as Jake settled onto the couch.

"Oh, about the same," Jake replied with a humorless laugh. "Frustrated. Exhausted. Sad. The usual, you know. Where's your trainee? I never see you without him."

Detective Banks smiled. "Shadowing somebody else now. I'm getting a new partner soon, but I'm on my own for the next week. I didn't need him today anyways. No need to take notes. This is just a check-in and a quick update."

"I appreciate that." Jake sipped his coffee. Damned if Liv wasn't right about the aeropress. It was so much better.

"Obviously the investigation is still active, but there's only so much we can do with zero evidence after two months. Every possible lead has been followed." Detective Banks frowned. "As you know, we've had a whole team working on this ever since Liv disappeared, the physical searches of the site turned up nothing. We've scoured all the traffic cam footage within a twenty-mile radius of the quarry for both before and after she went missing. We've exhaustively interviewed everybody — you, Mr. Evans, and all Liv's friends and family, plus all the homeowners in the quarry's vicinity. There's very little more we can do at this point. We're not giving up on Liv, but," he hesitated, "I'm going to be working on a new investigation with my new partner, as of next week."

Jake sat back with a deep exhale, trying to suppress a sense of rising panic. "So this is, what, a cold case? Already?"

Detective Banks gave him that sympathetic half-smile. "It's too soon to call it that, but we've exhausted our leads and resources. I'll still be the detective assigned to the case, and anyone can still call me with any new information that may turn up."

Jake gazed past the police detective at the beach print on the wall behind him. "I'm guessing, then, the searches on Kirk's house and car didn't show anything, otherwise we'd be having a different conversation."

"That would be a reasonable assumption," the detective confirmed.

"And I'm not under suspicion?"

Detective Banks spread his hands. "Impossible to define. In cases such as these, where there is no evidence and no apparent motive, suspicion lies everywhere and nowhere. We have no evidence you did anything to harm your fiancée. And you seem credible. Personally, I believe you are telling the truth. The problem is, Liv's disappearance is so inexplicable, so *in*credible, something must be off somewhere. I don't think it's you, but I've been wrong before." He uncrossed his legs. "I think the article about Liv in the *Atlantic* last week did you some favors, though. I wouldn't have recommended you giving that interview, but it seems to have paid off."

Jake nodded slowly. "Yeah. I was really torn about it, but my sister-in-law works in PR and crisis management, and she knew the reporter, said she'd be sympathetic. I hadn't told my side of the story to anybody, and I trust the *Atlantic* more than most, so . . ." He shrugged. "With all the stuff people were saying about me, it seemed time to defend myself. At least to make it clear you guys hadn't found anything when you searched my stuff. I was nervous the reporter would turn it around and do a hatchet job, but thankfully she didn't."

Detective Banks stood up, signaling his visit was over. "It was a gamble, for sure. Maybe one you should've run past me, but I'm glad it worked out. At least now the first Google results people see are an article that paints you as the grieving fiancé, instead of the key suspect. Hopefully things will quiet down for you online now."

Jake rose, walking with the detective to the door. "That would be nice. Not that it makes much difference to whether Liv comes back, which is the only thing that really matters. Honestly, I'm now more worried it could stop people being interested, that it will take her disappearance out of the public eye. People will forget about us, which could mean if anyone spots Liv, she's not so recognizable and they won't think to report it."

Detective Banks paused by the door. "No case stays front and center in the public eye forever, no matter how sensational. You got a ton of national attention, and this was as public as it gets. But, I'll be honest, it's up to you and the family now to keep Liv alive in the public eye. Look at other long-term missing persons cases. The families have set up websites, Facebook pages, blog posts that have been circulated on social media, crowd-funding campaigns for private investigator fees, that kind of thing. You'll probably want to do that and get a bunch of subscribers and followers while the case is still of public interest. You should work with your sister-in-law — she sounds like she'd be a real asset with this."

Jake shook Detective Banks' hand. "That's a great idea. Thanks, detective, I'll get on that. I'm sure Annabelle would help."

Detective Banks put a warm hand on his arm. "Take care, Jake. I'll keep in touch, and I'll let you know the moment I hear anything."

The police detective stepped down from the porch and Jake closed the door. He flopped down onto the couch and took a sip of his coffee.

A cold case. One of those unsolved missing persons cases that forever remained a mystery, and would get occasional media throwback coverage on significant anniversaries, but that was it.

Detective Banks was right. It would be up to them now. Jake was exhausted just thinking about it.

CHAPTER 26: OLIVIA

August 12

I lean out over the railing, contemplating the drop. The gray waters of Cape Fear River churn below me, mimicking the writhing in my stomach.

Cape Fear.

An appropriate name for my emotions, these days.

I recall an old horror movie of the same name, with Robert DeNiro going psycho on a boat, and shudder. That's more Jake's kind of film.

I pull myself up and take a sip through the tiny hole in the plastic cover of my takeout coffee cup. I close my eyes, concentrating as I chant to myself.

Mindfulness.

Live in the moment.

Feel the liquid in your mouth, taste the bitterness combined with sweetness.

Let it warm your throat.

Enjoy the hot sun on your face.

Listen to the chatter of the tourists, the strums of guitar from a busker in the distance.

Remember, it could always be so much worse.

I meditate for a while, getting out of my head, pushing negative thoughts away. Minutes later, I open my eyes. Do I feel different? Has it helped?

It's another hot day, and Wilmington's downtown Riverwalk is busy with tourists on vacation and local families on a day out. They're eating ice cream, walking dogs, pushing strollers. Normal things. Things I'll never have.

I've got the day off work, and I'd normally spend it reading by my mom and dad's pool, or lying on the beach. But I've been feeling claustrophobic at the house, with Mom's well-meaning attention smothering me. And at the beach, there's too much of a risk of running into Jake or Savannah, even on a working Friday. I'd even asked Dad this morning if I could take his boat out, as I've driven it dozens of times. But you'd have thought I'd said something obscene. He practically barked his refusal before storming out of the house with his golf clubs, leaving Mom startled in his wake. I guess as far as he's concerned, I've never been out on it before, and it's his baby.

I apologized to Mom, even though he'd way overreacted, and left as soon as I could, slipping straight out on the bike, riding hard, with no particular destination in mind.

I found myself on the River-to-the-Sky bikeway, riding the full hour into downtown Wilmington where I locked my bike up near 24 South, and splurged on the takeout latte I'm enjoying now.

I stretch, taking in the iron bridge that leads to Eagle Island as it glints in the sunshine. I stroll along the boardwalk toward it, past a little jewelry boutique, a touristy art gallery, and several packed restaurants. It's past lunchtime but I'm not hungry. The truth is, I haven't been eating much or sleeping well. I don't know what I'm doing here. What to do next.

I continue treading the planks until I get to a quieter spot, away from the main drag, where big houses stretch down to the water. There's a row of benches on the boardwalk in front of them. Choosing one, I take a seat, finish my coffee, and pull my journal and pen from my cheap canvas tote bag.

My journal has become the best way for me to organize my thoughts about what is happening. The only way. Without writing them down, those feelings are nothing but a nightmarish swirl in my head.

I pause for a moment, chewing the end of my pen, then begin to write.

I keep thinking about what I said to Jake on the beach that night. About being rejected by this world, pushed out by everyone and everything, like a failing transplant organ. A canker to cut out, a boil to lance. And as the pressure is getting more and more intense, the more I fail to find a place in this world. Unable to have a real relationship with my family, unable to make friends, or get a legal job. Unable to be with the man I love. I've tried it all, and nothing works here.

I don't work.

Like that boil, it's all coming to a head. Something's going to happen, and soon. I just don't know what that is, yet.

I've realized something, though, in the past week since I last wrote. What I truly want. And that's a breakthrough in itself.

I thought it was Jake, that I secretly wanted him to leave Savannah for me. I thought I wanted to find a way to live in this world as a fully functioning member of society, somehow, even if I was never able to get ID or Social Security. That's what I thought I wanted. But that night on the beach with Jake changed all that.

The thing is, the Jake in this world isn't MY Jake. He's a different version. A more messed-up one, because of my death and his relationship with his dad after that, although he's just as wonderful a man. But not my man. He belongs to somebody else now. Somebody who even seems to deserve him.

The Jake I want is MY Jake. The Jake I left behind in the world I belong in.

It seems unfathomable to me now, but the truth is I've spent very little time thinking about that world as a distinct and separate place from the one I'm currently in. I've been so anxious trying to make this world work for me, trying to find my place in it, that I've neglected my thoughts of the life I left behind.

If that reality is truly a separate place that exists in its own right, as I believe it is, then what about MY Jake? What happened to him, in that world, when I fell into the quarry lake on the day, nearly three months ago? Did I just disappear on him? Has he, have all my family, been looking for me? Am I a Missing Person?

I can't bear the thought of it — my real family, my real Jake — frantically searching for me, with no clues to my whereabouts, no understanding of how I simply disappeared. The wedding day's coming up in a couple of weeks. They must be devastated.

Or maybe I didn't disappear that day. Maybe I died in that fall, smashed on the rocks below. Just as I did here when I was twelve.

They may have already buried me, and be processing their grief. Maybe this version of reality is some kind of purgatorial afterlife, where I have to give this version of Jake the closure he needs before we can both move on.

Yes, I know what I want.

I want to go home. To my real world.

And if I'm dead in that world, then I want to be set free.

I can't keep doing this.

I can't keep living this half-life.

I have to lance the boil.

But how?

There's only one possible answer to that, an answer that keeps popping into my head over the past few days. If I can get home, and it's a big 'if', then I'd presumably have to go back the way I came. Through my own personal parallel-universe soft spot.

The quarry lake.

I look out over the river. I haven't been back to the quarry lake since the day I fell and was taken to hospital by, it turns out, Jake's dad's friend, Kirk. I haven't seen any reason to go. Now I wonder why.

Why haven't I returned to the place where all this started? Why have I been subconsciously avoiding it?

A family with two young kids strolls past me, the pretty blonde mom giving me a smile as the daughter skips ahead. The father is very tall and sandy-haired, a boy with a shock of platinum-white hair sitting high on his shoulders, clutching a toy monkey. They could almost be Jake and Savannah with their kids, in seven or eight years' time.

I need to leave. I need to let Jake and Savannah be happy together, without me around to complicate their lives, or confuse Jake any further.

I know I'd be leaving Mom and the rest of my family all over again, and Mom would be heartbroken for a second time. But she barely has more than the ghost of a daughter now. It's nothing like our real relationship. I'm not her Livvie. I can't be.

I have to end this.

But how? By going to the quarry lake? Deliberately flinging myself off the highest point on the cliff and hoping I end back with my Jake in my own world?

There's no way of knowing if that would work. And if not, it's surely suicide.

What's even more alarming is that doesn't seem like such a terrible idea.

At least this would all be over.

CHAPTER 27: OLIVIA

August 17

I stick my head through the bifold doors, my bike helmet over my arm.

"Mom? I'm heading to work."

No reply.

I can hear her voice in the distance. It's coming from the little study near the front doors. I step into the cool of the house. She's on the phone to somebody.

I fill my water bottle in the kitchen sink. I can just make out what she's saying, without intending to eavesdrop.

"It's worked so far, hasn't it? I don't see what the problem is . . . So, get creative with the books. It's only one server's pitiful pay, Juliette, I'm sure you can hide it from the auditors. For goodness' sake, put it down as supply expenses or something. There's no paper trail . . . I don't know. You're the one running a restaurant . . . But we had an *arrangement!*" Mom's voice rises. "Look, I don't want to have to go through with saying anything to Manuel, but let's face it, we both have our secrets, and you're leaving me with no options. That job is all Liv has. She has no way of earning otherwise, and it's the only thing giving her purpose . . . I'm sorry you feel that way, I really am . . . Juliette . . . Juliette?"

There's silence, then the stomping of footsteps coming toward the kitchen. Mom appears around the corner from the living room, and freezes when she sees me at the sink. My water bottle is suspended halfway to my lips.

I can't believe what I just heard.

"Mom?" I manage. "What the hell?"

My mother purses her lips, exhaling slowly before she says, too brightly, "Honey. I thought you were on your way to work already."

"Mom. Seriously. What the hell were you and Juliette talking about? Did you . . . Are you *coercing* her into letting me have this job?"

She sits on a stool at the marble kitchen island, her hands shaking. Suddenly frail.

I persist. "Are you threatening to tell her husband something if she doesn't keep me on? That's what it sounded like."

Mom looks at her hands. "I did something bad, Livvie. I asked Juliette to hire you, telling her you were my relation, but you didn't have ID or Social Security, and when I wouldn't tell her why, she refused. I knew you desperately needed a job to give you some purpose and a sense of independence and adulthood, and I was out of options.

"Juliette has been very unhappy with Manuel, and I knew she'd started seeing a guy on the side, one of the golf club pros. So I just dropped a hint that I'd keep her secret if she looked the other way about ours, and hired you under the table. I knew she was real short-staffed at the restaurant, so it didn't take much . . . *coercion*, as you call it." She doesn't look up at me for this entire confession.

I put my water bottle down. "Mom. That is *blackmail*. And you call yourself a Christian? I can't believe you'd do something like that. Juliette is a kind and generous woman, she's been a good friend, and you bullied her into giving me a job? It's totally unforgivable."

Mom raises her eyes in surprise. "She's also an *adulterer*, Olivia." She only uses my full name when she's really mad. "Juliette is far from perfect. And it was more of an . . . arrangement, I'd say. A *quid pro quo*. We both needed our secrets to be kept, to help each other out. And that's that."

I shake my head, bewildered. "But now there are auditors coming, and she's worried they'll find out I'm working there for cash?"

"It seems so." Mom's gaze drops again, as she fiddles with her heavy engagement ring.

I twist my mouth and take a gulp of water. It's pretty clear what I have to do.

"You should never have done that, Mom. I'd have never taken the job if I'd known what kind of position you were putting Juliette in. You know I wouldn't."

"I *don't* know that, Livvie," she replies in a cold tone. "I don't know what you're like as an adult. What your morals are, or where you'd draw the ethical line. I barely know you, honestly. You don't seem anything like the daughter I lost sixteen years ago."

I turn to leave, her words cutting me to the quick. "That's because I'm an adult now, Mom. I'm twenty-eight years old and you've been treating me like a pre-teen ever since I moved into the pool house."

Her shoulders shake and she buries her face in her hands. "Of course, I did, Livvie," she rasps. "I thought I had my baby back, at long last. But it's like you're not even her."

Despite the truth of her words, that I'm not her Livvie, I'm hurt. Still, I step around the island, place my hand on her back, patting her ineffectually.

"Mom. I know it's hard, but I have to go back to the restaurant. I need to tell Juliette today will be my last shift. I can't continue there, considering the position she's been put in, both with you and with the auditors. And you," I say firmly, "you're going to mind your own business and say nothing to Manuel, okay?" I hold up my hand as she goes to speak. "Quitting the job is my choice, so Juliette held up her end of the bargain. Deal?"

If there's one thing Mom understands, it's a deal.

She raises her eyes to me, stares, and nods. "What will you do if you're not working?"

I drop my water bottle into my purse and pick up my bike helmet. "You let me worry about that. I gotta go, I'm late."

I leave Mom to consider her sins as I push out on her yellow bike, racing to work in record time. The day is mercifully cooler than it has been, slightly overcast, and for once I'm not dripping with sweat by the time I arrive. I lock up, as usual, near Jake's condo, reasonably confident that at 11.12 a.m. on a Wednesday, he won't be home. I run up the steps to the pier, and push into the restaurant. Two customers are already standing at the front desk, being attended to by one of the young servers.

Kevin is behind the bar.

"Good evening."

His tone is sarcastic, although not as bad as usual. He's softened a little since Hayley quit two weeks ago, after Juliette gave her a much-needed dressing down for being rude to customers. But he's never going to be my friend. I don't seem to be doing that well in that department.

Deb is pouring ice water for the customers being seated in her section. She glances up as I approach. "What happened to you? You're never late."

I shake my head, grabbing an apron from the hooks. "Craziness at my house. Too complicated to explain. Is Juliette here?"

"Sure, more things I wouldn't understand," Deb mutters, but loud enough that I hear. "Yeah, she's in her office." She strides off to her customers.

I don't seem to be able to win with Deb. It's probably for the best that I likely won't see her after today. She"s made it clear she can't be my friend either. I have too many secrets.

There's nobody in my section yet, so I grab the chance to talk to my boss. I knock on Juliette's semi-ajar door, pushing it open when she looks up at me. She straightens, brushing her long gray hair off her face, and gives me a sad smile, as if she already knows what I'm about to say. Or as if she's about to fire me.

I hold up my hands. "Before you say anything, I overheard my mo — erm, Tilly talking to you earlier, and I had no idea she had put you in such an awkward position when she asked you to hire me. I'm so sorry. I'd never have taken the job if I'd known. I thought you were simply doing her a favor." I take a deep breath. Of course I should have questioned it. "I feel real bad about it. I think today has to be my last shift. I'm really sorry, as I know you're busy, with Hayley gone."

Juliette's smile widens. She's clearly relieved. "Thanks, Liv. I wasn't going to be able to keep you anyways, with the tax audit in two weeks. It's just too risky. I interviewed a few people after Hayley left, and I've got two servers starting this weekend, so I'll be okay. We'll miss you, though." She sounds sincere. "You've been an excellent server, and great to work with. I'm sorry it had to be this way."

"Me too. I can't believe that happened. . . Anyways, you don't have to worry about that anymore."

"Thank you. I've already had to quit book club. I can't face Tilly again. I think that friendship is over."

"I can imagine." I half-laugh, half-grimace. "Okay then. I'll get started and finish at five. Maybe I can get my last pay then?"

"No problem, Liv," Juliette says with a nod. "I'll have it for you ready."

I slip out into the restaurant, which is starting to fill with lunch customers. Deb raises an eyebrow at me as she posts an order for the kitchen. "What was that about?"

I bite my lip, grabbing an order pad. "Today's my last day. I just quit."

"You quit?" Deb's eyes widen. "Liv, why? You got another job?"

I smile at her, shaking my head. "No, I just had to. I got customers, Deb. Talk later, okay?"

But I don't get a chance to do so.

It's a busy shift, with tourists taking the opportunity of a cloudy day to spend hours inside the restaurant, first for lunch, then for afternoon snacks and ice cream for their kids. By the time 5 p.m. rolls around, the restaurant is still half-full, and the staff is swapping over for dinner shift. Except for Deb, who is pulling another double, covering the shortfall until the new servers begin.

I manage to grab Deb by the bar after Juliette hands my final pay. "I'm heading out," I tell her. "Just wanted to say bye. It's been great working with you." And I mean it. She's one of the few people who was kind to me.

Deb purses her red-painted mouth, her eyes on one of her groups, who are trying to grab her attention. She nods at them and smiles. "Best of luck, Liv." Her voice is low, and she doesn't look at me. "I really hope it works out for you."

"Thanks, you too." But Deb's already weaving between tables to her waiting customers.

I press my lips together and drop my apron into the laundry bin for the last time. I've already said goodbye to Juliette. The other young servers are busy with guests. Guess I'm done here.

Leaving the restaurant, I try not to feel depressed as I jog down the steps of the pier, crossing the sand to my parked bike. Have I really left such a minimal impression here? Will anyone miss me when I'm gone? Is anyone missing me back in my world?

The sky is darkening and, as I ride home, it starts to spit rain. I don't mind, though. It suits my mood.

Back in the pool house, I shower and change. Since breakfast, I've eaten nothing but a handful of fries on a ten-minute break, and I'm ravenous. I make my way over the terrace to the main house, where Mom is cooking dinner.

"Hi." I smile at her, hoping our quarrel from earlier will be forgotten. Especially now the job situation is resolved. "Can I help with dinner?"

Mom flinches slightly as she chops a tomato. "Sure," she replies, but sounds unconvinced. Clearly there's still a lot of awkwardness here. I guess suggesting that she was a bad Christian didn't go down too well.

"How was your shift? Did you speak to Juliette?"

I nod, grabbing a chopping board and a red pepper. I slice it lengthways, the way Mom likes it. "Yeah. I won't be going back. I quit, and picked up my final pay. So that's done."

Mom sighs, sliding the tomato expertly into the salad. "What will you do now? I can't get you another job," she adds petulantly.

"I know, Mom. I don't expect you to. I'm . . . not sure what I'll do, honestly. But things aren't really working out for me here." I add my pepper strips to the salad. "You want onion, too?" I reach for it, but she stops me, her hand tight on mine.

"Olivia. Never mind the goddam onion. What are you saying? You can't leave!" Her voice rises in pitch. "You don't have any options. You have no money, or only what cash you might've saved up, which would last you . . . what? A month? You've no means of survival if you're not living here with us. What are you thinking?"

I put my hand over hers. "Mom. I'll figure it out. Don't worry. I know I've been nothing but a burden on you since I came back. I want you to stop worrying. Please. Let's just eat."

She grips the side of the island, gnawing at her lip before admitting, "I do worry. I worry I'm going to lose you all over again, that you're going to do something to hurt yourself. It seems like you're checking out." Tears well up in her pretty eyes. "I'm scared, Livvie."

So am I, Mom, I want to say. But Dad wanders into the kitchen. His heavy brow raises as it takes in the scene before him, his wife visibly distressed, my hand over hers.

"What's going on?" His tone is curt.

Mom sniffs. "I think our daughter is leaving us again."

I turn to Dad. "I didn't say that, Dad. I quit my job at the restaurant today, and I don't know what I'm gonna do."

That's not entirely truthful, but . . .

Dad glares at me, seeing right through my bluster, the way he always does. "You've upset your mom, Olivia. That's unacceptable. No." He raises his hand, palm toward me. "I think you'd better not join us for dinner tonight. Take yours into the pool house for tonight, okay? Let your mom calm down."

Wordlessly, I obey, serving myself salad and a slice of grilled halibut and taking my plate across the terrace. Inside my room, I eat at the little table, watching my parents move around the kitchen through the two sets of large doors, the turquoise pool stretching between us.

I've never felt so distant from them.

Checked out, like Mom said.

Their lives carrying on.

It's as if I'm already gone.

CHAPTER 28: JAKE

August 8

Jake carried his surfboard across the sand, weaving his way between groups of early evening beachgoers. He was definitely feeling better than he had earlier that day. His surf had been a good one, and nobody he'd chatted with out on the water had said anything about Liv. Things were getting quieter on that front, which seemed like both a good and a bad thing.

There hadn't been any mention of Liv in the news for more than a week now. And that most recent story was the *Atlantic* article, which seemed to have served as a kind of punctuation mark on the whole debacle. The public frenzy and social media commentary had died down, for which Jake was thankful. Onto the next big story — another scandal about a TV mogul exposed for coercing an intern into oral sex in exchange for a staff job. And the only thing Jake had seen on social media about Liv in the past few days was the Facebook page Annabelle had set up.

'Find Olivia Grainger', it was titled, as if demanding a proactive approach from the public. There was also a Twitter feed, and an Instagram page on which to post reels made up of photos and video clips of Liv. His sister-in-law knew what she was doing.

Annabelle's plan for the Facebook page was to write occasional blog posts about the investigation, share the friendlier news pieces like the *Atlantic* story, keep the page's followers up to date on the search for Liv — what search there still was — and give them a platform to share any pertinent information. Not that there was much more news to share, or even any more police work going on, as far as Jake could tell.

Jake shook the salt water from his hair and strolled into Randy's surf shop. He'd barely slept last night, and had loafed around in his briefs all day, failing to focus on the book Ed had lent him. He'd given up around five, throwing on his board shorts and T-shirt, and stacking his board on the roof of the Audi for the first time in weeks. It had felt good to be out on the water again, the salt water cleansing the negativity and darkness from his mind — at least for a little while.

As he propped his board against a wall of wetsuits, he could just make out his cell ringing from within his locker. But he was too slow to pull the key off his wrist and open the door, and the melody stopped. A missed call from David, his boss. What did *he* want at seven in the evening?

Jake grabbed his stuff and headed back out onto the beach after giving Randy a departing salute. He sat on a bench among the grasses near the pier steps, momentarily watching the distant surfers who'd joined him a little later and were still out. Then he hit 'call back' on his cell.

"Jake, hey, thanks for returning my call."

"Hi, David. Sorry I missed it. I was coming in from a surf. What's up?"

His boss chuckled. "Yeah, I figured you'd be out on the water a lot these days. Not your usual time of day, though. You're a dawn patroller, right?"

"Yeah, but I have a lot of insomnia right now. My sleep patterns are shot to hell."

"Understandable. So . . . we haven't spoken for a while. I guess it looks like things have changed a bit since then. I figured maybe you'd want to start rethinking about coming back. I know I said we'd need you on leave for a while, but it could be time, now that the media attention has moved on. Have you thought about it? Working again?"

Jake pulled a lungful of seagrass air through his nose. "I haven't, David, to tell you the truth. I guess when I asked you last time, I was desperate for distraction, but you were 100% right to bench me. Even aside from the optics, I'd have been useless to you, a total mess. Which we can't afford with our clients. And I dunno, I might still be. It's so hard, I tell you." His voice thickened, but he pushed through it. "We'd've been getting married this month, in just over a couple weeks' time. I've got all these people on me about the wedding arrangements, and I don't know what to tell anybody. I'm not sleeping." He shook his head.

A distant surfer caught a racy barrel, and Jake itched to go back out. Nobody out there had questions for him about Liv, the wedding, or his responsibilities. "I don't know if this is a good month for me, man."

David paused for a moment. "I get it, Jake. I do. You gotta remember, though, we're running a non-profit here. And right now you're on leave at full pay. The college interns picking up the slack will be gone by the end of September, and we'll need to hire new counsel if you're not gonna be coming back."

Jake nodded, pushing his lips out. The wedding was one thing, the non-refundable honeymoon to Southeast Asia he'd booked from late August to late September was another. Could he go alone? Would it be good for him, a month-long soul-searching journey—maybe give him some closure? Or would he simply be miserable the entire trip?

"I need more time, David. Can you give me another six weeks, while the interns are still around? You don't need to pay me, if you can't keep doing that. Call it a sabbatical."

David took an audible breath. "Sure, Jake. But keep me updated. And I'm gonna put you on half-pay for the next six weeks, okay? I know it's tough without Liv's income, and that reno cost you guys a fortune," David added.

Jake laughed darkly. "Yeah, it was supposed to be an investment in Liv's business, as well as creating a nice home for us."

"I guess it raised the house value a lot, right? If you end up selling, you'll get all the money back."

Jake kicked some sand through his flip-flops. He really didn't want to do that. "Probably. It feels too soon to think about that. But the truth is, I can't afford the mortgage long-term on my income alone. That's another part of the equation in coming back to work. Long-term, it's either work for you and sell the house, or get a higher-paid job."

Silence for a few seconds. "Yeah. That sucks," David said finally. "Not great choices either way, and we'd hate to lose you. I'm sorry, man."

Jake rose from the bench. "You've been so cool about this, David. I appreciate it. I'll speak with you soon, okay?"

"Take care, Jake. Send my best wishes to the Graingers."

The Graingers who were barely able to look him in the eye right now, given the awkwardness over the wedding plans, let alone exchange pleasantries. Yeah, maybe not.

Jake picked up his board and strode back to the car, strapping the board to the roof. He was ravenously hungry, and there was nothing but dried-up parmesan and moldy olives in the fridge at home. But the last thing he wanted to do right now was go to a fluorescent-lit grocery store in his damp board shorts. Jake had been living on takeout for weeks and there was no reason to change that tonight. He could use a beer, though.

He drove off the barrier islands onto the mainland and over the little creek bridge toward his house. The parking lot at the marina was busy and, through his open window, ubiquitous country rock from the bar drifted in, along with the buzz of voices. Maybe it was time he showed his face in there. He hadn't been inside in months. Not since a beer-fueled date night with Liv in early May. Griff the bartender would probably ask after her, but apart from that, Jake should be okay.

He parked at home, ducking inside to change into dry jeans and a fresh T-shirt, and walked the five minutes back to the bar. It was busy and loud inside, but there was a single stool at the end of the counter in the corner where he should be able to sit in peace. He slipped into the spot before anybody else could get it, and caught Griff's attention.

The bearded, forty-something hipster sauntered over, a tea towel on his shoulder. "Jake! Good to see you, man. Wasn't sure we'd be seeing you again, with everything that's happened. How are you holding up?"

How are you holding up? Every time, that question.

"Hanging in there, man." Every time, the same reply. "It's been rough. Thanks for asking."

"Of course, buddy." He'd be calling Jake 'sport' next. "We've been following the whole story. It's a nightmare." As if Jake didn't know. "We're all really sorry about Liv. What can I get you? The usual IPA?"

"Yeah, and a bacon burger with fries. No onion. Thanks."

"You got it, champ."

Champ. *Christ.*

Jake had sat on this stool before, many times. This corner was a favorite spot of his and Liv's. It was the only area of the bar where they could squeeze really close together, side by side, sharing fries and a pitcher of IPA, and be mostly hidden from other customers. The further down the pitcher they got, the more their hands would roam each other's thighs, and the less appropriate their neck nuzzles would get. By the time they were at the bottom of the jug, Liv's hand would be pressed against the growing bulge in Jake's jeans, his hand slipping inside her shirt.

Many times, he'd had to hurriedly pay up and hobble outside, holding his baseball cap awkwardly in front of his fly, much to Liv's giggling amusement.

Sometimes they could hardly make it home — once they hadn't. She'd gone down on him behind the marina shed containing the rental paddleboards, Liv on her knees in the grass, Jake lolling his head back against the rough wooden siding, in heaven.

God, she was the greatest woman who ever lived.

Shaking the memory away, Jake sipped the beer Griff placed before him, and took out his phone. It was only to help him avoid eye contact with the jostling patrons around him, he didn't actually need to check anything. Sure, he had a few new emails about the wedding, including one from his cousin in Connecticut, but he had no desire to read them.

Still, it was either that or scroll through his Facebook feed, which mostly nauseated him these days, with all the faux joy of families posting vacation photos.

Elsa's first time kayaking! So sweet :)

He knew Elsa was a tiny monster — her long-suffering father, a buddy of Jake's from college, had told him many times.

Or he could browse the news, which he hated for not being about Liv, even though he always hated any stories that *were* about Liv, and the comments that accompanied them.

Not appealing.

His final option was to stare into the middle distance, maybe watch Griff going about his business behind the bar.

And that wouldn't be weird.

Emails, then.

The message from his cousin, probably the third show of support Pete had sent since Liv disappeared, was characteristically kind.

Jen and I are thinking of you, man. We canceled our flights and Wilmington hotel yesterday, which made us both feel terrible. Jen was in pieces. If there's anything at all we can do, I figure this month is probably the hardest one yet—

Jake screwed up his mouth. As he'd suspected, Tilly had evidently told the guests they should cancel their travel plans for the wedding, without asking him first.

Maybe she was right. It wasn't their relatives' fault Liv had disappeared. They shouldn't be expected to pay out to attend a wedding that probably would never happen.

A group of three frat-looking dudes and a couple of girls behind Jake laughed a unison roar about something hilarious. One guy stumbled backward into Jake's stool, just as Jake was taking a swig out of his glass, making him slosh beer onto his clean jeans. Jake turned to him with a scowl.

"Sorry, man," the guy turned to Jake, hands raised. "Did I make you spill?" He was young, bald, with huge shoulders. Not someone to mess with.

"Don't worry about it." Jake turned back to the counter, where Griff was setting a large plate of burger and fries in front of him.

The bald guy put a hand on his shoulder. "Hey, I know you! Okay, I don't *know* you, I've seen you. You're the dude with the missing girlfriend, right? You've been all over the news. Hey, guys, it's the dude from the news, you know, that story with the hot chick who disappeared."

"Oh, right, yeah," another guy said.

"Charlotte Grainger's sister," added another, turning to someone else. "You know her, don't you?"

Now they were all facing him. Jake could feel their inquisitive stares boring into the side of his head. He took a fry and munched on it, raising his eyebrow.

"Hey, man, they found her yet?" the bald guy asked Jake, removing his meaty hand.

Jake rolled his eyes but turned his head toward the guy, just a little. "Nope, not yet."

Two of the other guys, dark-haired jock types, were chuckling about something. "Probably did it himself," one of them muttered in the other's ear.

Jake screwed up his face. Maybe he needed to take this food to go.

"Gary, don't be an asshole, leave Jake alone," one of the girls in the group was saying, the tall blonde. She pushed the bald guy aside. "I know him. He's going through a hard enough time without being harassed by you guys, okay?"

Wow, she even knew Jake's name. He must be famous now. Famous for being a suspect in a high-profile missing person's case.

He slid her a quizzical glance. Oh, it was Charlotte's friend. Savannah.

She smiled, revealing the cute gap in her front teeth. "Sorry, Jake. My friends are douchebags." She scowled at the guys. "In my defense, they're really Kirsty's friends, not mine." She gestured to the girl with the streak of pink hair, and squeezed into the space beside him. "How've you been?"

At least she didn't say, "How are you holding up?"

Jake forced a half-smile. "Taking things day by day. You know. Seen much of Charlotte recently?" He purposefully changed the subject.

Savannah nodded. "Yeah, a lot. She's joining us tonight — just texted she's on her way. Oh, she showed me the 'Find Olivia Grainger' Facebook page you and Ed's wife set up — it's really good. I've shared it on my social, all our friends have. Seems to be getting some good attention."

Jake nodded. "Yeah, Annabelle's been great. She's kind of in charge of it, even though it's supposed to be from me and the Graingers. I'm no good at that stuff. She's been ghostwriting blog posts free of charge, making little reels, and she set up all the social feeds. Every little helps, I guess."

"Absolutely. And it's not little. I saw you guys have over a thousand followers on the Facebook page already. That's amazing." She seemed to expect some kind of reply to this, which Jake didn't supply. She pressed on. "Charlie also said you met with Burt and Tilly a couple weeks ago, to discuss the wedding." She shook her pretty head. "That must've been so hard."

Huh. Another person who probably thought he was nuts for not canceling the arrangements. It was none of her business.

"Yeah." Jake turned away, waving Griff down. He wasn't about to discuss his wedding, or lack thereof, with Savannah. And he couldn't face seeing Charlotte tonight. "I'm gonna pack this up to go, thanks, Griff." He picked up his glass and drained the last of his beer.

Savannah's face fell. "I hope you're not leaving on our account."

Jake pulled a twenty from his wallet. "Nah, just too crazy in here for me tonight." He lifted his uneaten burger and tepid fries into the takeout box Griff placed on the counter. "Tell Charlotte I said hi, when you see her. I'm sure I'll talk to her soon."

Savannah put a gentle hand on his arm, giving it an overfamiliar pat. "I will. You take care of yourself, Jake."

He squeezed his lips together at her in an approximation of a farewell smile, and pushed past her douchey friends.

"Take it easy, man!" one of them called after him.

"Try not to murder anyone on your way home," another guy called with a stifled laugh, just as Jake made it to the exit.

Jake stopped, his hand on the door's push bar.

It might feel really good to punch that guy right about now.

He rotated, slowly. The guys were glancing over at him, chuckling like kids, turning into each other, evidently a little nervous about his reaction.

Beside them, a group of thirty-somethings at a table were watching the exchange, their conversation halted. One of them lifted a phone, aiming the camera toward Jake. He was being recorded.

Fuck that.

Jake wheeled back to the door and shoved it open, to relieved chuckles from the jocks. He stepped out into the balmy night, gasping lungfuls of sweet-scented air. He hadn't realized how fast his pulse had been racing until he got out of there.

Dicks.

He'd thought — hoped — all that was over, now that the media attention had fallen away. That there would be no more baseless accusations directed toward him. But maybe he was wrong. Maybe he'd be under a cloud of suspicion for the rest of his life.

Would he ever be able to move on? Make new friends? Or even — *Christ* — get a new job, if that's what he needed to do to keep the house? Would a private law firm even hire him, after Googling his name? Thank God he hadn't just punched some asshole on a video that would end up going viral on social media.

He strode through the warm night. He could feel his heart rate slowing with each step. And he could smell Liv again. She was in the sweetness of the moist air, the green scent of the foliage mingling with the pale blue aroma of saltwater.

She loved this walk home. Loved the Spanish moss that hung heavily from the oaks that lined their street. "Quintessential Carolinas," she'd said once, dreamily, as they walked home from the bar.

That had been soon after they moved in, before they'd started tearing the house apart. She'd turned to him, excitedly. "Ooh, that's good. I mean, as a name for our home design." She always gave her interior design projects names such as 'Southern Comfort' and 'Beachfront on a Budget', and their own home was evidently no exception. Her ensuing blog posts about their renovation had been given titles like 'Quintessential Carolinas: Layering prints and textures' and 'Quintessential Carolinas: Mixing it up in the kitchen' — all accompanied by her own beautifully shot, light-filled photos.

Jake didn't know how she did it. She was a rare talent. She made everything perfect. Utterly whole.

And her absence rendered it all empty. Hollowed out. Rotten.

Including Jake's life.

His heart.

CHAPTER 29: OLIVIA

August 19

I wave from the sand as he strides toward me. His body tall and lean, deliciously tan. His hair as pale and blond as it gets from a summer out on the surf.

I don't take my eyes off him as he gets closer. This might be the last time we see each other, and I want to memorize everything about him. His slightly loping gait, borne of teenage years with awkwardly long legs. His firm jawline, those high cheekbones. The strong nose and deep brow. The soft, golden hair on his arms.

I don't know whether I'll be getting my own Jake back tomorrow, so I have to remember this version of him. Today is my last full day, in this world, at least. Maybe in any world.

He sits beside me on the sand, folding his legs just like mine.

"Hey," I say.

Jake smiles slightly. "Hey."

"Thanks for meeting me. I know you don't have much time."

He nods, screwing up his face as he glances at his waterproof watch. His eyes are reddening. He already knows what I'm going to say.

I can't look at him, or I'll start crying too. I gaze out at the ocean, where a group of surfers are drifting in the silvery swell.

"This is where I saw you coming in from the surf, that day I accosted you, and you had no idea who I was. I was sitting exactly here," I say it more to myself than to him.

He blows out a breath, saying nothing.

"You know I came to say goodbye, don't you, Jake?"

I see his nod in my peripheral vision.

"Where are you going?" he asks, his voice quiet.

I trace a circle, a tiny planet, a miniature universe, in the sand. "I'm gonna try to get back home. See if I can find a way back to my own reality. My own Jake."

His head snaps to me. "What? How, Liv? Your soft spot? The *quarry*?"

I shrug, still watching the surfers. "I don't know any other way."

"That's crazy, Liv. You won't . . . *jump*, will you, Liv? Swear to me you won't do anything to hurt yourself."

I turn to him. His lashes are damp, his face stricken. I place a hand on his bare knee. "I won't hurt myself."

That's only half a lie. I'm pretty sure that whatever happens, it won't hurt. Not for long, anyways.

"I have to go, Jake. I don't belong here. Yes, I belong with you, but another version of you, the one who loves only me. He's looking for me, Jake. I feel it. I have to believe it. And I have to try to get back to him."

Jake's face crumples. "I'll never see you again." He takes my hand in his and I squeeze it.

"No, you won't. But you have your answers, Jake. My death as a child was in no way your fault, and you can be secure in the knowledge that somewhere, in another life, I lived. You saved me, and I lived, and we were happy. And it means you are free to be with Savannah, to be a good husband to her, to love only her. It's much better if I'm not around for that. And you know I need to be with my own Jake. It's the only answer. You know it."

He drops his forehead onto my shoulder, breathing heavily. "I'm gonna miss you. I only just got you back. Apart from everything else, you were my best friend. The very best friend I ever had."

A tear spills down my cheek, dropping onto his flaxen hair. "I'll miss you too, Jake, so much. Even if I get my own Jake back, I'll always think of you, and wonder how you are." I sniff inelegantly, and he raises his face to me.

"This sucks." He gives a sad half-laugh, half-snort through his blocked nose.

I nod, wiping my face on my T-shirt. "Yep. But we'll both be okay. Come on, help me up." I hold out my hands and he rises, pulling me to my feet. "You'll be late to pick up Savannah for her birthday weekend, and you have a big day tomorrow."

"I guess we both do."

I smile at him, not letting go of his hands. "Have you got a ring for her?"

He tries to pull away at this, not wanting to talk about it. "Liv . . ."

"Jake." I hold his hands firmly, shaking them slightly. "I want you to be happy. If you love her, and you're going to propose to her tomorrow, I want to know that it goes well for you. Do you have a ring?" It takes everything in me to ask that.

Jake pauses, then pulls a tiny black box from his pocket. I raise my eyebrows. I didn't expect he'd have it with him.

"May I?"

He nods, looking away.

Inside is an oval engagement ring, a large stone surrounded by dozens of tiny ones. It's much glitzier than the simple square diamond my Jake bought me last year. But it's more Savannah's style, and it's beautiful in a different way.

"She'll love it," I tell him, closing the box and handing it back. "Go give it to her. And promise me you'll be happy, Jake."

His face breaks again, but he makes a conscious effort to keep his composure. "I promise, Liv. You be happy, too. Tell the other me to be good to you."

I stretch up on the sand and kiss his damp cheek, squeezing him for a moment.

Then I let him go and walk away, without turning back.

I'm too shaken to ride my bike home, so I walk it most of the way, trying to breathe through my sadness. After a half-hour of pushing it in the warm evening sun, I mount the bike, my tears finally subsiding.

One major farewell down.

Only my family to go.

Not long later, I glide into my parents' driveway. Charlotte's blue car is parked there. She and Taylor are here for dinner with Meemaw and Pappy, giving me one more opportunity to see them again. I push my bike through the side gate and leave it by the pool house.

"Auntie Livvie!" Taylor shrieks as I step into the kitchen. She flings her little arms around my legs, Muffin the bunny in hand.

One very important thing I will never get back, if I make it home. My gorgeous little niece.

"Hi, baby girl. Hey there, Muffin. I'm so happy you're both here." I smile up at Charlotte, who is watching her daughter with raised eyebrows. "Hey, Charlotte."

She smiles back, the first truly warm response I've gotten out of her since I arrived. "Hey. Looks like you're a hit now."

I laugh. "I think it was the cookies that did it."

"Probably."

We share a surprisingly amicable dinner with our parents on the terrace, Taylor insisting on sitting next to me. Mom looks a little strained around the eyes and Dad is quieter than usual, but we manage to keep up a conversation about their recent golfing vacation in Florida, and Charlotte's plans for a spa trip with girlfriends on Labor Day weekend.

"We'll take care of our beautiful grandbaby. We'll have fun, won't we, Tay?" There's an anxious note in Mom's voice. "Maybe Auntie Livvie will help out, too." She looks up at me, a question in her eyes.

She's asking if I'll still be around on Labor Day.

I break eye contact, sipping my glass of wine. I answer her question without saying a word.

Scraping back my chair, I rise, reaching for the dishes. "I'll clear the table."

Dad helps me gather plates and bring them into the kitchen, where he opens the dishwasher. He coughs, a telltale sign he has something to say. I rinse the plates as he stacks them into the dishwasher with a clatter, waiting.

"You sticking around, now the restaurant job is over?" Dad's voice is gruff.

I pass him the last plate. "Probably not, Dad. I need to go . . . go figure some stuff out."

He coughs again, heading out in the direction of the terrace. But he stops next to me, laying his hand on my shoulder and patting it, just once. "I can understand that, Livvie." And looking at him, I think he does. "It's been good having you with us. Even for this little while." He clears his throat, and steps outside without looking back.

Charlotte brings some glasses into the kitchen, a sleepy Taylor following her, thumb in mouth. "I've got to get this one home," she says. "It was . . . nice seeing you, Liv."

I don't want her to see my face, so I lean in for a hug, surprising her. Charlotte freezes for a second, then gives me a quick squeeze back.

"Good seeing you, too," I say to the side of her head. I drop into a crouch to Taylor's level, hurriedly wiping my eyes as I do so. "Hey, kiddo. It was wonderful to spend time with you. And with Muffin too, of course. Have a good sleep, baby girl."

I kiss Taylor on her soft temple, holding my mouth there for just a moment. I'll never see this little girl again. I rub her little back and stand, turning away, busying myself with clearing glasses.

"Safe drive home."

In a moment, they're gone.

I wipe my face and finish the clean-up, stepping out into the terrace. It's now mercifully dark, so my parents can't see the red rims of my eyes.

"I'm heading to bed, it's been a long day. Goodnight, Dad."

I won't be able to say goodbye to Mom tomorrow morning. She'd break down, beg me to stay, never let me go. Even though she knows I don't belong with her.

This is it.

I lean down and kiss the top of her finely haired head. "Thanks for a lovely dinner, Mom."

She takes my hand on her shoulder and looks up at me, sensing something is up. Maybe Dad said something to her about me leaving. She rises, pushing her chair away, and gives me a tight hug. Just like when I was little.

"You're welcome, Livvie, my love. Good night."

I hug her back. "Good night, Mom. Love you."

I gently pull away and let myself into the pool house, locking the door, and closing the blinds. My goodbyes done.

Even though I feel like something's breaking inside me, I don't belong here. I don't fit in. And maybe, tomorrow, I'll get my real family back. No Taylor, and that hurts, but a family who truly loves and wants me.

It's worth risking everything for that.

Isn't it?

CHAPTER 30: JAKE

August 19

What the fuck was that?

Jake groaned into his pillow, the light in the bedroom too bright through those damn gauzy curtains. It was mid-afternoon, and he was desperately trying to sleep the day away, having been awake all night. His plan was to sleep the next few days away until the Big Day was over.

There it was again. Knocking. On the front door. Shit.

Jake dragged himself out of bed, pulled on some shorts, ran a hand through his matted hair, and stumbled into the darkened living room. It was cooler in here, too. Maybe he should nap in here, where the window coverings were heavier.

He pulled open the front door. A middle-aged woman, wearing overalls emblazoned with hippy floral embroidery, and a beaming smile, stood on the step.

"Hello! You'd be Mr. Johnson, I'm guessing?"

"Uh, yeah." Jake just about stopped himself from yawning. "And you are?"

"Briony Ratchet, of Briony's Blooms. Is Olivia home?"

Jesus. Does this woman not watch the news?

Even though he longed for anonymity, it always amazed Jake when people didn't know the story of his missing fiancée.

Everybody in the world should know.

"No. She's not — not home. Can I help?" he added reluctantly.

"Absolutely!" She beamed again. "I have Olivia's bridal flowers for tomorrow. She arranged delivery for today, ooh, way back in April?"

Fuck, the flowers. Jake hadn't even thought about the flowers.

"—explained she'd need space in her refrigerator. Has she prepared it?"

"Uh, sure. There's plenty of space." Their extravagant, stainless-steel, double-door fridge, another thing Liv had insisted on, was virtually empty. It had been for weeks.

"Great! I'll bring them in. If you can leave the front door open and direct me to your refrigerator." The woman thudded down the porch steps to her small white van, with a floral motif that matched her overalls on the side.

What was he going to do with all the wedding flowers?

Watch them die slowly in his fridge. Then compost them.

Liv had started a little compost heap at the side of their yard, to which he'd managed to add the occasional orange peel since she'd been gone. It would be poetic to see all the bridal flowers rotting on there. A metaphor for his life.

Briony trotted into the house, carrying a magnificent circular bouquet of white roses and peonies, with silvery green foliage. He could just imagine Liv carrying it as she walked down the aisle toward him. The woman slid a box onto a shallow shelf in the fridge. "There are six buttonholes and three bridesmaid posies in here," she explained, as she turned to leave. "I'll just be back with the twenty pew-end arrangements."

What in God's name was a pew end?

Jake slumped onto the couch, leaving Briony to it.

She returned with two more flat boxes, which she had to rearrange some fridge shelves to accommodate. She seemed unimpressed with Jake's lack of interest, or assistance.

"These go on the end of the chairs on each side of the aisle, ten rows each side," she told him, even though he hadn't asked. "They're all on ribbons, so they'll be easy to fix."

"Great," Jake replied, looking at his phone, pretending to read. "Is that it?"

"That's it. Congratulations. I hope you have a wonderful day." The grin she'd greeted with him had long disappeared. "Say good luck to Olivia." Her face said: *She'll need it.*

Jake guided her out of the house. "Thanks. Take it easy." Before she could say anything, he closed the door behind her, a quiet slam.

Man.

He lay back on the couch in the cool, low light, picking up his phone again. He'd had several missed calls from Liv's mom over the past week, plus one voicemail and two texts, one from a couple of days ago.

Hi Jake, it's Tilly—

As if she didn't know her name would come up.

I called a few times and left you a voice message to see if you're doing OK. It's been very hard with the wedding date this weekend and I'm sure you're going through hell right now. I'd love to see you. Maybe we can support each other through these tough few days. Charlotte said a friend of hers ran into you and you seemed very down. Please call me back, I'm worried about you. Hugs, Tilly xoxo

He hadn't replied.
What could he say to her?

Hi, Tilly, yes, I know, I was supposed to be marrying your daughter in a glorious celebration of love and commitment tomorrow, but instead she's disappeared off the face of the fucking earth and we're all devastated, and the internet thinks I murdered her and somehow disposed of her body,

243

so now I'm a social pariah slash local joke, and I have thirty exquisite floral arrangements sitting in my fridge, and a wedding gown that will never be worn hanging up in my beautifully curated bedroom, in which I can no longer afford to live on my single income. But I can never get a higher-paid job because aforementioned social pariah, and I can't go back to my old job that doesn't pay enough unless I sell our home, which is the one place that makes me feel close to Liv, like she's still here, because I'm surrounded by her scents, and her fabrics, and her creative inspiration, except it also makes me miss her so much I want to stab myself in the chest. And I have absolutely no fucking clue how I can exist in a world that doesn't have her in it. You want to talk about that?

Jake threw his phone down on the rustic coffee table and let out a wordless yell into the vaulted ceiling.

It didn't help.

He buried his face into a silver velvet pillow, pulling the soft gray blanket over him, despite the warmth of the day. Maybe the couch would swallow him up. Maybe he could be absorbed into the very fabric of the house itself. Then he could haunt the next owners for all eternity, the house becoming renowned as the place where Jilted Jake, heartbroken groom, roamed the open living area every night, wailing into the ceiling.

Jesus.

His phone tinkled on the coffee table, taunting him with its unreasonably jaunty melody.

He sat upright and turned the phone over.

Burt Grainger.

Shit. Tilly was bringing out the big guns.

Jake blew out a long stream of breath. He'd have to talk to them sooner or later. Maybe now was as good a time as any to face the discordant music.

He hit 'Accept call'.

"Hey, Burt," he sighed.

"Jake. Thank goodness. We've been trying to reach you. Tilly's called you numerous times."

Three, but who was counting?

"Sorry, Burt. I know she's worried about me. I'm having a hard time right now, as I'm sure you all are. It's not easy to talk at the moment."

"We understand, son, but it's not just that. It's all these wedding arrangements. We've been inundated the past couple days with deliveries and set up — I mean, jeez, you didn't cancel *anything*, Jake."

No, I told you that.

"—got 100 white chairs in rows on the lawn, a pergola overlooking the creek, and a stage with a sound system on the side of the goddam terrace, for Chrissake. And the delivery guys have been insistent that because it's all paid for, they have to deliver, and they won't pick it up again until Sunday afternoon, as scheduled." Burt heaved an audible sigh. "I asked them not to set up, but they said it's up to either Olivia Grainger or Jake Johnson to tell them that, and if we didn't let them in the side gate, they'd dump the whole lot on our front lawn. And you know how well that would go down with the HOA. It's a *lot*, Jake. Too much."

Shit.

"—very upsetting for Tilly. Every hour, one more thing arriving that reminds her of the wedding that won't be happening tomorrow. Son, I know you're hurting, but you gotta make some calls . . ." Burt trailed off.

Jake leaned back against the pillow, fingers pinching his nose as he fought the nausea flooding his throat.

"Burt, I'm sorry it's upsetting for you and Tilly, I really am. I gotta admit I didn't think it all through when I took over payments for the wedding . . . how it would affect you guys, when the date finally came. I just didn't want to cancel, you know? I thought that even if there was the tiniest chance of Liv coming back, I wanted to have it all in place for her." He blinked rapidly, a tear sliding down the side of his head. "I couldn't bring myself to undo everything she'd put so much thought and energy into. I just couldn't do it, Burt."

"I get that, Jake. More than you know." Jake knew it took Burt a lot to admit that. "There was a huge part of me that didn't want to cancel my little girl's big day either. But our yard has been goddamn *transformed* into a wedding venue, and it's breaking Tilly's heart. I've got all the curtains closed. And I can only imagine what's going to happen tomorrow, when the caterers show up with all the food and drink. I mean, at the very least, you gotta call *them*, right? It'd be such a massive waste. I'm sure they're already working on the food. The cake will already be made."

Fuck. The food.

Jake pulled his thighs to his chest, resting his head on his knees. This was a nightmare.

Why hadn't he just canceled everything, like they'd asked?

It would have saved him a fortune, too. The rest of the payments had come off his credit card over the past couple of weeks, and he was now out nearly fifty thousand bucks. Pretty much all of his and Liv's savings.

"I'll call the caterers, Burt. I will. And I'll make sure the band and photographer don't show up tomorrow. I'm pretty sure you guys have already told all the guests and the officiant not to come. Can you live with the rest of the stuff, the chairs and the stage, until it gets picked up Sunday?"

Burt sucked his teeth. "Not really, Jake. Tilly is climbing the walls. I'm gonna have to take her away tonight for a few days, maybe until Monday. I'll book us a hotel upstate, there's a spa place she likes. Just be here Sunday to supervise the pick-up, okay? Make sure it's all gone. You still have Liv's key to our place?"

Jake nodded, although Burt couldn't see him. "Absolutely. The whole place will be de-weddinged by the time you're back Monday, I swear." His chest was tight. "I'm sorry, Burt. I really didn't mean to cause you guys extra pain, Burt. Please give Tilly my apologies. I was only . . . trying to hold on to hope."

"I know, son." Burt's voice had softened. "We're all still hoping — we'll always hope. Just because tomorrow isn't happening, it doesn't mean any of us have given up. We'll never stop looking for Liv."

Jake hadn't realized how much he needed to hear that. He felt a little bit less alone. "Thanks, Burt. You have a good trip."

Jake pressed "End call" and slumped into the couch cushions again, his thoughts racing. He'd call the caterers in the morning. All the food was paid for, so it may as well get prepared, and he was sure he could get it donated to the soup kitchen that his non-profit had ties to. Plus, he could probably get a refund on the unopened crates of drinks.

The main thing was Burt was right. Canceling the wedding wasn't the same as losing all hope Liv would be found.

And while Jake might want to die right now, he had to live.

For Liv.

CHAPTER 31: OLIVIA

August 20

I wake at dawn, before my alarm. My mind is already on full alert, my entire being tuned to the significance of today.

Today should have been my wedding day.

Today may be the day I die.

I sit upright, trying to control my breathing.

In for four.

Hold for a moment.

Out for eight.

Stay calm.

Just go through the motions. One step after the other.

No need to think.

No room for second-guessing.

I shower, wash my hair, and dress in my now favorite striped T-shirt, white shorts, and sneakers. Not that it matters what I wear today, as I'll have to strip off at the quarry lake. I need to recreate the conditions of last time as exactly as possible, and that involves being naked. I don't bother blow-drying my hair today. What's the point? This is not something I need to look good for. I just need to survive.

Or not.

I make my bed with neat edges and pack all my possessions into shopping bags, so Mom won't have to afterward. This will be hard enough on her when they find me gone. While I said my goodbyes last night, my family didn't know it was a final goodbye. I need to leave them a note. Something short but expressing two important things. That I love them, and that I'm not coming back.

I never imagined myself as the kind of person to write what is essentially a suicide note. And yet, that's what it might end up being.

I open my journal, turning to a clean page. What to write?

Dear Mom, Dad, and Charlotte—

A good start, Liv.

It has been wonderful spending time with you all over the past three months. I know it has been hard for you all, having lost me such a long time ago. I know it has been almost impossible to believe I'm even real. I want to thank you, with all my heart, for embracing that impossibility and showing me your love and trust.

I can't stay here, though. Although you have embraced me, this life has rejected me. I can never live here as a member of society. I can never really make friends, as my being here makes no sense. And the man I love is marrying somebody else.

Even writing that breaks my heart.

My only options are to be dependent on you, both financially and emotionally, forever, or be an outcast, living off the land or on the streets. And neither is viable for me. I value independence and comfort far too much for that!

So, while I know you won't understand this and I hate hurting you, I'm choosing to try to get back to the world where I do belong. I must try. I believe there's a world where other versions of you are looking for me, feeling the same desperate hurt at losing their daughter, only a grown-up me, and where Jake Johnson is waiting to marry me, not someone else. I'm sure you wouldn't deny them their Olivia back.

If my attempt fails, and you find my body at the quarry lake, I'm so sorry for the pain that will cause. I can only hope these extra few months with me have given you some closure over the death of your own Livvie Grainger, sixteen years ago.

Please know that I love you both and Charlotte deeply. I hope you believe that. Charlotte, I was so happy to meet my amazing niece, Taylor, who captured my heart, and is a true credit to your abilities as a mom. Please give her this stuffed bunny from me as a companion for Muffin—

I stroke the yellow-colored rabbit I picked up in town a few mornings back.

—her name is Cookie — and tell Taylor I'm going to miss her, very much.

Thank you for accepting me, and I wish you all nothing but joy.

All my love, always,
Liv xoxo

I rip the page out of my journal and place it on the bed, with the journal beside it for them to read, if they choose, later. Picking up the soft rabbit, I remove the price tag with my teeth and lay it carefully beside the note.

I stuff $100 into my purse, leaving the rest of my earnings on the little table — it's not as if I can take it with me into the next world — and check my watch. I booked a taxi last night for 8.10 a.m. It's picking me up at the Landfall Country Club so my parents won't be woken by the sound of the car outside. I don't want to see them. I couldn't face seeing them again.

I unlock the pool house doors with a slow click, careful not to make any sounds that will wake my parents, whose bedroom window looks over the pool terrace and the creek beyond. I leave the doors unlocked and creep past the pool, which is a still and inviting pale minty green in the morning light.

I pause at the side gate, casting my gaze back over my shoulder. Beyond the shimmering pool, the well-watered lawns are vivid green and sparkling with a dew that will soon burn off. Past the gardens, the long dock leads into the silver strip of creek, where a flock of seagulls swoop down onto the water. The gentle putt-putt of a small boat breaks the morning quiet and sends ripples toward the reedy shore.

This has been a beautiful place to live for a summer. If I manage to get back home, I vow to spend more time at Mom and Dad's place. More time with Dad on the boat. More time with Mom on the terrace. More time with Charlotte. I'll encourage my sister's dream to become a mother, rather than hint that she's too young, as I've always done before. I know now how spectacular she'll be.

I unlock the gate and let myself out, silently slipping my keys into Mom and Dad's mailbox at the foot of their drive. I walk the couple of minutes to the gate of the country club, and the taxi draws up.

This is really happening.

"Hi there," I say a little shakily to the driver, getting in the back. My insides have begun to churn, and I feel sick. "Head to Travers Lane, which is kinda between Rocky Point and Long Creek. Not the Travers Lane in Pollocksville," I add, as the driver tries to punch it into his GPS. "It probably won't be in the system. It's just a tiny rural track. Just head to Rocky Point, and I'll direct you."

"Okay, ma'am," the driver replies as he pulls off.

The fifty-minute drive is picturesque but agonizing. Every turn takes me closer to my fate, every bump in the road brings more nausea. I grip the sides of the passenger seat in front of me and focus on my breathing exercises again.

251

"You okay back there, ma'am?" The driver's watching me in the rearview mirror. He looks concerned. Probably worried I'll hurl in his car.

I let out a stream of air, and give him an unconvincing half-smile. "I'm fine. Take a right up here, please."

"This little track, ma'am?" he confirms. "I think it's a dead end."

"Yes, that's fine. Thanks."

Looking unconvinced, he drives all the way to where the track meets the almost-invisible trail entrance into the forest, and pulls to a stop. My heart is thudding.

"You on a hike today or sumthin'?" he asks, his gaze sweeping over me suspiciously. "Sure is a pricey way to get here."

"Something like that." I hand over the cash, including a generous tip — the last of my money. "Thanks. Have a good day."

I climb out and pull my purse onto my shoulder, leaving the perplexed driver to turn the car around, and drive away.

I push through the twigs that obscure the trail head, evidence that hardly anyone even knows about this overgrown trail, let alone the hidden quarry beyond the fence.

A moment of acute panic floods me.

I recall Adam saying the quarry was private property, when we first met, what seems like a lifetime ago. What if he'd also informed the owners of my accident, and they've since fixed the fence? What if I can't get through? I didn't even think to bring wire-cutters. I grimace, wishing I'd thought of this sooner. Dad has a pair in the garage. I could have brought them.

I force myself on to find the wizened tree that marks the point where Jake and I usually push through the undergrowth to the fence. In our world, we've marked the tree with an "X" on its bark, but I'm confident I'll know it regardless.

The undergrowth is thicker in this version of the wood, not having had me and Jake pushing through it for years, I guess. It's a struggle to get past the low shrubs and spiky branches to the fence. The image of Kirk the hiker carrying my naked, unconscious body through the bushes jumps into my mind. It must have been difficult getting me out through this terrain.

Eventually, I come face-to-face with the wire mesh fence. To my relief, the section we usually enter through is still unsecured.

So, Adam didn't rat me out to the owners. Kind, sweet Adam. I hope he finds a wonderful woman to make him happy.

I scramble through the fence, careful not to catch my clothing on the jagged wire, and within moments, the landscape opens up to the quarry. *Our quarry.* I am a bundle of nerves, and I really might throw up now. I stop for a second, suck in a big breath, then exhale before I step out onto the gravelly ridge.

It's now well past 9 a.m., and the sun is already warm. The water in the lake below me is the brightest turquoise I've ever seen it. It's dazzling.

And it's another perfect summer day in North Carolina.

A perfect day for a wedding.

Or to celebrate a proposal.

To jump off a cliff.

My heart begins to race again. *What am I doing?*

I climb the rocky ridge to its highest point.

The point where Jake always takes his running jump into the pool.

The point where I fell, both as an adult and as a child.

I remove all my clothes, deliberately folding them neatly, and laying them on the rock beside me, next to my purse. I don't need any of this now. Finally, I sit, cross-legged, on the cliff edge, and stare down into the water. All I can hear is the pounding of my heart in my ears. The flat rocks directly below me are both an invitation and a threat of what might be.

Life.

Death.

I close my eyes, feeling the sun on my face. One last meditation? I need to be calm when I do this, not on the verge of vomiting.

I don't know how long I sit there. Maybe it's twenty minutes, maybe close to an hour. It feels like an age. When my mind comes back into the world, and my pulse has slowed, I know it's time.

But how do I do this?

I can't take a running jump, I'd just land in the water and nothing would happen. And the rocks below are the key, I'm sure of it.

Dive onto them, head first?

That seems . . . painful. And potentially unpleasantly messy.

I clamber to my feet. I'm overthinking this. It has to be a fall, exactly like when I was twelve and almost died. And *did* die, in this world. And like the incident that brought me here.

I turn my back to the lake, and shuffle backward to the edge of the rock, where it meets the slippy rubble. It would be easy enough to fall accidentally. But this has to be *intentional*.

I'm telling the universe, all universes, that I want to go home.

I stretch my arms up to the glorious sun, then hold them out to each side. All it will take is a tiny lean back.

And trust.

I must trust in the universe to send me home.

I must trust I will see Jake and my family again.

I must trust I will survive.

I lean back, and in a moment I realize I am not afraid. The world is telling me: *Let yourself go. I've got you.*

I lean back further, further still, and gravity takes its course.

Time slows as I fall.

It slows enough for me to remember: *Oh yeah. This is what it felt like last time.*

It slows enough for me to smile up at the dazzling sun, warming my outstretched, naked body from above.

It slows enough for me to send my thanks to this universe for showing me what another life might be like, and how extraordinarily lucky I've been to have mine.

It slows enough to wish this world's Jake Johnson a lifetime of happiness with his partner.

I close my eyes, and it's my family's faces I see, including sweet little Taylor.

I keep falling. I open my eyes and I'm in darkness, punctuated only by white speckles. Bubbles? I go deep, deeper, deeper still. I'm cold but not uncomfortable, suspended in the infinite dark. The black water, if it is water, morphs into nothingness. A massive void of space. The bubbles now tiny stars.

One star is brighter than the others, diamond bright, pulling me toward it.

The nothingness becomes a sudden whoosh of movement. I'm in the blackness of the void, but traveling at great speed.

Upward.

Outward.

Through.

I break the surface in a massive gasp of breath.

I'm wet, naked, on a warm rock, under dazzling light. The sun beats onto my skin.

I roll onto my back, suck in another lungful of air, and scream the only word my scrambled mind can process.

A call across universes for my lost love.

CHAPTER 32: JAKE

August 20

Jake reached forward to crank up the air-conditioning. Along the leafy, rural roads, the light between the foliage created a strobing effect as the Audi sped past. It was almost hypnotic. Twice he had to brake suddenly as he came across an unexpected stop sign. It had been months since he'd driven out to the quarry lake.

Two months and twenty-four days, to be precise. He felt the need to be here today. It was the last place he'd been with Liv.

Last time, when he'd driven along these roads, Liv had been by his side, full of anticipation for their celebration. Then, the surrounding fields were lush and green. Today, they were dry, sandy, desiccated after a hot summer virtually devoid of rain.

That's what Jake's existence felt like these days. Water was life, and Liv his hydration. Without her, his world was barren.

He pulled down the shady track that led to the woodland, and parked next to the trailhead at the end, under a wide oak tree. He sat for a moment in the cool of the car, anticipating the day's heat hitting him like a mallet when he stepped outside, despite it only being 9.30 a.m.

This sweet car was another thing he'd have to give up before long — the exorbitant lease payments were out of his league on a single income. He didn't need two cars anyways. He'd have to use Liv's aging Kia and pray the roof rack fitted.

Jake screwed up his nose. It was impossible to comprehend the reality of life after today, what was meant to be their wedding day. The happiest day of their lives. Everything led up to this moment. And here it was.

Jake leaned and grabbed the bouquet of white blooms and silvery foliage from the passenger seat. He'd felt the need to do something symbolic with these flowers today.

He stepped out of the car. Jesus, it was hot. Beautiful, but hot. Clear skies, aside from some airplane trails overhead. And there was only a very light summer breeze. Like the day of the picnic.

A perfect day for an outdoor wedding.

He stepped through the trailhead into the darkened woodland. It felt cooler again. Jake almost smiled. He must make an incongruous sight, a six-foot-four guy in a Silverfish T-shirt and board shorts, carrying a bridal bouquet through a rough forest trail.

Not that anybody else was here to see him.

He was totally alone.

Here and there, brilliant patches of sun illuminated foliage like spotlights. One such beam settled on the gnarled tree with the X that marked the hidden turnoff to the fence and the quarry, about fifteen minutes from the trailhead.

Taking care not to damage the bouquet, Jake pushed his way through the shrubbery, which had been cut back during the police search for Liv. Still, new branches had sprung across since then.

After a few minutes he came to the wire mesh fence, which was now cut away entirely at this section to aid the search. There was still yellow police tape across the gap. He was surprised the landowners hadn't secured the fence — but then again, they'd always seemed to be absentee owners. Detective Banks had told Jake that he'd placed an international call to one of the owners to let them know what had happened, and they didn't seem to care.

Jake slipped under the police tape, emerging into the open air of the old quarry site. He felt a pang at its familiarity. How many times had he and Liv come here? How many happy times had they shared here?

The clifftop was hot and dusty but, as he stepped forward, the water below revealed itself. Turquoise from the quarry sediment, bluer than he'd ever seen it. Deliciously, invitingly cool, and beguiling. A person could lose themselves in that lake.

Jake gazed at it for he didn't know how long. Water is life. The water below was Liv herself, quenching him, soothing his desperate thirst. He longed to touch it.

But he came here for a reason. To say goodbye.

Goodbye to Liv? . . . No. Never.

Goodbye to his old life? . . . Perhaps. He needed some closure, some significant event to mark the first step in moving on. Whatever that meant.

There was another possibility. Goodbye to his life. How could he think he could live without Liv? What would that even look like?

Feeling his heart beginning to quicken, Jake stepped onto the highest cliff point, the one where he'd last seen Liv. He raised her bridal bouquet to his face, inhaling the sweet scent of the white roses, and laid it carefully on the flat rock. A memorial of sorts.

The lagoon was enticing. It seemed to be beckoning him down into the water.

Jake closed his eyes. As far as he could see, he had three options.

One: To walk down the access road and step into the lake, take a gentle swim, and soothe himself. But that didn't feel like a big enough event for a day like this.

Two: Take his usual running jump off the cliff to plunge safely into the deep end. That was certainly more exhilarating, more all-embracing than option one. But, after he emerged, nothing would have changed.

Three: Simply let himself fall.

Perhaps that was the only way to be with Liv. Down there, in a place where there was no space or time. He'd been telling himself throughout the past months that he had to stay alive, in case she came back. Now he had to face the possibility that she was never going to.

Maybe this was the only way to be with her forever.

He stepped forward, to where the rock met the gravelly cliff edge, and the scree slipped a little beneath his sneakers. His pulse was racing.

He lifted his gaze to the cerulean sky. The airplane trails had dissipated, leaving nothing but a faint white haze over the blue. The light was so bright, he was dazzled. He closed his eyes, and felt the vertigo of uncertainty wash over him. If he moved his foot, just a little, all his pain would be over. He could so easily fall before he'd even made the final decision to do so.

But the pain of his family, his loved ones, his friends stopped him. He surely couldn't do that to them. Could he?

Jake inhaled deeply, the warm air filling his lungs, then let out a primal holler into the void.

Suddenly he stopped. What *was* that? Overlapping his own yell, another cry, another voice.

A woman.

Calling his name.

Screaming it, from down by the water.

Liv.

CHAPTER 33: OLIVIA

August 20

The light blinds me. The heat sizzles, burning the moisture off my flesh almost immediately. Only my long hair remains soaked, spread over the flat rock.

There's a noise above me. The sound of scrambling. Loose bits of gravel fall from the clifftop and explode at velocity on the flinty surface beside me. The tiny bombs jolt me upright.

"*LIV!!! LIIIV!!!*"

A scream. A yell. My name. Over and over. From high above me. A voice from the heavens. I twist my naked body, raise my eyes to the sky, but the sun bounces off the cliff face, dazzling me. Still, I'd know that voice anywhere.

Jake.

It's Jake.

"I'm here!" I'm screaming, but it's only coming out as a croak. I can't see him, but he's coming. I can feel him coming. And his footsteps are loud on the clifftop. A shadow passes across the sun — a giant bird come to take me away? It swoops, gains mass, crashing into the water with a huge splash.

Jake.

He erupts through the surface, gasping, wiping his face.

He sees me and his beautiful, beloved face crumples. He sweeps through the water, hauling himself up onto the rock, flinging his soaking body at me. And I'm in his arms. I can't believe it.

He's shaking, sobbing, repeating my name over and over. And I realize I'm doing the same.

I hold him close to my prickled flesh, tighter than I've ever held him before. I won't let go. Can't. Is this real? No. I just flung myself off a cliff — I'm likely dead. And if I let go of Jake, he'll evaporate into the sun and breeze.

Or, maybe this is heaven.

I'm frowning as Jake lifts his face to me, holding my own between his hands, reaching up to push my wet hair back, searching my eyes as if looking at me for the first time.

"Baby, oh my fucking God. Liv . . . it's really you. You're here."

He kisses me, pushing his lips hard against mine, only to break away again, breathless. "Oh my darling. Jesus Christ, I thought I'd never see you again. Liv. *Liv.* Where've you been, baby? I lost you for so long. I've been going crazy. I nearly just killed myself. Fuck . . . Liv."

His eyes search my face, as if waiting for something. Suddenly, it occurs to me I haven't said a word to him yet.

Is a dead person supposed to talk to an angel?

I swallow, my ears popping like I've been in a submarine.

"Jake?" I manage, the word barely a whisper. "Are you real?"

He half-smiles, half-sobs, nodding, as he pushes my hair back from my face. "Baby. I'm real. *You're* real. We're together, finally. I can't believe it." He looks at me closely and I see, with a pang, how thin he is, the dark shadows beneath his eyes. He's suffered, too.

"My darling, where've you been?" His voice is a rasp. "We've been searching for you for months." He can't seem to stop touching me. But I'm the same. But I can't answer him. I don't know how.

"You're real. And I'm back. That's what's important," I whisper, my fingers against his cheek. He turns his mouth into my palm, his lips warm against my skin, the gesture heart-achingly familiar.

"Yes, Liv, my darling." His hands run over me, searching, probing. "Are you okay? Are you hurt? Can you walk?"

I glance over my body. Nothing seems broken.

"I'm naked."

He laughs at this. "Yes, my love. As the day you were born, and the most beautiful thing I ever saw. Ha!" He grins, looking like the Jake I know. "Oh my God, I don't care where you've been. You're back . . . And honey, you know what day this is?" His azure-colored eyes are alight with love. "It's our wedding day, baby. Our wedding day!"

I gaze back into blue eyes I know better than my own. This is *my* Jake. I'm really back.

A sob builds in me and shudders through my body, bubbling up in my throat and coming out as a cry. I squeeze him, clinging to his body in my sudden torrent of tears. I have absolutely no idea how I'm going to explain my disappearance to him, or to my family, but I'll have to find a way.

"Baby, I got you," he's saying. "I got you. We're together now, nothing else matters, and nothing is ever going to keep us apart. I swear to you, Liv. I swear."

He holds me until the shaking subsides, and I bury my face in his neck. He smells of himself — saltwater, coconut, and pinewood. I kiss the soft skin under his jawline, moving my mouth around to meet his, devouring him, blending myself with him until we're a morphed blur of passion. I need us to become one being.

I break free, holding his cheeks in my hands.

"It's our wedding day," I repeat back to him.

He laughs again. "Yes, baby, that's what I said. It's our wedding day."

I lift my head, shriek a laugh up to the sky, and look into his clear blue eyes.

"Then let's get married."

* * *

"Just . . . tell me again. I know you told me already, but it makes no . . . Tell me again, okay? From the beginning." Jake settles down beside me on the couch, turning his body towards mine. He's wearing nothing but a pair of grey boxer briefs, given that he immediately stripped out of his wet clothes as soon as we arrived home, after some pretty intense and distracted driving. I'd had no clothes at all when he found me, so he had wrapped me in a picnic blanket for the drive and I'd had to run inside, laughing, when we made it back to the house. And then . . .

I pull my plush bathrobe around my chest, and tuck my feet underneath me as I sink deliciously into the soft corner pillow. Damn, I've missed our home so much.

Smiling at Jake's still-bewildered expression, I touch his arm. "I know, I know. It's impossible to believe. It's impossible that it happened. Yet it did. And I'll tell you again, the whole story, as many times as you like. But . . . what time is it now?" I look at the mantel clock, but it's clearly stopped, its hands at five past seven. I turn back to him with a smile. "Jake, I still fully intend to make it to this wedding. If being away from you this summer has taught me only one thing, it's that I'm totally, one hundred percent, *certain* that I want to marr—"

Jake's phone cuts me off. He rests one hand on my bare foot as he answers, beaming back at me. "Jake Johnson . . . yes . . . right . . ." His brow furrows slightly. "Wow. Is she okay? . . . Oh. Oh, good. Well, thanks for getting them the message. And they're on their way now? Awesome. Thank you so much. Hey, before you go — can we trust your discretion on this matter? We really don't want the media to get wind of this today, given the . . . We appreciate that — thanks so much."

He hangs up and turns back to me. "Your folks' hotel, calling me back. They said your mom was told the news you'd been found while she was on the massage table — apparently she leaped up and immediately passed out cold. But she's fine now, they're already on their way back, and

Burt called the officiant, so we're all set for 4 p.m. Charlotte can be here in an hour, she's ditching her shift at Zara's, and . . ." he checks his phone, "it's only 12:15 now. We have some time." He leans across the couch to kiss my temple. "Tell me again, honey. I do believe you, I swear — I just need to . . . understand. It's like . . . a kind of *wormhole* between alternate realities? And . . ." he lets out a perplexed laugh, "you ended up in a world where I'm dating Charlotte's friend?"

I chuckle at him, an eyebrow raised. "Oh, yeah, I figured you'd be interested in that part. Yes, you're even going to propose to her — in fact, I encouraged you to. Well, you know. The other you. She's actually kinda nice. Anyways . . . from the start. So. After I fell, I woke up in hospital . . ."

* * *

Doing up my dress in our bedroom, Charlotte's hands are shaking so much she can barely push the tiny buttons through their tight loops. She hasn't stopped sobbing since she arrived at the house an hour ago.

"Char, I know this is a lot, it's totally crazy, but we've only got thirty minutes before we have to go to Mom and Dad's. I love you for caring so much, but we've still gotta do my hair and face."

She sniffs inelegantly, managing the last button, and turns me around to hug me for the seventeenth time. "I love you so much, Liv. I can't believe we got you back, today of all days. I have no freakin' idea what the hell is going on, or where you've been all this time — nothing makes any sense. But I'm just so happy you're here."

I kiss the top of her head. "Like I said, all that in due time. It's just . . . *really* hard to explain." I laugh. "I mean, impossible. And right now, we've got a wedding to get to."

Jake is outside the bedroom door, speaking loudly and excitedly on the phone to Nicole. "Right?! . . . Yeah, I know, totally incredible . . . Exactly . . . No, no, we'll bring your bridesmaid dress to the house — Sara's too. Just meet us at the Graingers in a half-hour, forty minutes max, okay? Ceremony's at four. And just tell everybody you can get a hold of that they're welcome. A bunch of the guests won't be there because they obviously cancelled their travel plans . . . But obviously not to let the media know until we tell them later — we don't want a circus today . . . Yeah, we can't believe it either. I know! So unbelievably happy. It's a total miracle, and I don't even believe in miracles . . . No, and what's crazy — I mean, it's all crazy — but . . . I never cancelled any of the wedding arrangements, it was all paid for already, so it's literally going ahead just like we originally planned. Caterers, flowers, jazz band, everything . . . I even kept our honeymoon to Asia booked, in case I decided to go alone, and now we can still go . . . I know, right? Okay, I gotta run, and so do you. See you there. Yes!"

Charlotte pulls up my blow-dried hair into a casual bun and fixes it in place, some tendrils falling down the sides. "Will this work? I don't have time to do anything super fancy." She twists a pretty wire hair accessory with glass-bead tips around it.

"It's great, perfect. I don't want anything too formal."

I apply my rush-job bridal make-up with a trembling hand as Charlotte slips into her own aqua-colored brides-maid dress and freshens her tear-smudged make-up.

I rise and hug her yet again, carefully this time, then pull back to look at her shining face. "Thank you for helping me. You're the best maid of honor ever. And I know we have to run, but I want to say something to you first." I smooth down her rich brown hair. "You're also the best sister ever, and one day you'll be an incredible mother. Whether that's some time soon, or whenever it may be. You'll be wonderful."

Charlotte gives me a puzzled smile, and another tear forms in the corner of one of her hazel eyes. "Oh, Livvie. Thank you. That's . . . just the sweetest. So will you, one day. When you and Jake are ready — maybe after a bit of traveling, right? But come on, now, don't get me blubbering again — we need to get you married. Ready?"

"Yep. We're as ready as we need to be. Crap, we still have to get all the flowers out to the car. Can you grab Sara and Nicole's dresses?"

Charlotte stops me as I try to open the bedroom door, listening to Jake making another phone call to his brother. "He can't see you in your wedding dress!" she exclaims, her eyes wide. "It's bad luck for the groom to see the bride in her dress before the ceremony."

I laugh, taking my sister gently by the shoulders. "Screw that. We've had enough bad luck for a lifetime already. I'm not letting that guy out of my sight ever again. And you just try telling him to drive to Landfall in a separate car — see how well that goes down."

She holds up her hands, the draped teal dresses slipping down her arm. "Fair enough."

Jake is pacing the living area, devastatingly handsome in a cream linen suit and pale-blue tie, chattering excitedly to his brother. It seems Ed has managed to get hold of their father on the golf course, despite his cellphone being off. Jake's dad is best man, and someone from the clubhouse had to run all the way to the 13th green to tell Ted that I'm back and the wedding is still on.

Charlotte passes me the bouquet Jake had rescued from the clifftop and grabs one of the flat flower boxes, juggling the two bridesmaid dresses over her other arm. "Tell Jake to get the other boxes," she says, scurrying out to load them into her car.

Jake finishes his call and turns to me.

"Holy shit," he says.

"What?"

He steps towards me, studying my dress, my hair, my face. "You're breathtaking. An angel. My angel." He reaches an arm around my waist and tugs me closer.

I kiss him, ever so gently, leaving only a tiny layer of gloss on his lips. "I am indeed *your* angel. Always."

He twirls a tendril of my hair around his finger. "You won't leave me again, will you?"

I reach up to stroke his soft blond crop. "Never again, my love. I promise. As long as you promise not to leave *me*, given that I obviously sound like a total nutjob right now."

He laughs, shaking his head. "It's all pretty wild — I mean, ridiculously wild — but I do know for sure you're not crazy. I told you that I believe you, and I mean it. That's what happened."

I nod. "Thank you. And even though *you* know the truth, we'll have to figure out a much more convincing story to tell everybody else about what happened to me. Including the media, if they're as interested in me as you say. But we don't have time for any of that right now. We have a wedding to get to."

Jake runs a finger down my cheek. "We do. And I refuse to lose you, ever again. We'll figure the rest out. It's you and me, forever."

I touch my lips to his once more.

"Then let's go."

THE END

AUTHOR NOTE AND ACKNOWLEDGMENTS

I wrote this book, *The Love I Could Have Had*, in the summer of 2020, while I was furloughed from my media day job. I had not yet sold my debut, *The Love of My Other Life* — in fact, I'd only just signed for that novel to be represented by an agent in New York. I was off work for several months, unwilling to start looking for a new career move, knowing I'd either get my job back or I'd be fully let go and paid severance.

This gave me the extraordinary opportunity of having six months, from April to September, to do nothing but write, with zero guilt. *Bliss*.

While everybody else was juggling pandemic-induced nightmares of working from home and managing online schooling for their kids, or worse, I was going for long sunny walks to think about my next stories. Emboldened by the offer of agency representation, I figured I'd work a nine-to-five, Monday-to-Friday schedule as a full-time writer — it could be my only chance to do so before retirement! I decided to write as many manuscripts as possible in the free time I had, however long that would be.

I wrote three manuscripts that spring and summer. Two are very different in theme from my debut novel, and have yet to see the light of day (but may be resurrected later

— TBD). The third, written in the height of summer, was the manuscript that became *The Love I Could Have Had*. I wrote this book as a very deliberate follow-up to *The Love of My Other Life* — in no way a sequel, but an exploration of the same themes — in case we got lucky, and my debut sold. Maybe there would be an appetite for more multiverse romance, if the first book did well!

However, with this new novel, I wanted to flip the concept of my debut on its head. Instead of our protagonist waking up in a universe where she has (almost) everything she ever wanted, what would it be like if she found herself in a world where she had literally nothing? And I'm not talking merely about poverty — I mean nothing at all, not even an identity. Well, that could only happen if she didn't exist as herself in that world — either she'd never been born (which was my first instinct) or, worse, if she had *died as a child*. So, there were people she might encounter who knew who she had been, had loved her as a child, and had wondered about what she might've become if she'd lived. Plenty of scope for drama there!

And what would happen in the world she'd left behind? With no alternate body to swap with (unlike my debut), she would simply disappear. And with missing people come police investigations, and national headlines, and public accusations. I loved the idea of giving a kind of *Gone Girl* twist to this story, with my secondary narrative from the distressed fiancé Jake's point of view.

I also knew that this story could end up feeling a lot heavier than the fizzy delights of my first novel, which is all luxury Manhattan real estate and champagne parties. So, I decided to set the new book in a popular coastal town — Wilmington, North Carolina — across the course of a heady summer. And I could make sure there were lots of surfing scenes, seafood dinners, and vacation vibes to give it that beach-read feel. Hopefully I managed to balance the darkness with enough light (and, of course, that incandescently happy ending).

With that concept in place, the novel just about wrote itself—I plotted it all out in a week and took four more weeks writing it, full-time, from start to finish. However, it took me two more years (because of the Big New Job that I took after my layoff) to get it redrafted, beta-read, redrafted again, and polished enough to show my agent. Thankfully, she loved it, and passed it to the team at Joffe Books, who had published my first novel. They also said yes right away, and here we are.

Speaking of, I'd like to extend my warmest thanks to them. To Victoria Skurnick, my fabulous agent at Levine Greenberg Rostan in New York, who gave me the kick up the butt I needed to finish editing this book in time for a summer 2023 publication. And to Kate Lyall Grant and the whole team at Joffe Books, who have supported my work so kindly and worked so hard to get this beach read turned around for a summer release, satisfyingly one year after my debut. Also, many thanks to the numerous beta readers and other members of the writing community who provided input — your support is always invaluable.

Big hugs of gratitude to the incredible women who have given me their friendship and encouragement throughout the years, to whom this novel is dedicated — Shona, Sarah B, Libby, Becky, Jo, Rach, Sarah J, and Nic. Love you long time.

And finally, to my family. I have had the extraordinary luck of having an incredible family whom I love dearly. Mum and Ian, whose timeless love story blows any of my plots out of the water. My big brother Rich, his wife, Emma, and the girls, who are an amazing example of making the life you want happen.

And lastly, to my sister, Alice, her husband, Kieran, and the great loves of my life: my nephews, Oscar and Felix. Thanks for being even better than *Frozen* at showing me that true love isn't always about romance.

THE JOFFE BOOKS STORY

We began in 2014 when Jasper agreed to publish his mum's much-rejected romance novel and it became a bestseller.

Since then we've grown into the largest independent publisher in the UK. We're extremely proud to publish some of the very best writers in the world, including Joy Ellis, Faith Martin, Caro Ramsay, Helen Forrester, Simon Brett and Robert Goddard. Everyone at Joffe Books loves reading and we never forget that it all begins with the magic of an author telling a story.

We are proud to publish talented first-time authors, as well as established writers whose books we love introducing to a new generation of readers.

We have been shortlisted for Independent Publisher of the Year at the British Book Awards three times, in 2020, 2021 and 2022, and for the Diversity and Inclusivity Award at the Independent Publishing Awards in 2022.

We built this company with your help, and we love to hear from you, so please email us about absolutely anything bookish at: feedback@joffebooks.com.

If you want to receive free books every Friday and hear about all our new releases, join our mailing list: www.joffebooks.com/contact

And when you tell your friends about us, just remember: it's pronounced Joffe as in coffee or toffee!

ALSO BY C.J. CONNOLLY

THE LOVE OF MY OTHER LIFE